THE
FAR SIDE
OF THE
DESERT

Also by Joanne Leedom-Ackerman

Fiction

No Marble Angels

The Dark Path to the River

Burning Distance

Nonfiction

*PEN Journeys:
Memoir of Literature
on the Line*

Stories and essays
included in:

*The Journey of Liu Xiaobo:
From Dark Horse to Nobel
Laureate*, editor Joanne
Leedom-Ackerman with Yu
Zhang, Jie Li, Tienchi
Martin-Liao

*The Memorial Collection for
Dr. Liu Xiaobo*, editors Chu Cai
and Yu Zhang

*Short Stories of the Civil Rights
Movement: An Anthology*,
editor Margaret Earley Whitt

Remembering Arthur Miller,
editor Christopher Bigsby

*Snakes: An Anthology of Serpent
Tales*, editor Willee Lewis

Electric Grace,
editor Richard Peabody

Beyond Literacy,
editor Patton Howell

*Fiction and Poetry by Texas
Women*, editor Janice White

*The Bicentennial Collection
of Texas Short Stories*,
editor James P. White

*What You Can Do:
Practical Suggestions for Action
on Some Major Problems of the
Seventies*, edited by *David
McKay Company*

THE
FAR SIDE
OF THE
DESERT

A NOVEL

JOANNE LEEDOM-ACKERMAN

OCEANVIEW PUBLISHING
SARASOTA, FLORIDA

ISBN 978-1-60809-535-3

Published in the United States of America by Oceanview Publishing

Sarasota, Florida

www.oceanviewpub.com

10 9 8 7 6 5 4 3 2 1

For Peter who always believed in me

THE WAKING

Of those so close beside me, which are you?
God bless the Ground! I shall walk softly there,
And learn by going where I have to go . . .

Theodore Roethke
"The Waking"

ACKNOWLEDGMENTS

The Far Side of the Desert has been read by friends and family over many drafts and many years. Their insights helped me shape and craft the story and assure the accuracy of the research. First among them was my husband, Peter, who encouraged me my whole career. He always claimed he was "just a reader," not a writer, and I shouldn't put too much stock in what he thought, but I did. I couldn't help it. I thank him in my heart every day.

My two sons, Nate and Elliot, always read with care. Elliot, who is himself a beautiful writer, offers insightful literary observations, and Nate, a mathematician and one of my biggest fans, responds enthusiastically, then tells me if the logic of the story falters or an inconsistency arises.

There have been many friends—writers and readers—whose responses and various expertise have helped, including family Judy Tyrer and Beverly Campbell; Mary Locke, a most valued first reader; Hans Binnendijk; longtime friends and colleagues Julia Malone, Robin Wright; and Azar Nafisi, Eric Lax, Deborah Jones, Sheila Weidenfeld, Lynn Goldberg, Krishen Metha, Lee Lowenstein, Gilly Vincent, and the late Judith Appelbaum, whom I miss; and Kamber Sherrod, who has helped in so many ways. Thank you!

My literary agent, Anne-Lise Spitzer, has offered friendship, insight, and the determination to find a home for *The Far Side of the Desert*. She succeeded with the fine team at Oceanview Publishing. Thank you to Patricia and Robert Gussin, Lee Randall, Faith Matson, and all those at Oceanview who bring care and high professional standards to the process.

Finally, thank you to the readers, current and future, who take the story into their hearts and imaginations and make it their own, thus expanding the life and reach of the book.

PART
ONE

PART
ONE

CHAPTER ONE

July 2007

A MOORISH KING AND QUEEN bobbed momentarily above Samantha Waters's scrambled eggs as if waiting to be fed. Outside the second-floor windows of the Hostal dos Reis Católicos, 12-foot puppets of kings and queens and devils and saints peered into the dining room then lurched away toward the square. Samantha leaned over the balustrade and filmed the festivities on the plaza below.

"Let's go, Monte," she urged her sister who was hunched over the wooden table with a plate of pancakes. "We can get coffee on the plaza."

Outside, the smell of coffee and fresh almond cakes rose from pushcarts as pilgrims hurried past shaking tambourines, beating drums, and filling the morning air with sound. Somewhere bagpipes played. The sun was already baking the cobblestones in the square where tables and chairs had been set up.

"It's too crowded," Monte complained as they merged with a stream of dancers and musicians. "This is a security nightmare!"

"It's a festival!" Samantha spotted an empty table and tossed her black straw hat over the heads of other spectators to claim it. They'd arrived late last night, she from London and Monte from the U.S. Embassy in Cairo. At breakfast they'd read the guidebook, which explained how a monk in the 9th century had discovered the body of the Apostle in a vault in the King and Queen's home village. The village had been celebrating its destiny ever since.

"Remind me why we came here?" Monte blinked into the sun. "We're not Catholic. Are you doing a story?"

"We used to live in Spain. I thought it would be fun to come back."

"We lived in Madrid, not Galicia, thirty years ago," Monte said. "You're doing a story. You're always doing a story."

A correspondent for the International News Network (INN), Samantha conceded the point. "But not today. I'm hoping Cal will get here too." Their older brother was flying in from Washington en route to a magazine assignment in Turkey. "It's beautiful here and filled with history," Samantha added.

"Everywhere in Europe is filled with history. Cairo is filled with even more history." Monte pulled off her khaki jacket, rolled up her shirtsleeves, and unbuttoned the waistband of her slacks, which was pinching her.

"I wanted to see you before you disappeared on your new assignment," Samantha said. She watched her sister who seemed more irritable than usual. Monte's pixie-like features were still young, but she'd put on weight, and her pale brown hair flared into gray arrows at her temples. Monte was thirty-seven, married with two children; Samantha, still single, was almost forty but looked like the younger sister. Samantha waved for the waiter threading among the tables. "I also wanted us to cheer up Cal before his divorce, though none of us knows how to take a vacation."

Monte pointed to the massive baroque and Romanesque cathedral across the square, its twin towers rising over 200 feet like giant dripping sandcastles framing the façade. "How do they know it's the real body of the Apostle in there?" she asked.

Samantha read from the guidebook: *"A hermit saw lights and heard music in the woods and found the body. Ever since, Santiago de Compostela has been the destination for pilgrims on their journeys of faith."*

"Faith in what?" Monte asked. "Even you don't have faith in two-thousand-year-old bones."

"No, but I have faith in festivals." Samantha smiled an easy smile. Monte frowned. "People want to believe in something larger than themselves, Monte."

"Maybe, but that doesn't mean something exists." Monte fanned herself with a folded newspaper as the sun rose above the Cathedral's spire. She slid out of her heavy leather sandals and set her bare feet on top of them. She glanced up at the sound of a helicopter circling above.

Around them tourists in shorts and tee shirts weaved among the super-size puppets whose wood-framed costumes balanced on the pilgrims' shoulders. The crowd looked like a gathering of medieval giants and midgets. A twelve-foot devil in a smiling white mask strode past with a troupe of musicians and sat a few tables away. Suddenly the street exploded with more tambourines, drums, horns, and laughter from people dressed in 15th century tunics. From the backpack at her feet, Samantha extracted her small video camera and began to film.

"So, you *are* doing a story," Monte said.

"Just taking footage." Samantha planned to stay after the Festival to research a story on drug and diamond smuggling along the Camino de Santiago, but she didn't want to tell Monte and disrupt their vacation. "I'm feeling pressure at work," she said. "Younger reporters are shadowing me, and the network is getting new management that doesn't care what I've done in the past." She set down her camera. "But this weekend I'm not working. I want us to have time together. I want to hear about your new post. Do you even speak Indonesian?"

"I'm studying, though frankly I'd rather be studying ancient Greek."

Samantha laughed. "You did that in college, didn't you?" She remembered their father's objection and bewilderment when Monte went off to Harvard and majored in ancient languages. "You planning to liberate the Parthenon?"

Monte smiled for the first time, her small mouth revealing a slightly crooked front tooth. "Someday I imagine myself sitting in a hut somewhere in old age reading the wisdom of antiquity in the original with the ocean lapping outside my door."

Samantha stretched her long legs into the plaza then pulled them back when a pilgrim tripped over her sandaled foot. "I can't imagine anything beyond next Wednesday."

"What happens next Wednesday?"

"That depends on what happens Tuesday."

"Don't you ever get tired of the pace?" Monte fished an ice cube from her drink and rubbed it along her neck which was turning pink.

Samantha took off her straw hat and handed it to Monte. She pulled her hair up into a ponytail off her neck. "Yes, but I don't know how to stop right now, though someday I'd like to have a child and a family."

Now Monte laughed as she put on Samantha's big-brimmed hat, which fit Samantha but dwarfed her. "That would slow you down. You have a father in mind I should know about? Any relationship over a few months?"

Samantha's blue-green eyes momentarily lost focus, and she frowned. "That's unkind. No one since Evan." She looked back out on the square.

"I'm sorry. I forgot. You never talk about him."

Because you're full of judgement, Samantha wanted to say, but she didn't. She just didn't talk about her partner who'd been killed last year filming in the hills of Afghanistan.

"Thank you for bringing us together." Monte amended and raised her glass for a toast.

They sat watching the square in silence as a band with drums and tambourines started playing. Two tables away a man from the hotel with unruly gray hair sat down and tipped his cap to them. Samantha nodded. Monte didn't acknowledge him, but Samantha thought she saw him. Across the square the devil put on his white mask and weaved toward them.

"How does Philip feel about moving to Indonesia?" Samantha asked.

"He's not thrilled." Monte lowered her sunglasses and covered her eyes.

"You want to talk about it?"

"No." Monte glanced up at the helicopter still circling above the clock tower then looked back at the crowds dancing along the cobblestones.

The devil stepped over to their table and extended his hand to Samantha. "Dance?" he asked.

Samantha glanced at Monte, who was closed off now behind dark glasses, her arms folded around herself. "Do you mind?" Samantha asked.

Monte peered at the figure silhouetted against the sun. "You don't know him," she warned.

"I won't be long."

The devil guided Samantha to his table where he handed her a purple-and-gold costume, which she slipped over her head and onto her shoulders, and she disappeared, transformed into an eight-foot-tall queen.

Monte signaled to the waiter and ordered another lemonade. How like her sister to dance off with a stranger, Monte thought. Samantha, with her teal-colored eyes and cascade of chestnut hair, lived the rarefied life of an attractive woman, even on the front lines of the news. To Sam, everyone was a story, or a character in a story she would tell. "People are not as bad as you think they are," Samantha told her just this morning when Monte cautioned about the man at the hotel who'd made a point of sitting next to them at dinner and at breakfast. "Give him a break," Samantha'd said. "He's probably just lonely."

"He doesn't look the lonely type," Monte answered. Her job at the State Department was to monitor insurgent movements and terrorist organizations, a job that had grown almost impossible. It was her job to know how bad people could be, and religion only inflated differences, and pilgrimages and festivals such as this one infused people with a belief that God was on their side.

*   *   *

The sun shifted behind the clock tower. Monte took off Samantha's hat and set it on the table. She slid her sunglasses to the top of her head. She was glad to have a few moments to herself. Yesterday her husband had told her he wasn't following her to Indonesia. They'd been sitting at the kitchen table after lunch. "But it's a big promotion," she'd argued. "It will mean a raise."

"You didn't think it necessary to consult me?" Philip asked, hunched over his plate, elbows on the table, his eyes cast down at his food.

"We agreed my job took priority. You can audit government accounts anywhere." As she spoke, she heard her father's voice arguing with her mother as his career in the Foreign Service bounced their family around the world.

"We'll talk when you get back from your sister," he'd said.

"How can I go now?" For the first time she noticed Philip's brown hair receding and saw his long-suffering eyes hardened. "It's a little late to be telling me this." Her own voice hardened. When he didn't answer, she asked, "Are you leaving me?" He still didn't answer, and his silence unnerved her. The longer the silence took root, the surer she grew that she'd missed some essential point. "Who?" she demanded. "Who is it?"

Philip stared at his plate, looking miserable but also removed from her. He got up and cleared the dishes from the table.

"Who?" she'd demanded as their five-year-old son, Craig, came into the room to say the driver had arrived to take her to the airport. She swept Craig up in her arms, hugging him to her. "I'm not going!" How could she leave now? How could she leave her son and daughter?

"Go. We'll talk when you get back. Nothing will happen before then," Philip said.

So she had come not to disappoint Samantha and her brother. Her brother's marriage was capsizing, and now she wondered if her own marriage was unraveling. She'd called home last night but talked only to the children. Philip wouldn't leave her, she reasoned. These were the battles of a marriage. She would deal with them when she returned.

* * *

"May I join you?" The man from the hotel stood in front of her blocking the sun. He put out his hand. "Stephen . . ."

"Oh . . . hello . . ." She glanced toward the square where the crowd had closed. "I guess . . . if you like. I think I've just lost my sister." She could see only the white-faced devil and a moving purple shape she thought was Samantha.

"She may be gone for a while," Stephen said. "They're dancing off around the church."

There were now four devils and at least three bobbing heads in the same queen costume. Monte could no longer tell which one was Samantha.

"I'd ask you to dance," he said, "but I don't like crowds. You can never be sure when they might get out of control, and then there you are trampled in the middle."

"My sentiments exactly."

"The crowds aren't so large yet but be careful on Sunday. Stay on the edges." Stephen took off a red Universidad de Sevilla cap, which uncovered his full head of scrappy white hair.

"You've been to this before?"

He set down a cup of espresso he was holding. Monte didn't want him to join her, but Samantha had told her she'd been rude to him this morning. He leaned back in the folding chair. He wore blue jeans, a short-sleeve khaki shirt untucked, and thick brown leather sandals with rubber soles. He looked like an aging academic until he pulled a pair of aviator sunglasses from his front pocket and put them on.

"Are you American?" she asked. His accent sounded American or Canadian, but he could also have passed for a local. In dark glasses, his tanned skin aglow, he looked younger and more attractive than he had at the hotel. She noticed his hands—graceful in the way they moved, and his skin was not old. She guessed he was sixty, but now she wasn't sure.

"I spent my early years in America." In his front shirt pocket Monte noted a small pad of paper and a pen, the kind she was used to seeing in her brother's shirt pocket and in her sister's purse. "I'm doing research."

"On?"

"Civilization. Or rather civilizations. This was a crossroads and a battleground of civilizations, you know."

Monte couldn't remember when she'd last chatted with a stranger with no agenda of her own. "Are you a writer?"

"I write articles and books to pay for my habit of history, though they rarely pay enough." He gave a self-deprecating smile, revealing a dimple on his right cheek. "You know the history here?"

Monte opened her hands, palms up, inviting him to continue.

"In the 8th century, the Moors swept through and destroyed all the churches except for the tomb of the Apostle. Legend has it that the Moorish commander came upon an old monk in prayer and spared him and his church. That was where the Apostle's body was later discovered, though some say the discovery was a hoax to attract business and tourists. The Moors enslaved the citizens who didn't flee and made their new slaves carry the bells of the church back to the Commander's base where they melted them down and made lamps. When the Christians overran the Moors centuries later, they made the Moors slaves and forced them to carry back the lamps, which they recast into bells."

As if on cue, the bronze bells in the cathedral tower chimed high noon, *clang . . . clang . . . clang* ringing through the plaza and across the hills, announcing the day was half done.

"Is that true?" Monte asked.

Stephen smiled. "True? It is believed. An industry has grown up around it. Inquisitions were held here based on a collective view of truth. Christians threw out the Moors and the Jews so their version of truth prevailed. Truth goes to the teller."

"So is that now you?"

Stephen leaned forward and touched Monte's hand on the table in a friendly gesture she didn't think she'd warranted; she had an odd sensation he knew her. "Depending on what I tell." He added, "Some people are expecting a miracle here. It's nonsense, of course, but the pageantry is worth seeing."

"You think it's nonsense?"

"Does that offend you? Are you Catholic?"

"No." Monte reached for her lemonade, removing her hand.

"Well, I do find it nonsense and offensive to see old women prostrate themselves, kissing stones, thinking they'll find spiritual power in bones and relics and icons of the past, but people have been coming here for the last half millennium defying my rational view of the world."

Stephen lifted his sunglasses and looked around for the waiter. His shoulders were broad, and he raised his arm with the assurance of a man in charge. When he turned back, his dark eyes met Monte's and held her gaze for a moment as if he were memorizing her face.

"There must be 20,000 people here." Monte averted her eyes. She found his attention disconcerting. Was he flirting with her? She could barely remember what that felt like. She wondered for the first time if her husband was still her anchor. Her son and daughter; they were her anchors.

"The crowds will double on Sunday . . . But ah . . . here comes your sister." A devil and queen were winding their way against the crowd toward the table. "I'll leave you now." He replaced his cap, and before Monte could introduce him, he faded into the crowd.

"Oh good, you had company." Samantha lifted the queen's head off her shoulders, shaking out her hair. "Was that the man from the hotel? What's his name?"

"Stephen something."

"Well, this is Eri," Samantha introduced the stranger with black hair and blue eyes, who was watching the man who'd just left.

"Do you know that man?" he asked.

"We met at the hotel," Samantha said.

Eri nodded to Monte then took Samantha's hand. "I'll see you again." And he left, making his way into the square with the queen costume under his arm.

"Let's go," Samantha said.

"But the pageant's just getting started."

"I need to talk with you in private."

As they moved onto the plaza, Monte noticed Eri also preparing to leave. Farther down on a side street she saw Stephen. She thought he was watching them. At least he was standing in front of a shop window showing more interest than she suspected he had in silver jewelry.

CHAPTER TWO

"YOU REMEMBER ALEX SERRANO?"

Samantha and Monte settled back in the hotel dining room by a casement window flung open onto Obradoiro Plaza. The hotel sprawled on the northern edge of the square, built from slabs of golden granite by Ferdinand and Isabella, King and Queen of Spain. It had been a hospital in the 15th century, but now was a luxury hotel, advertised as "the oldest hotel in the world."

"Alex Serrano from the American School?" Monte asked, pulling a plastic bottle of hand sanitizer from her purse and washing her hands. She considered this friend of Sam's from high school in Brussels where their father had worked at NATO headquarters. Alejandro Serrano—tall, chubby, smart—with a crush on Sam. "You worked on the newspaper together."

"Yes. Well, Eri is his friend."

"Of Alex Serrano? Where is Alex?"

"He's here."

"Alex Serrano is here? Did you know that when you arranged this trip?"

"Alex used to talk about this Festival. I saw his name on a list of peace negotiators talking with the Basques in San Sebastian, which isn't too far from here, so I emailed him, telling him we were coming."

"Why didn't you tell me?"

"What difference does it make?"

"I would have liked to know all the facts."

"There are no facts. Eri said Alex couldn't come into the square, but he told me we should go back to the hotel. There are some security concerns."

Monte forked a lamb sausage, suddenly annoyed that her sister had her own agenda here and had pulled her away from work and family. "What kind of concerns?"

"He couldn't tell me, but he said the hotel would be safe."

"You know that that's not true," Monte said. She dipped her bread into the sauce of the chicken and couscous. "If there's trouble, a 5-star hotel is not a safe space."

Samantha pushed her hair from her face. "You're right. I'm sorry."

Monte wasn't used to her sister apologizing. She softened her tone. "When does Cal get in?"

"Soon, I think. He had a last-minute meeting with Carol. Their divorce is almost final, but I think he's still hoping to win her back."

"Why on earth? She left him and the children for another man."

"Failure of imagination," Samantha said with sympathy for her older brother who had always championed her causes.

"Cal told me his divorce was an occupational hazard," Monte said. "I told him a person is either faithful or not. That's character, not occupation."

"Half the foreign correspondents I know are divorced," Samantha defended.

"Half the foreign correspondents you know aren't faithful to their marriages."

"That's probably true. Dad would agree with you."

"Coming here I was remembering how Dad used to make us all go to Sunday school because you wanted to go," Monte said. "Cal thought Sunday school was make-believe; I thought it was boring, but you believed everything."

Samantha squinted at Monte, for a moment remembering her little sister with scrappy pigtails and hand-me-down pinafores siding with Cal against her for the first time. Samantha waved her fork like a wand. "You learned Western religious thought and the literature of the Bible even if you didn't believe anything."

"And I learned I was adopted." Monte's green eyes steadied on her sister.

Outside, Samantha heard the crowds and the music swelling as the festivities moved into full swing. "That was your punishment for mocking what I believed and for siding with Cal." Samantha speared a cube of pineapple from her sister's plate. "I was only eight," she defended herself.

"You convinced me that Mom and Dad had bought me when they were in Prague from gypsies who'd stolen me from my real parents."

"And you believed me and quit eating and got so sick, I had to confess what I'd done so you wouldn't die." Samantha picked at the fish on her plate as she and Monte repeated this story like a folktale that bound them. "Dad told me if I ever lied like that again, he *and* God would punish me. I spent the rest of my childhood feeling guilty over you and trying to take care of you." Samantha offered a half smile. "To this day, I don't think I've been cruel like that to anyone, at least not intentionally."

"Really?" Monte frowned as if reviewing the record. She pushed aside her dinner plate and started on a platter of pastries. "Well, I'm sure I have."

* * *

The air changed first. A sudden stillness like a cloud passing before the sun, quieting the room. A vibration rose through the music and noise from the plaza outside. Samantha and Monte felt the intake then the burst of air. Shrill cries echoed in the distance like a flock of frightened birds. Hotel guests, leaning out the windows to see and hear the festival, pulled back. At first slowly and then quickly, the scene below accelerated. People from the side streets rushed into the square. The immediate space around Samantha and Monte sped up as guests moved into the dining room.

"Get away from the windows!" someone shouted. Others hurried to the windows to look out.

Samantha and Monte heard the word *bomb*. A bomb had exploded on a side street. Monte quickly calculated how they could dive under the heavy oak table, but at the moment there was no visible threat.

The maître d' moved from table to table passing out checks as if his greatest fear was that guests would skip out on their tabs. "Remain calm . . . remain calm. Sign your bills. Go to your rooms."

In the lobby rumors quickly spread that three . . . no, five . . . no, eight people had been killed and dozens injured by a car bomb.

At the front desk Samantha asked for their keys. She was also handed a slip of paper.

Arrived early. Gone to the square to find you.

Love,
Cal

She pulled out her phone and saw the same text from her brother. She called his number, but no one answered. "We're at the hotel . . ." she started her message.

"Let's go to the bar," Monte suggested. "It has access to the square if we need to get out of here."

"Meet us in the hotel bar," Samantha added. She also scribbled a note and asked that it be put into Cal's box then she texted him. Samantha's mind was already racing. Was this a single incident or a wider attack? She remembered Casablanca—fourteen bombers in four locations. "I need to report this," she told Monte as she looked around for who she could interview.

"Let's stay in the hotel . . . for now," Monte said. "We don't know who's out there." Monte had her own protocols.

"I'll film from the terrace . . ." Samantha hurried to the patio off the bar while Monte grabbed a booth in the bar and dropped her bag, jacket, and Samantha's hat on the table near the door. She slipped her wallet and passport into her pocket. She needed to check in with the Embassy in Madrid, but the phone lines were jammed, and the internet connection in the hotel was almost nonexistent. She tucked her phone into her side pocket then joined Samantha on the deck where Samantha was already filming. Not everyone on the plaza knew a bomb had gone off so some were still dancing. In the distance a procession of pilgrims wound their way to the cathedral. News of the bomb apparently hadn't reached them either. Suddenly sirens shattered the air.

"Another bomb must have exploded in the south." Stephen stepped up beside them.

Samantha turned her camera in that direction. "How do you know?"

"That's where the police are headed." Stephen pointed, touching Monte's shoulder.

"Our brother's out there," Monte said, unsettled by his touch. Given a choice, men always focused on Samantha.

"I wouldn't worry," Stephen said. "Journalists know how to take care of themselves, but you should go inside." He rested his hand lightly on the small of Monte's back as if to guide her.

"How do you know our brother's a journalist?" Monte turned around.

"You told me."

"When did I tell you?" She wondered if Samantha had told him.

"I've got to send this film." Samantha moved to the table in the mahogany bar. At the other end a cordon of men entered, including Eri, who'd shed his devil suit and now wore green and brown camouflage fatigues. "Excuse me." Samantha headed toward Eri.

"Don't go!" Monte said.

"I'm just going to the business center. I'll be right back."

Stephen smiled as she left, but when he saw Eri and the other men, he said, "We need to get out of here."

As Monte settled into the red velvet booth, he took hold of her arm and lifted her from the seat. "Now!"

Monte pulled her arm free. "Who are you?"

"Security. If you don't go now, you'll be a hostage." He kept his eyes on Eri, who had just spotted Samantha as she took his picture and paused to talk with him.

"Whose hostage?" Monte resisted Stephen's arm around her shoulders. "I can't leave my sister!"

"She's left you. If you don't get out now, you can't help her," he whispered, steering Monte toward the rear door. "I'll come back for her." More men in camouflage raced into the bar through the door they were exiting. Two men positioned themselves as guards outside. "We need to get you out of here," Stephen added as though he knew who she was and who she worked for.

Monte had been airlifted out of situations before and flown to a secure location. "Who are you working for? Spanish security? U.S.?" Monte demanded as Stephen propelled her up a metal staircase toward the roof faster than any sixty-year-old man she'd ever met.

"Yes," he answered.

When they arrived on the roof, Stephen pulled out a walkie-talkie and whispered into it as they crouched behind a chimney. Monte opened her own phone and pressed #3 *Send*—Samantha's number. She wanted to tell her sister to get out of the hotel so she wouldn't be taken hostage, but no one answered. Even if they couldn't talk, Samantha would see that she had called. She hoped Cal's instincts would keep him from rushing back into the hotel.

A helicopter hovered above the rooftops but banked left and flew away. Monte glanced over the red tiled roofs at the pilgrims and tourists scattered on the plaza below. The sun had slipped behind the cathedral. She needed to get back to Samantha and find Cal. She turned toward the stairs as three men appeared on the roof and went to each corner. At first shadows obscured their faces, but then in the fading afternoon light, Monte saw the faces were obscured not by shadows, but by masks.

Only then did she—expert in insurgencies, trained by the U.S. government—understand that it was not Samantha being taken hostage, but herself.

CHAPTER THREE

"Have you filed yet?"

Cal came up behind Samantha in the business center where the servers were down. She was digging through her bag for her local contact so she might send the breaking news video that two—or was it three?—bombs had exploded in the square and side streets in the middle of the historic Festival of St. James. At least twenty-three people were reported dead, Eri had told her, and more than one hundred wounded, though she hadn't verified the figures. The number would rise if a third bomb was confirmed. Other journalists would soon pour in, but for the moment she had a jump on the story. The attack was bigger than the story she'd come to research or maybe it was part of the same story.

"Cal! Thank God, you're safe. When did you get in? What's happening in the square?" Their vacation was over before it began. The attack would send the three of them into professional mode. She was already putting events in categories and scenes and questions, reducing the chaos to a three-minute "Breaking News" flash. "I want to go back out, but I need to get this video sent."

"Slow down." In jeans and white shirt with a pad and paper in his hand, Cal scanned the room with owl-like eyes behind black-framed glasses. "Where's Monte?"

"I left her in the bar."

"I didn't see her there. We need to get out of here. Troops are rolling in on the main roads. There may be other bombs. The hotel could be a target."

"I need to file."

"The servers and phone lines are down here, but there's an American post nearby. You can file there. Let's get Monte."

They made their way through the crowds in the lobby, back to the bar. "She was over there." Samantha pointed to their table by the door where her sun hat and Monte's canvas satchel still held their space. "She was here just a minute ago."

"Maybe she left already," Cal said.

"I don't think she'd leave without telling me." Samantha pulled out her cell and saw Monte had phoned, but when she called back, she got Monte's voicemail. "Where are you?" she whispered, watching soldiers entering the bar. "Cal's here. We're headed to the American post. I've got your bag. We'll slip out the back door and look for you."

Guests were rushing through the halls in tight clusters. At the front desk people were shouting for directions. "Where's the embassy? U.S.? France? England? Norway? Japan? Where is our embassy?" But there were no embassies or consulates in this medieval city.

Samantha and Cal waited by the back door, but when Monte didn't show, they snaked their way through the streets to a modest building already filling with Americans and a few Europeans. Monte was not among them.

Samantha explained to the receptionist that she was a news correspondent, and he let her use an aged computer; but the transmission was so tenuous, she finally called into the studio and reported live by phone with a thumbnail picture of herself on the screen.

At least two car bombs have exploded at the historic Festival of Saint James in the capital of Spain's northwest Galician region. Police have surrounded the famed Obradoiro Square and Santiago de Compostela's majestic World Heritage Cathedral as random gunfire continues to ring out. According to an American consular official, the death toll has risen to at least 30, including six of the attackers with more than 120 wounded. No one has yet claimed responsibility though it is assumed the bombs were set by separatists or terrorists, the categories interchangeable for the Spanish government. No one yet knows if the motive is religious, political, or economic . . .

Samantha and Cal went outside and looked up and down the street for Monte. "She was with a man we met earlier at the hotel," Samantha said. "Maybe they're together."

"Who was he?"

"Stephen something. He never told us his full name." Samantha again tried to return Monte's call. Next, she called her friend Alex Serrano, now a Spanish diplomat, who said he'd meet them for breakfast at the hotel. In the meantime, he'd check with his sources for Monte. They shouldn't worry, he assured. Monte probably got caught up in the crowds. He'd have his people check the hospitals in case she'd been injured. She was probably back at the hotel now that the streets had been cleared. She could join them for breakfast. Samantha called the hotel, but the lines were busy. When she finally got through to Monte's room, no one answered.

"Something's happened to her," Samantha said. "She would have checked in."

"You know anything about the man she was with?" Cal asked.

"He showed up in the dining room, then in the plaza and later in the bar and sat near us. He spoke perfect English."

"We need to report her missing," Cal said. "The U.S. Embassy in Madrid needs to know."

*   *   *

Samantha and Cal returned to the hotel by way of the square where they looked for Monte and also interviewed people. Cal was filing a report for *The Economist*, and Samantha had to file an update. The plaza was nearly empty now except for soldiers and police patrolling the cobblestone streets and a few tourists wandering out of bars that had stayed open. Samantha and Cal showed people a picture of Monte that Sam had on her phone, but in the chaos, no one had noticed a 5'2" brown-haired American woman with green eyes, a slightly crooked front tooth, wearing a khaki pantsuit and white blouse.

At the hotel, police had set up a cordon because of the many distinguished guests. As Cal stopped to question the guards, Samantha hurried inside where she retrieved the large wood-handled key to her room. Monte's key was still in the box. She sprinted up the wide mahogany stairs. In her room velvet curtains closed out light, and only a night-light illumined the space. The same dim glow came from Monte's adjoining room.

"Monte . . . !" She switched on the chandelier. The queen-size bed, the dark wood dresser and desk, which seemed so elegant when she checked in twenty-four hours ago, now seemed foreboding. "Monte . . . ?"

She hurried through the connecting door and flipped on a standing lamp. Monte's nightclothes were folded on the green velvet chaise in the corner. Monte's suitcase sat closed on the luggage stand. In the bathroom, housekeeping had laid out Monte's toiletries—toothpaste, toothbrush, powder, lipstick, hairbrush—on a white hand towel. Samantha caught her breath. Monte had not been back to her room, not even to brush her teeth, which she did three or four times a day.

CHAPTER FOUR

Whop-whop-whop-whop-whop-whop. The whir of helicopter blades was the last sound Monte heard. Water in the distance was the last view before the sedative coursed through her, and she passed out.

Monte had trained for this contingency years ago when she'd taken an assignment in a region where kidnappings were common. *Stay calm. Don't react. Don't appear afraid. Or angry. Or desperate. Focus on whatever will keep your mind in control—an object, a scene, a person.*

Monte woke up repeating this training to herself. She was strapped into the rear of an old Land Rover, the seatbelt cinched tightly across her shoulders, her hands bound by hard plastic cuffs in front of her. She was barefoot. Where were her shoes? The floor was hot. The metal on the floorboards burned her feet; even the floor mats were baked in the sun. She lifted her feet slightly to cool them. What had they done with her sandals? At least they hadn't bound her feet. She might still be able to run . . . but where? Over hot pavement and sand without shoes?

She focused on Stephen—was that his real name?—sitting in the front seat. The back of his head was no longer gray, but black. On the floor, like a large, deflated animal, lay a gray wig. No one noticed that she was awake. She again closed her eyes, feigning unconsciousness so she could listen to the three men. She recognized Stephen's voice first. He was speaking Arabic and French, both languages she knew. She kept her head down on her chest bobbing as if she were sleeping. Squinting through closed eyes, she watched for any familiar landscape passing by, but she saw only sand-colored stalls, a palm tree, a low cement building. Was it an apartment building?

What did they want from her? She was a political officer for the U.S. Embassy in Cairo—at least that was her title. Who did they think she was? What did they think she could do for them? She lifted her head to see better.

The guard beside her shouted to the front seat. *"Heeya saahi!"*— She is awake!

The car pulled off the road into a barren lot. Stephen, looking twenty years younger, came around to the rear of the car and opened the door.

Do not look or sound afraid, Monte told herself. She squinted away from the bright sun. She tried to focus on this man she had met at the hotel and befriended on the plaza. "I don't have any money if that's why you've taken me," she said. "And there is no one who will pay money for me." She wondered if this were true.

Stephen handed her a cup of water, cradling her head with his hand to help her drink. He wiped the excess water from her chin with his fingertips.

"I'm sorry we've intruded on you this way," he said. "It is not personal or for money—at least not for ransom, not yet. But you should be glad to know that you do have value." He pushed back the hair that had fallen in a sweaty string onto her face. With both hands, he swept her hair behind her ears with a gentleness that surprised and confused her.

"We have several more hours," he said, "so please get as comfortable as you can."

"I need to go to the bathroom." She toughened her voice in case he'd sensed a fleeting submission. She would survey the landscape and determine how to escape. She had to get back to her job and to her children. She couldn't let them take her.

"I'm sorry, we can't let you do that. We will refrain from giving you any more to drink or eat so you can, I hope, wait."

"What if I can't?" she asked aggressively.

"Well, we will all have to endure whatever indiscretion you show," he said. "Perhaps I should give you another sedative." He called to the front seat and was handed a first aid kit.

"No . . . no . . . no. I can wait," Monte said. "If you could just give me my shoes. The floor is hot."

Stephen pulled out a hypodermic and covered her head with his hand, holding it as he shot the needle into her arm. "I'm afraid we can't give you shoes . . ." Those were the last words she heard.

CHAPTER FIVE

THERE WAS NO EVIDENCE of Monte. Samantha took a leave of absence from her network; Cal did the same. They stayed in Spain where they interviewed the police, the soldiers, bus and train personnel, military, pilgrims, and others along the Camino de Santiago. They moved out beyond the city and took detours through the fishing villages along the Galician coast, showing pictures of Monte as they searched for her trail.

They went all the way to the granite cliffs of Finisterre, the ultimate destination for intrepid pilgrims and the Camino's final point. The cliffs faced west over the Atlantic. Here the ancient Romans had thought the world ended, a spot they called the Cape of Death because the sun died here and because ships wrecked on the rocks that jutted out in a finger hook into the sea. The Romans saw nothing westward and imagined nothing but terrors so declared *Non plus ultra*: *There is nothing beyond.*

As Samantha stood staring at the endless blue Atlantic, she had a sinking feeling that there was nothing beyond. She and Cal had been at work for two weeks, interviewing dozens of people but uncovering no useful clues. For all her training, she didn't know how to find her sister. Her brother-in-law, Monte's husband, was taking care of their two young children in Cairo and told her that was all he could manage. He was an accountant, not an investigator, he said. He sounded almost angry at Monte for disappearing.

Farther down the rocks, Samantha saw a group of young people, who told her they were pilgrims who'd come to this spot on the day of the Festival to burn their old clothes and show their willingness to start anew. In the early evening the day of the attack they said they were sitting in new tee shirts and jeans on the rocks sharing wine and bread when they saw a helicopter fly out over the ocean.

"We didn't know there had been an attack," said one. "We watched the helicopter circling in the dying sun, like a dark angel. Then it flew south."

"We took it as a sign," another pilgrim said.

"A sign of what?" Samantha asked.

"That something was out there."

*　　*　　*

The news stories about Monte's disappearance proliferated around the globe:

U.S. DIPLOMAT MISSING
KIDNAPPED? DEAD?
WHERE IS ANNE MONTGOMERY WATERS?

Samantha and Cal worried that the publicity was counterproductive, especially the comparisons to Cal's friend Allen Roy, a journalist who'd been kidnapped and executed two years before. The video of his beheading had been released to maximum impact after the frenzied publicity following his disappearance.

Samantha and Cal didn't share their anxiety with their parents, who didn't share theirs. Everyone was trying to be brave, but

Samantha feared that the very power their family was connected to put Monte at risk.

Cal arranged a family conference call to review what they'd learned. Because their father had been in the Foreign Service and served twice as an Ambassador and their grandfather had been a Deputy Secretary of State and even their great-grandfather had served in Congress, the family knew and could call upon power brokers in Washington and other world capitals. The level of their contacts imposed a public decorum on them. No one wanted to fall apart in public or even in private though Samantha knew from her grandmother that her mother had broken down at the beauty parlor when a stranger said she was praying for Monte. "Quit praying!" Lacey Waters had reacted. "She's not your daughter!"

"Oh dear," Samantha said, understanding the strain this put on her mother's sense of decorum and privacy. "Mother needs you."

"She's got me," her grandmother said. "Me and Lala." She added their great grandmother. "That's why we're still here, I'm sure."

Cal asked Monte's husband, Philip, to join the conference call. But when he phoned in, Philip said, "I don't know anything. I've got my hands full with the children."

"Of course," answered their father, who took the lead on the call, though Samantha and Cal were doing most of the investigating.

"If it was the Basque separatists, they're like renegade children," Edgar Waters began. "They blow things up—buildings, trucks— but usually give warning and don't target civilians though hundreds have been killed over the years. ETA is dangerous, but far less dangerous than Al Qaeda. If Al Qaeda has taken her, we can only pray there are some religious among them who won't hurt a woman."

"But why would they take her?" their grandmother Marjorie asked.

"We don't know that they did," their father answered.

Cal reported on the pilgrims' sighting of a helicopter. "We don't know that Monte was on it, but if she was, it means they quickly took her away."

"ETA and Al Qaeda don't usually have helicopters, do they?" asked their mother, who, in her early career, worked in intelligence in the State Department.

"The police and military have the helicopters," said their great-grandmother, who watched spy dramas on television. "Money is passing hands. Take my word. They want money!"

"But no one has asked for a ransom," Samantha reminded everyone. "No one has even contacted us."

Samantha's normally robust voice lost volume. She pushed the mute button on her phone so her family wouldn't hear her despair. They were counting on her, but in the early morning hours she lay in the dark, her eyes moist, trying to hear where Monte was. Was Monte calling out somewhere? Monte had to be somewhere in the universe if only Samantha could hear.

CHAPTER SIX

STANDING ON THE hot pavement outside the white stucco hotel, Safir Brahim read the courier's message: *Send the girl. Return home.* At the bottom sprawled a hand-drawn *E* with a circle and a slash through it.

About bloody time, he thought. Two weeks ago, he'd smuggled Monte onto this remote headland in the Western Sahara, this outpost wedged between the ocean and desert. As a boy he and his brother used to visit on school holidays and play on the rocky beaches where the desert sand and dust swirled, where iron-filled rocks made compass needles spin erratically, where the northeast winds blew in all seasons as the current accelerated down the shoreline. The coast was legendary for shipwrecks. Underwater reefs rose close to the surface, and waves thrashed and small fish swam in the shallows as large fish fed on them. Cape Bojador was a way station on the road to Dakhla or Nouakchott, Mauritania. The dangers here had caused ancient mariners to claim a sea monster dwelled beneath the surface.

Safir had chosen this inauspicious city, whose Arabic name, Abu Khatar, meant "the father of danger," because his father's uncle once lived here when Spain, instead of Morocco, was the colonial power. His uncle still had interests in a fish processing plant and two apartment buildings. Monte was locked in a third-floor back room of one of those pink stucco buildings, the windows sealed, and a mattress on the floor. An old ceiling fan stirred the hot, stale air. His great uncle now lived in Vigo, Spain, on the Galician coast, and his properties were run by locals who didn't care who came and went and didn't ask questions.

Standing in the sun on the pavement, Safir read the courier's message again then went inside to write a reply. He had no way of communicating directly with the Elder, who allowed no phones, no computers—nothing that could be tracked. He knew already he'd made a mistake taking Monte, but the only way he saw to proceed was by going forward. He expected to release her soon. He'd been careful not to interact with her further. He knew he'd have to go into hiding for a while, but no harm had come to her. If she was released unhurt after two weeks, he reasoned the hunt for him would taper off, and he'd drift to the bottom of a long list of wanted men. He planned to live incommunicado for the next few years anyway while he wrote his book about the Elder, a book he would write under his Moroccan name, Safir Brahim, not the name his Spanish father had given him—Stephen Carlos Oroya.

*   *   *

Safir's journey here began five months ago when he climbed into the back of a battered Land Rover. After a fourteen-hour drive into the desert, he was pushed through a doorway of a red dirt room.

"Have you ever killed anyone?" asked a white-robed figure peering through a slit of a window. The man turned slowly. His gray-red hair was tied back in a ponytail. A full rust-colored beard flecked with gray, the shade of the peeling walls, masked his face except for his forehead, flat nose, and bead black eyes. His left eye drooped.

"I've never had the chance," Safir answered. Swallowing dust that stirred in the hazy light, he began to cough.

"You were trained by the U.S. military. Didn't they teach you to kill?" The man spoke a deep, guttural English.

Safir needed water, but no one offered. "I was never in the line of fire."

The man moved toward him, walking with a slight limp, then sat on a pillow at a low table and gestured for Safir to join him. From the shadows another man emerged wearing a pale beige suit even in this hot, airless room. Safir lowered himself onto the pillow, grateful to be sitting on something that didn't move. From his battered satchel, which had been searched four times, he pulled out a tape recorder and a pad of paper.

The man they called the Elder, whom Safir had been hunting through North Africa, held up his hand. "There will be no interview."

"But . . ." he started to protest.

In the doorway guards held Kalashnikovs over their shoulders and knives sheathed on their belts. Safir touched his meager black beard and moustache that he'd grown for the occasion as if dressing for a part. He wore local dress, loose cotton shirt, and drawstring pants that obscured his muscular build. In his waistband he concealed a thin wire of tensile strength that could slit a man's throat.

"I was told we would talk," he said.

"We will talk, but you will not write or record." The Elder waved to the boy closest to the door. "Get our guest tea," he ordered in a language Safir recognized as Berber. The Elder set a cloth pouch of pistachios on the table between them. "Here . . ."

Safir drew from his satchel a plastic folder with a dog-eared magazine inside. "You have seen this?" He held up the article he'd written that referenced the Elder. "I want to write your full story."

The Elder smiled, his thin lips parting slightly. "Were you trying to flatter me? Instead, you have exposed me. I have brought you here to tell you to stop."

"I would like to write a book—your book," Safir coaxed. He'd practiced this speech. "I'd like to be your—"

"My Boswell?" The Elder laughed, a ragged laugh. "You know I studied in England as a young man. You know I spent my school years at British boarding schools and was dismissed from the London School of Economics. But do you know I have thirteen brothers?" The Elder turned to the pale-suited man at the table. "My friend here also studied at the London School of Economics and went on to read law so that he might assist me. He tells me you have worked in the financial markets?"

Safir hesitated. His life in the financial world was as Stephen Oroya and was long over except for managing his own money.

The Elder cracked pistachios in his thick, muscular hands, hands like a wrestler's who could choke the air out of you. A small hill of shells piled between the three men.

"Why did you quit?" the Elder asked.

"I had made enough."

"I have never met a man who has made enough money," the Elder said.

"I don't believe him," interrupted the man with short peppered-gray hair.

"I made enough so I didn't owe anyone." Safir met the other man's pale blue eyes, noting his manicured nails.

A teenage girl in jeans and a loose white cotton tunic entered and set a tray of tea on the table. The heat and dust wrapped around Safir, making it hard to breathe. He sipped the warm bitter tea, which gave no relief for his thirst.

"Do you have a family?" the Elder asked.

"No."

"You have a mother, I am sure. And a father? Have you made enough for them?" The Elder's lazy eye closed, but his remaining eye held Safir in its focus as if pinning down an insect.

Safir sat forward. He wanted to reclaim the agenda. "I do have a friend with a firm. I invest with him."

"And how do these investments do?" the Elder asked.

"We make a 10 to 15 percent return a year." He was taking a risk talking about money lest they seek a ransom for him, but he thought perhaps this might be a way into the Elder's world.

"I don't believe the return," the older man said.

Safir focused on the man's prim mouth. "I could show you . . ." He pushed up his loose sleeves and smiled a salesman's smile, revealing a dimple in his right cheek. He understood the selling of financial products, though making money had never been his primary ambition. His ambition was to have enough so he could do what he wanted and not have history bury him as it had buried his brother, who'd died in prison in the Western Sahara. He opened his pad. "If I had a computer, I could be more specific, but you can check the returns." He addressed the man in the corner. "I didn't hear your name."

"Rainer." The man's accent was German or Austrian. "Anton Rainer."

"So you believe in the capitalist markets of the West?" the Elder asked. "Yet you write about insurgencies that would bring them down?"

Drawing a knife from his robe, he began cleaning dirt from beneath his nails.

Safir heard malice in his question. He reached for a handful of nuts and ate them slowly, glancing at the boys in the doorway who looked as if they'd just as soon kill him so they wouldn't have to drive him back to Agadir.

"The markets are global," Safir said. "They are no longer owned by the West."

Rainer nodded.

"If your returns are correct, if Rainer finds you are correct, we will put money with you and your friend," the Elder said.

Safir sat forward. This was an unexpected and possibly perilous turn. "You want to invest with me?" He knew, or suspected, the Elder ran a criminal enterprise that must have sizeable funds and served political movements Safir wanted to penetrate. "What about the book I want to write?" he asked. "Can we work together to write your story?"

The Elder set his knife on the table. In a voice between a whisper and a hiss, he said, "You were not brought here to interview me, but so that I might interview you. If I invest with you, you will earn a commission and be paid well and be connected to me. That is the first step to see if we can trust each other."

Safir glanced about the small stuffy room and into the next room—a meager kitchen with a wood-burning stove built into the wall. "How much money are you talking about?"

The Elder nodded to Rainer as if returning to a prior discussion. "We would start small with perhaps a million dollars," Rainer said.

"Why do you want to use me and my friend?"

"If your returns are in fact as you say, they are admirable," Rainer answered.

"You and your friend are not known," the Elder added. "That is to our advantage. You will report to Dr. Rainer."

The Elder wasn't offering him a choice. It was a major risk. First, he'd have to convince his friend Kenneth. And yet no one had ever gotten this close to the Elder.

* * *

Three weeks before the Festival in Santiago de Compostela, four months after he first met the Elder, Stephen Oroya visited Kenneth Shawcross's home overlooking Gibraltar Bay. As Kenneth studied the accounts Rainer had provided, Stephen examined a gilt-framed painting above the fireplace—the Rock of Gibraltar floating in a powder-blue sky on an azure sea. On the mantel beneath stood an antique clock adorned with a nubile girl, a young Venus or was it Eve holding an apple? Beside that stood two miniature sculptures of crusaders in chain mail, one in a white tunic with a red cross, hoisting a flag, the other in black chain mail. Kenneth and his wife collected and sold these memorabilia in the antique shop downstairs that she'd inherited from her father. The accumulation and clutter depressed Stephen.

Kenneth looked up from the papers. "I thought you said we'd earn a quick 60-100,000 quid. Now we're handling $25 million, and they want us to handle over a hundred million dollars? We have to report that."

"Not yet." Stephen sat on the Victorian sofa opposite him. "He's just starting to trust me."

"Don't be naïve," Kenneth said. "He's laundering money. He doesn't trust you. And I hope you don't trust him."

"If we do this, I'll be able to get into his camp soon."

"Do you know where these funds come from?" Kenneth asked.

"Not entirely, but I will."

"What happens if we lose money in the investments?"

"We can set up separate accounts for him."

"Double books?" Kenneth rubbed his palm over his balding head and took off his tortoiseshell glasses.

"You can show profits whatever happens in the markets, and you can also show the authorities that you were sequestering suspicious funds." Stephen's quick dark eyes met Kenneth's.

"Why not just tell the authorities what you suspect?"

"The authorities may be part of the problem."

"Doesn't his man check and audit the accounts?"

"Yes, but he's lazy. As long as I operate in a way he understands and we report good results, he'll go along, at least till the end of the year. He lives in Dubai. Meanwhile we'll collect commissions. Maybe you can actually keep some of these antiques Irene likes." He gestured to the mantel. "And take a vacation! The two of you have been running your grandfather's investment firm and her grandfather's antique business your whole lives while your sons are off enjoying school in London."

"Actually, Oxbridge," Kenneth said with pride.

"Both of them?"

"Michael goes to Cambridge in the fall, and David is at Oxford."

"Congratulations."

"All right, six months," Kenneth said. "So, what happens next?"

"I start growing my beard again. We're meeting in two weeks when he tells me his second condition before he'll bring me to his camp."

Irene stepped into the room carrying a silver tray. Stephen rose to help her set the tray between them. "Kenneth tells me you've taken up flying," she said. Stephen took a plate from the tray and selected tea sandwiches. "I've always wanted to fly," she added.

Kenneth looked over at his wife of twenty-two years. "Since when?"

"You don't know everything about me," she answered coquettishly, though to Stephen nothing was coquettish about her in her flowered polyester dress, thick ankles, black shoes, and graying hair.

"I'll take you up some time," Stephen offered, "though I'm only licensed for light aircraft, but it's lovely flying over the desert."

"Where are you living these days, Stephen?" she asked.

"Here and there . . . you know, wherever I find the most trouble." He smiled, showing his dimple.

* * *

Safir handed his typed response in an envelope to the courier: *Let me release her. The press has complied with stories. The Spanish markets have fallen. You have made your profit and your point. I'll leave her at Tenerife.*

Two days later the reply came with the same message: *Send the girl!*

At midnight men in hooded shirts pulled a van up to the pink apartment building where Monte was held in a back room. They blindfolded and handcuffed her and drove her away while Safir slept down the road in a hotel with air conditioning and a slight ocean breeze.

The next morning when he arrived at the apartment, Monte was gone. "Where is she?" he demanded of the three teenage boys left behind.

"They took her away."

"Who took her?"

"Men came and took her away."

"Bloody hell!" Safir searched the building, the parking lot, the town. "Bloody hell!" he kept saying to himself.

Finally, he returned to Agadir, where he pretended to live, and he waited. He read the papers, which continued to speculate on Monte's whereabouts, even local papers. The story was bigger than he'd anticipated. He should have taken a less-known woman. He'd been trying to impress the Elder who had instructed him: *Go to the Festival, choose a hostage, an American woman. We will let her go after a few weeks, after we have profited and shown what we can do. Fear is our weapon. It gives us power.*

Safir hadn't known there would be an attack at the Festival, but when it occurred, it gave him cover. The Elder's men helped him get away. The Elder wasn't responsible for the attack, he said, but he knew it was going to happen. Safir wondered how the Elder knew and how he played off his networks. Soon he hoped to get close enough to find out.

A week after Monte was taken from the apartment in Cape Bojador, Safir received word: *Credentials accepted. We will come for you.*

CHAPTER SEVEN

MONTE STAGGERED OUT of the Land Rover that had driven her from the blacked-out room in Cape Bojador deep into the wind-swept desert. Sand stretched in all directions, brown rolling hills of sand falling into flat parched plains of gray gravel with a few small trees and shrubs. She noted a fierce outcropping of rocks cutting through the land. There were no roads here, no paths to this place, only the tracks from the car and the fading footprints of camels, all of which would disappear with the first wind.

She'd been on the road at least twenty-four hours, pummeling over sand and dirt at speeds that terrified her. At first, she tried to remember turns and sounds, but finally she gave up and tried instead to sleep, hoping she would survive the journey.

When someone finally pulled off the cloth covering her eyes, light assaulted her. A dozen men in dusty pants and robes argued nearby in Arabic and in a language she didn't recognize. Stephen was not among them. As much as she'd cursed Stephen, she trusted him when he told her he would release her soon. But now here she was in the middle of nowhere. A hundred meters away flaps of large sand-colored tents fluttered in the hot breeze and next to them all-wheel-drive cars and rows of camels. The tents held ten to fifteen people; she saw only men except for one old woman who stepped out of a tent to witness her arrival.

Someone clipped off her plastic cuffs and shoved her stumbling in cheap bedroom slippers into a small tent next to a garbage dump. Inside, a mat spread in one corner, two sleeping bags, an abandoned backpack in a heap on the tarp, a low wooden crate, two dirty blue cushions. In an attached lean-to, a makeshift toilet dispensed lye over a bottomless pit. The heat was overwhelming. Her heart was beating fast. Was this the hovel where she was to stay? By the tent flap sprawled a canvas bag of water with two plastic bottles in the dirt. She'd have to ration the water. How long would they keep her here? Who else had been here? Would she be moved . . . or executed?

"Help!" she wanted to shout, but there was no one to help her. She looked around for an escape. She longed suddenly for her own cramped bathroom where she and Philip elbowed for space at the sink in the morning and alternated who got the hot shower. She ached for her children, longed to give them their warm baths in the evening. Emma still cuddled with her, but Craig at five was already turning into a young boy and was starting kindergarten any day. She'd miss his first day at the American School in Cairo. She longed for her home so desperately that she felt physical pain, a constriction around her heart.

The first night in the tent, Monte tossed between a restless sleep and panic. She smelled the offal of the camp—camel dung and human waste and meat gone bad—when suddenly she felt a man's foul breath beside her. He stuffed a rag into her mouth. She couldn't see him in the dark but felt his fingers fumbling to pull down her pants. She tried to struggle, but another set of hands held her down. The man mounted her, thrusting a flaccid penis between her legs. He probed, pushed, pressed until it finally stiffened and entered her like a small weapon forced around and around inside her. "Whore . . ." he muttered in low guttural English. "You whore . . ." He couldn't come and kept pressing harder and harder until finally he let out a moan. When Monte tried to resist, he took his knife and drew blood from the flesh of her neck. He ordered the other man to follow him. Twice his size, this man climbed onto her and was at first gentle with her, at least by comparison, but then he drove into her with the force of a missile all the way up her spine until she thought he would snap her in two. She struggled not to lose consciousness.

For the next week the man and his companion entered her tent each night and entered her body. She lay in dread all day, inert, wounded, drained by the suffocating heat. Her hair matted against her head, gritty with sand and sweat. She tried to remember her training, but nothing had prepared her for these assaults. She tried to plan an escape, but two guards sat in front of her tent. Where would she go? There was only empty desert all around. As she lay in the heat, she dreamed of the desert on the edge of Cairo where tourists rode camels around the pyramids. She once rode a friend's white stallion in the desert, galloping across the sand at sunset, a pyramid in the distance. "If we keep going, where will we end up?" she asked. "Libya," he answered. She returned to his home on the edge of the desert, exhilarated from the ride to find Philip on the terrace deep in conversation with her friend's wife.

The next night when the men entered her tent and climbed on her, she tried to return in her mind to the horse galloping away, but instead she thought of Philip with her friend's wife, all the occasions she'd seen them talking together—the young French wife lonely in Cairo—and Philip, her own quiet, accommodating husband. She tried to flee in her mind while her body endured each night. One night she managed to reach Paris in her mind where she sat in a café drinking espresso and jus d'orange pressé and eating a baguette with raspberry jam. She walked the length of the Champs-Élysées and sat for her portrait on Montparnasse until a woman in the shadows stole her purse and a man abducted her, and she returned hard and spent to the desert.

Monte thought about ending her life, but her children kept creeping into her thoughts and wouldn't let her go. She saw Emma twirling in a new yellow dress Philip bought her. "Daddy, will you marry me?" she asked. Craig told her she couldn't marry her own father with such authority that Monte wondered when he figured that out. She tried to think about Philip too, but she couldn't hold him in her mind without wondering if someone had wedged into their marriage.

As the first week passed, Monte began to lose her ability to think. She'd start a thought, then doze or veer off in panic. Finally, one evening in a burst of action, before the men came into the tent, she took her sheet and slipped out the rear where she dug a hole near a scrub palm tree. She didn't know if they'd find her there and drag her back in and beat her or even kill her; but she sensed they wouldn't violate her in the open. She felt safer under the light of the moon. To her surprise no one came for her.

Stephen showed up the next day and found her dirty and huddled in her hole, wrapped in a sheet under the scrawny tree. When he saw her, his expression recoiled, and anger swept over his face. When she told him what had happened, he stormed off. An hour later he returned. He told her that she would not be touched again. He told the Elder and his men that she was his and negotiated for her protection. He didn't tell her what he negotiated.

"I won't let that happen again," he promised.

"You're not here," she said. "You don't have the power."

"You must come inside the tent. You'll be released soon," he assured. "You were never to have been brought here."

"You'll have to drag me kicking and screaming and bind me to get me in that tent," Monte answered in a voice barely a whisper. She huddled in the corner of her sand berm with her two plastic bottles of water. In the morning she'd slip under the back of the tent to get the bowl of porridge and bread that was left for her and in the evening she retrieved the lentils and rice.

"You can't live out here," Stephen said. "I'll protect you."

"I am not yours!"

Stephen returned three days later with Tayri, an elderly Berber woman whose brown skin was wrinkled and baked by the sun. Her black hair, streaked with gray, cascaded onto her narrow shoulders. Monte stared into her dark probing eyes as Tayri climbed into the bunker of sand and took Monte's hand.

"*Vous êtes une femme avec un destin*," she spoke in French. "You are being prepared, though you feel you are being punished. You will find courage and lead others."

Monte didn't know who this woman was or what destiny she thought Monte had. Monte wondered if she was crazed. Tayri stared deep into her eyes and continued in French, "There are scorpions and vipers in the desert. You will die if you stay here. You must come inside. I will stay with you." Tayri gave Monte her hand and lifted her from the hole.

* * *

"Why did you take me?" Monte asked Stephen the first time he came into the tent. Until then he'd only talked with Tayri outside.

In Cape Bojador he'd checked on her twice a day but never came into the room. Tonight, he sat on a dusty pillow in the dark. She watched him as he looked around at the sleeping bags on the ground and at the wood crate that served as a table. The tent rose just four feet from the earth except at the center so he couldn't stand upright. There was no light, no ventilation.

Monte sat cross-legged opposite him. She noted a curly black beard now spread on his face. She didn't hate him as she hated the men who'd raped her, but she wanted retribution. At the same time, she needed him as an ally.

Stephen pulled a scented candle from his pack and lit it, setting it on the crate between them. Monte wore the same khaki slacks and white shirt from the day she was abducted. She'd lost weight and her clothes hung off her hips and shoulders. She washed them and herself once a week, but water was so scarce that she and her clothes remained grubby. Her hair was tied back with a string she found and now cherished for it allowed her to lift her hair off her neck in the heat.

Outside the tent Tayri stood in the moonlight, silhouetted against the canvas. Monte wondered if Tayri was giving them privacy or taking an excuse to get air.

Monte had been in the camp over a month and in captivity seven weeks. She counted the time by the fullness of the moon. Most nights she stepped outside to look up at the moon and remind herself of a world beyond. Her guards allowed this liberty; they were usually mildly stoned by then. She didn't know how they got their drugs, especially the khat, this deep in the desert.

"Who are these people?" she asked Stephen. "Will they kill me? Please tell me." No one talked to her. No one told her anything. She wrapped her arms around herself. It was cooler tonight and dark earlier. It must be almost October. She had no one to answer her

questions. Stephen had kept his promise, and the others had stayed
away. Tayri said she didn't know the answers though Monte suspected she knew more than she was saying. Tayri treated her stream
of questions like metaphysical inquiries, answering, *"Ça sera
revélé."*—It will be revealed. Or, *"Tout dans son temps."*—All in its
time. When Monte expressed a hope of any kind, Tayri blessed it.
"Enshallah."

When Stephen didn't answer, Monte asked, "How long will Tayri
stay?" She didn't know what hold Stephen had on this woman or
what debt she might be paying him, but Monte was grateful for her
quiet company.

"Is there anything you need?" Stephen asked.

"I need you to let me go!" she declared and stared at him directly
through the shadows and tried to meet his eyes which continued to
avoid hers. She noticed his gaze fall on the two tin bowls and plates
lined up on the ground and the plastic bottles next to them. She and
Tayri tried to keep the space neat, but the sand and dust were relent-
less. Depending on the wind's direction, the smell of refuse was
overwhelming. Tonight, the wind blew away from the camel pen
and trash pit. Usually, they wore cloths tied around their faces to
filter out the stench and the sand.

"You will be released soon," Stephen said as he had before. His
deep-set hazel eyes finally met hers in the flickering candlelight.

"Can you bring me books?" Monte asked.

"Yes. I can do that." He seized the request.

"A Greek dictionary . . . ancient Greek if you can find it." For a
moment she let go her total despair and allowed herself to want
something she might have.

*   *   *

The next time Stephen visited, he entered the tent with an armful of books, which he dumped on the crate in front of Monte, including a worn ancient Greek dictionary. He also gave her a flashlight. She had been captive over two months. Seeing him stirred her anger and also her relief. Except for Tayri, he was the only company she had. "Why did you take me?" she asked again.

"You earned me credibility."

"Credibility with whom?"

"The man who runs this camp." Stephen appeared more relaxed tonight as he settled on the pillow by the crate. He handed her a spare set of batteries.

"Is he the one who raped me?" She had figured this much. She repressed her anger so she could gather information the way she used to do in the streets and markets of Cairo. She was a professional, she reminded herself; she must act like one. "What does he want? Why do you want credibility?"

Stephen spread the books on the table—an old paperback of Shakespeare's tragedies, John Milton's *Paradise Lost*, a battered edition of the first volume of Herodotus, a worn edition of *Oeuvres de Robespierre*, *Arabian Days and Nights* by Nagib Mafouz, and two thriller paperbacks in Spanish. He appeared to be waiting for her to thank him, or at least acknowledge, this small library he'd brought her.

Instead, she demanded, "Who *are* you?"

Stephen touched his beard with his fingertips. He stood and moved to the center of the tent. "That is not your concern. You will be released soon," he said, and he left.

When Tayri returned, Monte asked if she'd heard anything about her release.

"Ce n'est pas le temps," Tayri answered.

"Then when is the time?" Monte asked in French. "How much longer?"

"He is trying," Tayri said.

*   *   *

The only visitors to Monte's tent beside Stephen were her guards who shoved in food twice a day. The other men in the camp lived in tents a football field away. She was relieved they left her alone, but she feared the time would arrive when they came for her despite Stephen—or maybe with Stephen—to take her away to kill her, perhaps for the cameras.

To manage her fears and wrest control of her thoughts, Monte set out a routine each day, rising before dawn and exercising in the middle of the tent while Tayri slept on a sleeping bag in the corner. Before the sun came up and the heat suffocated her, she did sit-ups and push-ups and stretches. She often felt queasy in the morning, but she made herself exercise before eating the bowl of watery, tasteless porridge that was pushed through the tent flap. She then read at the table the books Stephen had brought. She started with Robespierre, the French revolutionary who espoused freedom and equality, universal suffrage, abolition of slavery, and the end of the death penalty at the same time he executed without trial the King and used terror as a tool to eliminate the aristocracy and his enemies.

As she read, she watched a sand lizard in the corner that mutated during the day to the color of the sand. At night it grew darker, its color regulating its temperature, turning dark to absorb heat in the cool evening and fading into almost translucence at noon. Tayri told her the lizards that ran through the sand were harmless, but the snakes and scorpions could kill her. Each night Monte shook out her mat looking for snakes and scorpions.

When the heat of the day grew unbearable, she and Tayri slept, and the lizard burrowed into the sand. Monte usually awakened an hour or two before the sun went down and studied the ancient Greek vocabulary she once mastered as an undergraduate. She practiced by reading the first volume of Herodotus, which Stephen found for her in the Greek—an unexpected gesture. She appreciated the discontinuity of her study and her circumstances, but she was trying to hold onto something familiar, even an irrelevant skill in a dead language.

In the evening, she and Tayri shared at their makeshift table a meal of rice or pasta, sometimes lentils, sometimes bread and an occasional orange. Monte refused to eat the random meat offered— goat or dog or maybe rat. Rice wouldn't kill her, but rotten meat could. She was fed a subsistence diet, not more than 900 calories. She left a lentil or two for the lizard that walked along the rim of the crate looking for scraps. She'd never liked pets, had resisted Samantha's cats and dogs and parakeets, but for the first time she wanted to relate to this other creature. She studied it, trying to find a connection.

Tayri spent her days sewing and embroidering a very long piece of cloth as though content in this small, precise work that one day would be . . . what?

Outside the tent in the distance, Monte occasionally heard cars and even an airplane arriving and voices shouting, but she was too far away to make out the words. She stayed inside during the day so no one would be reminded she was there. Her fate, she assumed, was in Stephen's hands. Tayri said Stephen was trying for her, but trying what?

Only with Stephen could she talk, and that fact unnerved her. She knew the signs of Stockholm syndrome. Stephen assured her he was not her captor, but as far as she saw, he was the link to her freedom.

"Why did you take me?" she repeated her question the next time he came. He brought her a white kaftan she could wear instead of her fraying slacks and shirt. Her clothes had grown more uncomfortable. The loose full-length dress would give her freedom of movement and allow air to circulate around her, but she left the dress on the crate unopened in the cellophane package while he was there. She didn't thank him. He was the one who kept her here, or at least hadn't succeeded in getting her released. She'd been captive over three months.

"You raised the stakes," he answered, leaning on the pillow, a folded sleeping bag propping up his elbow.

"Have you asked a ransom for me?" she asked. "How much? You know the U.S. government won't pay, and my family can't pay." Her family could pay or raise the funds, but they would likely feel obliged to follow the government's directive. She wondered who was negotiating on her behalf and who was searching for her. She knew at any moment the men in the camp could come in and kill her, or a Special Forces team could sweep in and rescue her. Yet as time dragged on, she feared she was left there to exist by herself. "What were the stakes?" she asked. When Stephen didn't answer, she asked, "Is Robespierre your role model?"

Stephen smiled as though following her line of reasoning. "This isn't about me. And Robespierre miscalculated history."

"Of course it is about you. You are the reason I'm here. You gave me these books, which I assume are yours or books you've read."

"Or books I found at a local bookstall." He smiled again. Even with the full beard, his smile brightened his face.

"Where would that bookstall be?" Monte asked.

"There are many bookstalls . . . even bookstores in Ouagadougou, Nouakchott, Timbuktu, Niamey, and in Tamanghasset."

"You won't tell me where I am?"

"Better to live in your mind. It's safer there. I'm trying to ensure you're left alone to do so." That night he didn't say she would be released soon.

CHAPTER EIGHT

"WE HAVE TO PREPARE for the worst, Sam," Cal said.

They were sitting in a pub down the road from Samantha's South Kensington flat. Outside, London's late afternoon shadows closed in. The air was chilled, but inside a fire blazed for the few patrons.

"It's been over three months. Nobody has contacted us or claimed credit. We're still not even certain she was kidnapped." Cal dumped ketchup on his plate of fish and chips. His hair was uncombed, in need of a trim.

"I'm sure she was taken." Samantha hadn't touched the omelet in front of her. She'd been unable to eat a full meal since Monte disappeared. "And I am *not* prepared for the worst. I can't accept the worst!"

Cal touched his sister's hand to steady her. "Monte is a pro. If she was kidnapped, she'll know what to do. She probably speaks the language."

Samantha poured them both more coffee. "Is this you preparing me for the worst?"

"It's me being schizophrenic. I spend half my time these days trying to give Mom and Dad hope, then I go home and make dinner for my daughters and pretend life without their mother is fun, and they are at least luckier than their cousins whose mother has disappeared. I crash alone in my study each night imagining the worst for everyone but only after I've gone through all my notes about Monte to see if we've missed anything. By the way, you look terrible."

"Did you fly across the Atlantic to cheer me up?"

Cal smiled. "I'm on my way to Pakistan to cover the state of emergency there."

"How can you do that? I'm having trouble covering anything. My producer told me the other day the news waits for no man or woman."

"He didn't say that?"

"He did."

"Idiot," Cal said. "But I can't afford to stop working with two daughters and an ex-wife to feed so I'll get to interview Musharraf while looking over my shoulder for terrorists. It's a snake pit there."

"Be careful."

Cal leaned toward Samantha in the wooden booth. An old-fashioned gas lamp cast shadows between them. "You too."

"I'm thinking of going to Cairo to help with Emma and Craig. Lala called and told me I should go."

"She called me too. She said my girls could stay at their apartment anytime. She said she and Marjorie have bought *Bedknobs and Broomsticks* and *The Sound of Music* and have Scrabble and Monopoly." Cal and Samantha both smiled; they had the same broad grin.

"I call Philip once a week," Samantha said, "but he won't talk about what's happened. Maybe I should go home to D.C. instead."

"Go help Philip. And you must eat!"

Samantha pushed her omelet around the plate then took a bite and spread grape jelly on a cold piece of brown bread.

"I'm sorry to leave you with this," Cal said.

"Just come back. I may be in Cairo if I can buy time from my producers. I've told them I'm on to a story about drug and arms smuggling. That always keeps them interested."

"Is there a story?"

"I've uncovered some leads as I've investigated Monte, though in West Africa, not Cairo. But everything connects."

*   *   *

Samantha lay awake in her flat overlooking Queens Gate listening to the late-night patrons coming out of the pub on the corner. She dozed then woke again to the sound of the street cleaners' trucks swishing down the road before the sun came up. She was leaving for Cairo in a few hours. In the corner of her bedroom sat her packed suitcases. She hadn't seen Monte's children in almost a year. She wanted to be a better aunt. Losing Monte held up a mirror, and she wasn't entirely happy with what she saw. When her partner Evan had been killed last year, the same mirror showed her hurrying around the globe but missing her life. The month before, she had canceled a trip with Evan because of a story she could no longer remember. He'd said he had something to ask her, and she'd worried he was going to propose.

"Do you love him?" Cal had asked when they met on a flyby at Charles de Gaulle airport, Cal on his way back to D.C., and she en route to . . . where?

"I don't know. How do I know?"

"You know," Cal answered. "That is the one thing you have to know even if it doesn't last."

That she didn't know, had never known, worried her in a corner of her being she mostly ignored, though lately the question stirred. Evan's sudden death had knocked her off her base like a speeding truck in the dark without headlights, sideswiping her after it leveled Evan 3,500 miles away in the mountains of Afghanistan. That speeding truck with no lights had now veered again and taken Monte.

*   *   *

Samantha arrived in Cairo on a late November afternoon and moved into Monte's gated apartment on a tree-lined street. She slept on a brown fold-out sofa in Monte's study full of books and papers. She'd never stayed in her sister's house before. She always stayed at a hotel with a business center.

Each morning she rose early to make breakfast for the children. After school she took them to get treats or to the park and on weekends they'd go to Old Town Cairo and to the pyramids. Wherever they went, the children asked her to tell them stories. "Tell me a scary story," Emma, age three, insisted. Craig, who was five, helped create the villains in the stories. Emma and Craig featured as the heroes. They invented Baboosh, the crazy camel; Scratch, the mean cat; Gravlox, the green monster; Audrey, the peacock; and Upton, the dragon who hid behind curtains spying on everyone. Samantha provided the narrative, instructing on how to avoid, tame, and prevail over scary and unexpected creatures in the world.

At dinner Philip presided at the kitchen table. He'd put on weight, and his thinning hair made him look older than he was. He ate too much bread and drank large quantities of soda. She didn't know Philip well and hadn't really tried to know him. She knew he was proficient with numbers and balance sheets.

"How was your day?" he asked the children each night.

"Tell me a scary story," Emma replied.

"I don't know any scary stories," he answered.

Emma turned to Samantha. "Tell me a scary story."

"She has an insatiable appetite for stories," Samantha said.

"It's her way of coping, I guess," Philip said.

Samantha had never heard Philip tell a story. She asked the children if their mother told them stories. "Sometimes," Craig answered.

Nobody talked about Monte. Samantha was the only one who mentioned her name, which she did several times a day.

When the children were at school, Samantha pursued her own story. She was following the lead on a Cairo banker—Emile Lafourche—whom she suspected of facilitating illegal arms and drug trades and money laundering. His name appeared on a list of participants at a technology conference that she arranged to attend. She met him in the lounge.

He smiled at her behind fashionable Olin sunglasses. He was wearing an expensive light gray suit and a yellow silk tie. She started off with an easy question about the financial worlds of Cairo. He answered in a patronizing tone. She tried to watch his eyes as he spoke, but he never took off his sunglasses.

"How prevalent is smuggling in Egypt?" she finally asked.

"What kind of smuggling?"

She kept her tone innocent. "Illicit flows of diamonds, heroin, cocaine, arms."

He waved to the waiter for the check and handed him a wad of bills, telling him to keep the change. "If you tell me how to contact you, I'll see what I can find out." He stood.

"I'll contact *you*," Samantha said.

He pulled out a silver card case and handed her an embossed business card.

When she phoned his office the following day, she was told he was traveling. She left her number. She tried a second time, then a third. From a former employee Samantha had secured a statement from the Cairo bank showing large sums of money coming in then quickly being transferred to accounts in Cyprus and Dubai without proper documentation. When the employee had questioned the transactions, he'd been let go.

Samantha went to the bank, an old stone building in downtown Cairo among the Parisian buildings with cast iron balconies and balustrades. The receptionist made a call, then reported that Mr. Lafourche was out of the country. When Samantha asked when he was expected to return, the receptionist, without checking, said he was out of the country indefinitely.

At dinner Samantha asked Philip if he would look at the bank statement and talk her through it as it might relate to Egyptian customs and taxes.

"That's not my field," he said. "You'll have to find someone else." He was rushing the children through dinner.

"Is anything wrong?" she asked.

"I need to go out later. Will you be here for the children or shall I get Farha?"

"I'm here if you need." She tried to catch his eye, but he avoided looking at her as he cut Emma's dinner. "Are you sure nothing is wrong?"

He looked up then and met her question. "A great deal is wrong, starting with the absence of their mother, but we have to cope."

She noted he said "their mother," not "my wife" or "Monte." She glimpsed the strained edges of her sister's marriage.

*   *   *

Before Christmas, Philip told Samantha that she needed to leave. They were sitting in the narrow living room after the children had gone to bed. The room was crowded with bright pillows on the floor and toys tucked in every corner. Philip got annoyed at the disorder in the rooms, but he never got angry at the children, only at the housekeeper.

"I appreciate what you're trying to do," he said, looking her straight in the eye now, "but you're taking work from Farha, and she's complaining. The children are becoming too dependent on you. When you leave, it will be even harder for them."

Samantha sucked in air as if she'd been hit in the stomach. She started to protest, but she saw Philip grimace in anticipation. She saw how much he was holding back. "I have to find a way to go forward . . ." he said, ". . . in case she doesn't return."

"I feel guilty," Samantha confessed. She hadn't said that to anyone but Cal. "I'm the one who insisted Monte come to Spain. I left her while I went to file a story that day."

"We all feel guilty,"

"You're not guilty."

Philip leaned forward and poured them tea. He was wearing jeans and a loose gray shirt, the kind worn by shopkeepers in the bazaar. "We're all guilty." He didn't explain.

"I'll move out next week," Samantha said. "But I'd like to stay nearby. I'm working on a story."

"I can't tell you where to live."

CHAPTER NINE

MONTE HAD BEEN in the camp fourteen weeks when Stephen visited the next time. He brought her a copy of a book he'd written—his master's thesis at university. She opened the thin volume *Chaos and Old Night: A Study in the New Revolution*. She checked the title page—by Stephen Carlos Oroya—and the copyright page: published by a small reputable London publisher.

"You're an academic revolutionary?" she asked. "You've stepped way over the line here, you know."

"Read my book, then we can argue."

She read the book that week. She found it derivative: a rehashing of arguments about colonialism's hold through financial and security structures—banks, police, and military—which kept citizens in the colonial orbit. There were a few luminous passages, including his insistence that religion and politics should be kept separate. This argument undermined the profile she'd been forming of a jihadist. Finally, he questioned the whole underlying premise of the state as an organizing principle.

She studied the photo on the jacket taken more than a decade before, a picture of a handsome man in his late twenties with dark curling hair. He was smiling in front of a bridge, having set down his marker on the planet of ideas. She wondered if he had anyone else to talk to. She also wondered if he realized he'd now given her tools to find him should she ever get away.

*   *   *

Stephen started coming to the camp every week with the supply run and stopping by Monte's tent in the evening after his sessions with the Elder. In between visits Monte's anger at him simmered, but when he was there, she had someone to talk to. They talked late into the night about books as if they were graduate students, though she didn't forget where she was and who was responsible for her being there.

During the rest of her time, even with her reading and studying, her mind wandered. She reviewed her abduction over and over, tried to put together clues she'd missed. She'd been preoccupied that day with the argument she'd had with Philip before she'd left home. His refusal to follow her to Indonesia took her by surprise. She'd missed, or ignored, the gulf growing between them, telling herself she was too busy, that they were too busy, telling herself it was a phase of marriage, that Philip should be more understanding. As her career accelerated, he'd grown remote, almost passive. Maybe it was too exhausting being married to her. Why hadn't she asked to speak with him that night when she'd phoned home? Pride. Why hadn't she confided her troubles to Samantha? Again, pride. She always wanted to look good in her sister's eyes. She'd spent so much of her childhood living in Samantha's shadow, trying to please her sister and her parents, that she felt free to be herself only after she'd married and moved away.

But she still was trying to prove herself. But to whom? Her job and family had been her anchor and now both were taken from her. In this desert wasteland no one knew her or cared about her or her family, and all her dramas seemed petty excuses for her appalling lack of judgment that day. Had she gone with Stephen because he'd favored her over Samantha? It was an alarming thought, but she didn't dismiss it entirely. She had acted unprofessionally, and she blamed herself as she knew others would blame her.

In the tent she'd found an abandoned knapsack with a Bible and an old French geographic magazine that had an article on the Sahara. She wondered who had been there before her. Another hostage? In the Bible, Moses fled to the back side of the desert and hid there, tending his father-in-law's flock after he'd killed the Egyptian soldier. But Moses's desert was the Sinai, not the Sahara. The Sinai was 130 miles across, not 3,100 miles. The Sinai was 23,000 square miles. The Sahara was over three million square miles—3,360,000 square miles—according to the magazine. The Sahara spread over eleven countries. Monte had some sympathy for Moses. The back side of the desert was no-man's- or woman's-land. No flocks could have survived where she was. There was no Mount Horeb, only an outcropping of rocks and shifting dunes in the middle of a continent where occasionally nomads still passed on camels the same way they'd traveled thousands of years ago. Monte longed for a connection. She longed for the burning bush and the blinding light.

*   *   *

It was the end of November, almost Thanksgiving in the U.S., Monte calculated. The days had grown cooler, the temperature no longer above one hundred degrees. She heard cars and planes arriving more frequently, mostly at night. In the distance she heard weapons firing, usually in the mornings. She'd been captive eighteen weeks. She'd asked Stephen what went on in the camp, but he didn't tell her. She wondered if some operation was being planned.

Though she continued to exercise every day, she felt weaker. Her bodily functions had been erratic since she'd been here. She began skipping the afternoon nap. After Tayri and the guards fell asleep, she slipped out and sat at the back of the tent overlooking the camp, blending in against the canvas. Could she escape? Where would she escape to? She had no idea where she was or how far away a village or an oasis was. She asked Tayri who said she didn't know. Monte still had some faith that Stephen would get her released or that a Special Forces team would swoop in and rescue her. As she sat outside in her loose kaftan with her sheet wrapped around her shoulders to protect her from the sun, she sweated and watched over the bleak landscape while the camp slept and the sun beat down. The camels sank to their knees. She dozed against the tent, tucking herself into the corner that cast a shadow.

One afternoon she heard the buzzing of an aircraft even before she saw the wings of the plane emerge from the blue-white sky. It landed half a mile away. A man in a white robe rushed out limping between tents, rallying the other men, who hurried to meet the plane. Some men jumped into cars; others mounted the camels. All had crates already loaded as they advanced toward the landing strip. They returned an hour later without the crates, but with other baggage, including bundles of branches. Monte now at least understood how the khat arrived. She assumed the bundles contained other contraband.

That evening Stephen appeared at her tent. She'd taken her weekly sponge bath in the late afternoon so she was freshly scrubbed with the bar of lemon-scented soap he'd brought her. Her light brown hair was also washed with the soap and rinsed to the extent possible with the one plastic bottle of water she allowed herself each week for bathing. Her hair fell straight to her shoulders. She was wearing the white kaftan he'd given her. She sat barefoot on the tarp, her flimsy bedroom slippers tucked at the edge of the tent. She didn't know what had happened to her sturdy leather sandals.

Stephen seemed preoccupied. She wanted to ask what had happened in his meeting with the Elder as if he and she were friends or even spouses at the end of the day. "How was your day?" her son Craig used to ask with mimed maturity, and her daughter Emma copied him, asking: "How was your day?" when Monte and Philip came home from work in the evening. Hearing them now in her head, she felt a sudden pain. She wanted to hold them, to hold someone, but the emptiness stretched before her.

Stephen lit a scented candle and set it on the crate and settled next to her. Each visit he brought her some small luxury. Tonight, he gave her a box of mint tea and a tin of cookies, which she shared with Tayri, who took hers outside. Monte could see in Stephen's eyes, which darted around to the desolate corners of the tent, that her extremity unsettled him. She doubted he'd thought through the consequences of abducting her. She suspected the consequences were not in his control, and that frightened her. At one level he was at ease with her as if he understood who she was and where she came from while the others, including Tayri and her guards, looked at her as though she were from another world, which is how she saw herself. But she and Stephen were also playing a game. Through him she glimpsed her exit, but she had to play her very few and weak cards strategically. She'd been in captivity over four months. Soon it would be Christmas.

He'd told her he was writing a book about the Elder. Abducting her had gotten him access to the camp and to the Elder, but her captivity was only to have been for a few weeks. She knew this was not the full story, but that was all she'd managed to extract so far.

Stephen heated the water for the tea in a tin bowl over the candle. Outside, a camel bellowed in the distance. Stephen had trimmed his beard, which allowed the shape of his strong face to emerge. His black hair curled like a bramble on his head. He was wearing a navy dashiki and loose cotton pants. He'd taken off his sandals and set them at the edge of the tent beside her slippers. Their bare feet touched lightly on the tarp. He had bought her lemon-scented hand cream along with the soap on his last visit, and she'd rubbed it sparingly onto her feet and calves and hands which ached for moisture. Her small toes stirred at the touch of his and didn't move away.

"Were you here for the shipment that came in today?" she asked.

"I came with the plane."

"What else was on the plane?"

"Better not to know," he answered.

"Do you know?"

"Not everything."

"I assume guns and drugs going in different directions?"

"The less you know, the safer you are," he said.

"Are you safe? Are you part of the traffic?" They talked in low, conspiratorial tones, their feet moving casually against each other. They hadn't touched like this before. Monte felt a small release just to be touching another human being.

"I'm watching," Stephen said. "Something is being planned. But the Elder will open up to me only so far."

"What do you think it is?"

Stephen handed her the tin bowl of tepid tea with a weak peppermint flavor. "We see the world very differently," he said. For a moment she thought he was talking about her. "How does that happen?"

The question seemed naïve to Monte. "You must not have had brothers or sisters," she said.

"Once I had a brother."

"What happened to him?" Stephen didn't answer. Instead, he put his hand on her leg and left it there. She shook her head no.

"Are you sure?" He waited, his hooded eyes pulling her into his gaze. When she didn't answer, he moved his hand slowly up her leg, his fingers caressing the inside of her thigh. What was he doing? She felt disembodied as if she were watching herself from the outside at the same time she felt her breath quicken. Did she even occupy herself anymore? His advance arose so unexpectedly she couldn't calculate. He raised her kaftan and slid his hands up her thigh and up her hips and her waist with a tenderness that surprised her while Tayri sat, a looming silhouette against the tent outside in the moonlight. He opened a sleeping bag on the ground. What was he doing? Monte watched herself lie back with him. With hands gentle, yet sure, hands like wings, he swept over her body, which she barely recognized as her body anymore, and suddenly a warm, fierce wind lifted her from the earth. How could she allow him to have her? Did she have a choice? He was her only chance at an exit. Could they trade favors? She wasn't sure she could hold herself together to be this calculating. Why was he doing this? What did he want from her? She shut her eyes and tried to leave her body as she had done before. But he wasn't raping her. He was making love to her, addressing each vibration as though his sole purpose was to give her pleasure. She gasped, surprised that she could still feel pleasure and terrified by what she felt and where she flew with him, to a place she'd never been. She would use him as he was using her, she told herself.

CHAPTER TEN

SAMANTHA TRANSFERRED TO the Cairo bureau in January and rented an apartment near the children in the Maadi district, greener and less fraught than other Cairo neighborhoods and not far from the American School. Most nights she lay awake staring through her apartment window at the dim lights on the road, listening to cars honking in the distance and dogs barking. She no longer believed, as she had as a child, in a great beneficent Being keeping track of everyone scurrying around the globe; but as she lay there, she allowed herself to hope, and longed to know, an immutable power aligning the universe and keeping her sister safe.

She saw Emma and Craig on the weekends and often on Tuesday nights when Philip asked her to babysit. She didn't know where he went and she didn't ask.

Finally, he volunteered, "I have a bridge game with friends from the Embassy." He didn't look at her when he spoke, and she wondered if that was really where he went, then she scolded her suspicious mind. She'd been a journalist too long, she thought.

"I've never been any good at cards," she said.

"Neither was Monte," he answered.

"Neither is Monte," she corrected.

*   *   *

At work Samantha had tracked down information on a bank head-quartered in the Bahamas, part of a wider empire of an Egyptian businessman. She'd uncovered documents and a source who said millions of dollars from heroin and cocaine trafficking were being funneled through this bank to leaders in Hamas and Al Qaeda, and possibly even to Hezbollah. Hamas and Hezbollah might be mortal enemies, but it appeared they shared bankers and middlemen. She was coordinating her research with a fellow reporter in Nassau. In Pakistan, through his military contacts, Cal confirmed heroin routes out of Afghanistan into Pakistan then to Egypt and finally into Europe.

Emil Lafourche, the banker she'd met earlier, worked for a different bank, but Samantha had been shown corresponding transactions between the two banks and suspected he was involved. When she attempted to follow up with him, she was again told he was out of the country; however, she'd spotted him at a reception at the French Embassy. He left before she could corner him.

Two nights later she saw him at an outside café near her apartment with two men. Was that a coincidence? She didn't believe in such coincidences and made the judgment not to confront him there. She slipped in the back entrance of her building and called her producer in London with whom she'd worked over a decade.

"Get yourself security, Sam!" he ordered. "These people wear suits, but they're dangerous. Don't mess around. You think they're connected to your story or your sister's disappearance or both?"

She hadn't mentioned Monte, but Colin knew everything she did these days had a potential link back to her sister.

"I don't know. Trafficking and money laundering are everywhere, like a membrane suffocating the globe. Cairo is one of the nodes. I know there's a criminal network here with money from cocaine, heroin, and arms being washed through the banks. I know some of that treasure is being funneled to terrorist groups."

"Get yourself security!"

Samantha shared some of what she'd uncovered with Philip and asked if he could help her interpret the financial documents she'd gotten a hold of. Instead, he said, "I don't want you taking the children out anymore. It's too dangerous."

"I would never let anything happen to the children," she protested.

"You don't know if you're being watched. You won't see it coming."

"If I'm being watched, I shouldn't come to your home either," she said.

Philip agreed. He said they could meet at the American Embassy on Saturdays. Samantha wanted to protest, but she felt chastened. She hadn't assessed the risk to the children, but Philip had.

"I've applied for a transfer back to the States," he told her. "We're leaving as soon as school is out."

CHAPTER ELEVEN

MONTE DECIDED TO TRY an escape. She slipped out of the tent after Tayri and the guards fell asleep. She ran in the direction the planes came in, ran through the night across the desert, looking for a place to hide. The night was pierced with light, lavish with stars. She had no shoes, only the thin cloth slippers she'd been given from a cheap hotel. The slippers couldn't protect her feet from the stones and gravel or the burning sand when the sun rose. She held a sheet around her shoulders. The air was chilled but would quickly heat with the sun and burn her skin.

She kept looking up at the stars as she weaved over the land seeking shelter. Under her arm she carried two plastic bottles of water, but she knew the water would last barely a day. Her eyes scanned the horizon searching for anything . . . an oasis, a caravan to pick her up and take her to the nearest town . . . how far was the nearest town? She didn't know where she was. She turned north because she could locate the North Star and wanted to aim in some direction; otherwise, she might move in a circle and return to camp; but north may not be the safest direction. Depending on where the camp was located, she could be facing hundreds of miles of desert. Ahead of her was dry, barren land and an endless road to nowhere.

She'd fantasized this escape for months, but now that she'd crept from the tent and plunged across the hard scrabble out of sight, the escape was terrifying. She gasped for breath; a pain shot through her side. As she ran, she lifted her eyes to the moon. Once, she and Emma and Craig and Philip had gone into the Sahara at the edge of Cairo on a moonlit night to visit the pyramids. Her children and her family—all those she'd left behind—could look up at this same moon. She triangulated, sent her thoughts to the moon so they could all meet there.

To find her way she also looked for birds. She'd read that if she was lost, especially in the desert, she should look for birds and follow their flight for they would lead her to water. She searched for birds passing before the moon, but she could see none. Were there birds this deep in the desert? Nothing stirred. The vastness of the land dwarfed her as she wandered over the rocky gray sand, over rolling brown sand. As the sun crept toward the horizon, the sky grew pink. Tayri had told her to put pebbles in her mouth or to chew grass to stop thirst, but there was no grass here. She found three smooth stones, which she slipped under her tongue. She also remembered to breathe through her nose and keep her mouth closed and not to talk, though there was no one to talk to. The silence of the land was complete. There was no stuttering gunfire as there had been at the camp. There was only the quiet, listening universe. Was it listening? Was anyone listening?

She sucked her stones and plunged toward the horizon as a red rim emerged in the dark sky, which now flamed red and pink and orange. The huge yellow sun crept up slowly and then blazed above the edge of the earth, filling her with awe even as she ran in fear. The sun rose in all its splendor, indifferent to her drama on the ground. With its light she expected a four-wheel drive vehicle to appear at any moment with men pointing AK-47s at her and shooting her down like an animal. If she were killed, at least her captivity would be over. Or perhaps she would bake to death, lost forever to her children. She couldn't let that happen. She moistened her lips, sipped the water she'd brought. The sun pressed down, burning off the air. If she could find a finger of shadow, she could curl up in it and rest till evening, but there was no shade anywhere. The soles of her feet began to bake. Months from now would she be found shriveled on the sand?

Then, over the horizon on a camel, riding alone, a figure appeared with the sun at his back. By the way he held his body, upright, confident, swaying with the beast, she knew it was Stephen. Others were out searching in their four-wheel-drive cars, but he had set off on his own. She stuck out her thumb like a hitchhiker—a bad joke. His camel kneeled on its front legs, and he pulled her from the ground onto its back.

"You fool!" he shouted. "They want to kill you. I argue to keep you alive, and this is your gratitude? They will chain you up now!" Was he angry because she would be killed or because she had run away after he'd seduced her, after she'd failed to resist him?

She spat out the stones. "Gratitude? For what?" He was the one who'd brought her here. She understood they wanted to kill her because she knew where they were, because her purpose, whatever it had been, was served. She held onto him from behind, her body pressed against his as the camel lumbered across the land. She was so tired, she rested her head on his back and breathed in his dusty clothes and the pungent odor of the camel. "Why do you keep me alive?" she asked.

"I never intended for you to die," he said as they swayed on the camel, its huge feet padding over the soft sand.

"What did you expect from these men?"

He turned partly in the saddle and unwound the white keffiyeh wrapped around his head and face to protect him from the sun and sand and gave it to her. "I call them *Les Guerriers de l'Enfer*. I will bankrupt them, but it will take time." She leaned against him. "I don't know what they are planning, but something. I need you to help."

"Safi . . ." she called him by this name Tayri used for the first time as if exhaling air. "You will be destroyed."

On a map back at camp he showed her how far away she was from any civilization, how impossible was an escape. He spoke quietly in English as Tayri remained outside. He told her about the accounts he was running for the Elder and told her that he needed her to cooperate to buy time so the Elder wouldn't close the accounts and move camp. They sat together on the two pillows with the rough wooden crate between them.

"What do you know about him?" she asked as he watched her, not with pity but with attention.

"He is smart and cunning, the son of an English mother and Libyan father. His mother died when he was eight. Her family sent him to boarding school where he was teased because of his limp and because rumor was that his father had four wives. They called him 'the Goat.' He saw his father only twice a year. He failed out of university because he spent more time protesting than studying. When he finally left England and his mother's family at nineteen, the smart, argumentative William Foxhall—the name on his birth certificate—disappeared forever.

"His father introduced him to a Bedouin leader, who took him in and trained him in the ways of war. He helped the leader run a training camp for budding revolutionaries in Africa, a camp through which some of the future despotic heads of state emerged. He helped develop ways of financing the operations. Along with an Austrian friend from university, he organized trafficking businesses including drugs, arms, and gems. When his father died and his patron was assassinated, he started his own camp. He was often paid with the resources from the dictator's country. He and his partner also ran a business on the side, skimming profits from their suppliers. He hasn't told me this, but given the figures and his paranoia about others knowing his accounts, I'm fairly certain that's what's going on. That's why he came to me and my friend to invest his money—to grow it and to wash it. It pleases him to be making money in the very markets of those he would destroy."

"What exactly do you do for him?" As Monte listened, she shredded a packet of tissues Safi had given her, creating a small pile of confetti on the crate. When Safi reached for her hand to stop her, she folded her hands in her lap.

"We set up offshore accounts and investments. He pays us commissions from the profits, a complicity he insists on as protection and a sign of loyalty. I must show my loyalty or be killed." Safi met her eyes with a deadly serious stare.

"The Elder is not Al Qaeda?"

"He's ecumenical. Some who come through the camp are Al Qaeda, some Hamas, occasional ETA, former GIA and even Hezbollah though not at the same time. Also new aspiring leaders in West Africa train here, though mostly this is a fueling station where they make deals for the weapons they need. Arms are traded for drugs, which are transported to different destinations, mostly to Europe. There's also traffic in diamonds. Whatever premise your revolution is based on, whatever reason you want to disrupt the systems of the West—and that includes traffickers—you can work with the Elder."

"That is the worst nightmare!" Monte sat forward on her pillow as if in a briefing session about to plan strategy. Her mind turned instinctively to what assets—military and civilian—were available to stop him.

"The locals keep their distance," Safi said. "The Elder pays them off. He's a kind of Azazel."

"Don't be a romantic." Monte challenged the use of the mythical outcast in the desert, thrown out by God.

"He sees himself as Goliath."

"Why hasn't he killed me?"

"He may yet, or at least try, but I've argued for your life. You amuse him, or my request amuses him, for the moment. He sees it as further leverage on me."

"What about the negotiations for my release?"

Safi hesitated. He glanced out the tent flap and frowned. Monte followed his gaze and saw three figures moving across the rocky ground toward them. "There are no negotiations," he said. He looked back at her. "No one knows where you are or who has taken you. The Elder hasn't made contact or asked for ransom."

"What?" Monte's eyes opened wide trying to see Safi more clearly in the shadows. The black hole she feared suddenly expanded before her. "Why not?" She saw the men moving closer. Her determination to resist drained as she grasped that no one knew where she was, that no one was coming for her.

"He likes the anxiety he's caused, exposing the impotence of those who think they are all powerful. But I will get you out," Safi said without conviction.

"When your work is done!" Monte reacted. "I am your hostage after all."

"No," he replied quietly, "you're not, but I want to get you out alive."

"They will find this camp," Monte said.

"I doubt it. We're in a geological aberration here. Those big rocks all round are highly ferrous, defying navigation instruments. On satellite photos, this area appears only as a blur."

"We must be in some country . . . Libya . . . Algeria . . . Mauritania . . . Mali . . . Chad . . . Niger?" Safi had shown her only a geological map of the vast Sahara and a dark smudge where they were.

"I won't let them kill you."

"I don't believe you." Her voice vibrated as she grasped the truth that all Safi's assurances about her release were lies. She couldn't manage him, and she didn't trust that he could manage her captors.

The Elder arrived then at the tent with his partner and bodyguard and ordered Safi to go. To Monte's surprise and sudden panic, Safi left. What was she thinking? He was not her ally. He worked for the Elder.

The Elder stepped over to her, and in one gesture he stripped her of her dress. With a yank of her right arm, he tethered her with a chain to the tent pole so that she could move only four feet in any direction. "This is what we do to runaway whores!" he said.

It was the first time she'd confronted him in the daylight. In spite of herself she was trembling before him while the other two men looked on. She wanted to scream and fight him, but she couldn't mobilize her will, and she knew she'd make her situation worse and give him the pleasure of her fury so she buried her rage and submitted.

Another man peered into the tent, took a full look at Monte, then reported to the Elder that Safi urgently needed him. As the Elder and his partner turned to leave, he told his bodyguard to finish what he had started. Once the Elder was gone, the man picked up her dress and handed it to her and left without touching her.

*   *   *

It took Safi four days to secure her release. She was only partially dressed during those days since she couldn't put her chained arm into her kaftan. She also couldn't get to the hole to relieve herself so Tayri had to help her. When Safi finally appeared in the tent and unlocked the cuff, she didn't ask, or even want to know, what he'd had to promise, or if he even had to promise. She wasn't convinced that he wasn't in agreement with the punishment.

He sat down across from her and handed her a box of soft tissues. He didn't touch her. She no longer believed her life mattered to him. In the long nights and days on the chain, she'd determined that she would gather all she could about the Elder, and she would defeat him. Safi still remained her best hope, so she said nothing.

"I will help you escape when the time is right," he repeated.

She didn't answer. She took one of the tissues from the box and wiped the sweat from her forehead and eyes. She was three and a half months pregnant then, but she'd grown so thin and her body had no regular rhythms since she'd been kidnapped, so she didn't yet know.

*   *   *

Monte huddled in the middle of the tent as the sandstorm blew through the afternoon. The winds threatened to uproot the tent whose pole shook in the earth and whose canvas sides strained at their moorings, flapping like giant birds—*whopp-whapp-whopp-*

whapp—resisting the wind, which at any moment might lift the whole structure and everything inside, including Monte and Tayri, and fling them across the land. Sand blew through the cracks. Even the tightest seals couldn't hold. A coating of grit covered everything. Monte had endured sandstorms before when she lived in Egypt and Tunisia, but none like this. Out in the desert there were no buildings, no trees to shield her, just the fragile canvas of the tent. She suspected this was the beginning of a harmattan that would blow south for days into West Africa.

Safi ducked into the tent as the sun set and the wind accelerated. He was now trapped with Tayri and her. He'd brought Monte another white kaftan tonight to augment the ripped one Tayri had mended and her tattered shirt and pants which now restricted her. As the winds blew, she and Tayri and Safi crushed closer together and wrapped themselves in two sheets with threadbare towels over their heads. Tayri lay down inside her sleeping bag, her hair tucked inside her towel, which she used as a pillow, and she fell asleep.

Safi and Monte crowded together with the only other sheet binding them. Neither could sleep with the winds howling and the ropes beating against the poles and the camels bellowing outside. They sat burrowed into each other to shield themselves from the sand, a single flashlight shining between them.

"The gods are angry tonight," Safi said as the wind roared like a train across the land.

"They take their time," Monte answered. "They should be angry all the time. I am."

"You are not a god." Safi pulled out a cloth bag of dates and offered it to her.

His banter offended her, but she still needed his company. "I thought you believed in only one God."

"I don't believe in anything, though I would like to, unlike you, who are content to see yourself as the center of the universe." He said this almost with affection.

"Is that the debate tonight?" She spit a date pit into the sand.

Safi had been visiting every few days now after he interviewed the Elder and reviewed accounts with him as if he felt the need to watch over her. She'd been in the camp almost six months. She'd lost weight, but she was also aware of thickening again around her waist, and her breasts were heavier. She feared she was pregnant. She hadn't said anything to Safi, but she thought Tayri had noticed. She still relied on Safi to protect her from the other men, but men had started to come and look into her tent, sometimes just to stand and stare at her. She felt her heart race each time as she tried to ignore them. Tayri would shout at them until they went away, but one day she feared they would not leave. Was this why she'd accepted Safi as her lover? She argued with herself continually that she was betraying her marriage and her family, and even her country unless she found a way to gather information. On the other hand, she calculated her chance of survival, even with Safi, was less than thirty percent.

As she and Safi huddled in the center of the tent, Monte asked, "What did the Elder tell you today?"

The two of them traded information, passing secrets that were not really secrets between them. Safi told her the Elder's connections with terror networks, the Elder's side deals with the diamond, drug, and arms traffickers. She told him organizational structures of the U.S. security services, all of which a diligent researcher could find on the internet. She told him government tracking techniques to catch money launderers, which were also accessible if you did the research and most of which he already knew. The information she revealed kept her alive, he told her, for he shared it with the Elder and Rainer, the Elder's Austrian business partner. It was a perverse dance between them, a schizophrenia—lover and informant— which they shed in the dark when Safi's surprising force and gentleness carried her out of the camp and out of herself and held her aloft, at least for a while, before she returned to the earth and the hard ground. "So, what is the debate tonight?" she repeated.

Safi reached into his pocket and handed her a page of text in ancient Greek:

οὐ γὰρ ἔδωκεν ἡμῖν ὁ θεὸς πνεῦμα δειλίας ἀλλὰ δυνάμεως καὶ ἀγάπης καὶ σωφρονισμοῦ.

She studied it in the faint light: "'*God hath not given us the spirit of fear; but of power, and of love, and of a sound mind.*'"

"True or false?" he asked. He pulled their cover tighter around them, sealing their space from the wind and the sand. The storm momentarily quieted though the wind still blew.

"Irrelevant," she answered, "unless I can access the power."

"What if it is there for the taking?"

"What if nothing is there?" Monte countered. Her head fit into the curve beneath his shoulder, and she allowed herself to lean into him.

"Then you've closed off possibility. I think you are too smart for that."

"Were your parents Christian?" Monte asked. "It is unexpected that you quote scripture."

"My mother read the Bible and the Koran to us. I spent my last two years of high school with the Jesuits, who taught me to reason. My reasoning led me to reject them and their assumptions of power and religion intertwined with the state."

"And your brother?"

Safi had mentioned his brother only once, but tonight as the storm renewed its fury outside and he held her against his chest, his head resting on the top of hers, he answered, "My brother fell under the wheels of the state. He died in prison in a corner of hell. According to his friend, he simply ran out of air to breathe."

In the dark confined space of their bodies, Monte couldn't see his face. "Will you tell me more?" she asked.

His head pressed against her hair. The story he recounted flowed directly into her ear as if there were no separation between them. "He was an artist. He drew a map of the Western Sahara and hung it in an exhibition. Someone said it showed sympathy for the rebels, and the police picked him up with his friend, who was a poet. His friend didn't know what happened to Daoud, my brother. But his friend was made to lie naked on a board, his hands and legs tied. They beat him with electric cable connected to a car engine. People whipped his legs, ice cold water was thrown over him, then his head was pushed into a bucket of bleach. A few months later he said he felt like his mouth was full of ants, and all his back teeth fell out. Finally, he confessed to whatever they wanted.

"Daoud didn't show up for two more weeks. They were put in a cell together two meters by two meters, along with six other men. They had to take turns sitting and standing and sleeping. They were told they were brought there to die. Outside the cell each day were shrouds for those who had died in the night. They were told this would be them.

"They weren't allowed to write or paint, but they did. If they were caught, they were tortured, my brother's friend told me. One hour a day they were let into the prison yard where they looked for scraps of paper; they'd write with coffee grounds. They'd tuck the writing into their belts or around their wrists like bracelets. Sometimes they used the half bar of soap they were given each month to wash their clothes. They wrote plays and poems on their trousers, then memorized each other's words before they washed them away. Daoud drew pictures of their words with twigs of charcoal.

"My brother's friend gave me a plastic bag with a drawing in it of a lion Daoud had made for one of his poems. I stared at the yellowed scrap with lines smudged beyond recognition and tried to see in it my brother, but I saw only despair.

"After ten years the king granted an amnesty. Daoud's friend was released, but Daoud had died two years before. The police told his friend that if he talked about what happened, he would be considered a threat to national security and treated worse than before so he never talked. No one talked. When journalists asked to see the prison area, they were told it was a nuclear zone. Daoud's friend went into hiding. There have been more amnesties, but still people don't talk."

Safi turned his head from Monte's ear. "At night Daoud comes to me. He sits on my bed or at my desk and smiles as if amused by the rest of us. 'Safi, life is not so serious,' he tells me. 'It is much more beautiful than you think.'"

Monte remained quiet, letting Safi's story settle. Finally, she demanded, "After what happened to your brother, how could you have brought me here?"

He didn't answer. He drew the sheet over their heads, shrouding them in a space of their own. He eased her to the ground. He held her hands above her head with one of his hands, pinning her shoulders. He kissed her forehead then her lips. He slipped his other hand beneath the loose kaftan and opened her legs. He whispered to her, but she could barely tell his voice from the wind. He held her firmly as he lowered himself onto her. She struggled to get her arms free, and when she did, she reached up and touched his face. He came to her, and then she to him as the wind moaned around them. They never talked about their trysts in the dark. She no longer knew if she had allowed him or he had taken her, and she never asked the question of free will.

Suddenly the wind quieted. The roar fell away so quickly that the silence aroused Tayri who sat up. "C'est fini?" she asked.

Monte and Safi lay side by side under the sheet, breathing together. "Je pense que oui," Monte said. "Yes, I think . . . perhaps."

PART
TWO

PART

TWO

CHAPTER TWELVE

"So, what happened?" asked a woman in a gray silk suit, her white hair spun in a bun at the back of her head, her jaw sculpted at the edge of a knife.

Samantha reached across the table set with green and white patterned china and silverware for at least four courses and retrieved a popover from a silver basket. They were sitting in the marble entry of the Georgetown home of former Ambassador Donald "Bud" Tremont. The entry and dining room had been transformed into a garden with trellises and vines and flowers and rented chairs and tables with grass green tablecloths. Samantha wondered why they hadn't seated everyone in the garden instead where a full moon bloomed. Standing discreetly at the edge of the gathering with earbuds and cords curling down their necks, four dark-suited Secret Service men watched over the party, which included two current U.S. Cabinet Secretaries, a Supreme Court Justice, several Senators and Congressmen, Ambassadors, and selected media. Out front, black limousines and SUVs crowded the street.

"I was in the country as an unofficial observer for restarting peace negotiations," said the slightly balding man in a paisley tie sitting next to Samantha. "I'd taken the weekend to go to the Festival, then the bombs and shooting started."

A birdlike young woman on the other side of Samantha said, "I was a student and also came in just for the Festival."

"What are the chances of that?" asked the woman across the table.

In the idle chat between the asparagus soup and arugula and goat cheese salad, the three strangers discovered they were all at the Festival of St. James in Santiago de Compostela when the violence broke out last year. The woman across the table, who wasn't there, asked the waiter to remove the arrangement of lilies so they could see each other better. "How likely is that?" she repeated.

"Washington is a small town," said the diplomat, who'd introduced himself as Cooke Reston. "We're in a war zone one day then at a party in Georgetown the next. I was sent home after the attack. The negotiations collapsed entirely."

"I took the first flight out I could get," said the backpacker, who'd introduced herself as Mimi Tremont, the grandniece of their host.

"Was Bud the ambassador there?" asked the woman across the table whose place card read "Janet Spears," *the* Janet Spears, political commentator on National Public Radio.

"He was Ambassador to Morocco and Tunisia, but never Spain," answered Cooke Reston whom Samantha suspected her mother had seated beside her since his tapered finger wore no wedding ring.

"What about you?" Janet asked her. "Did you stay?"

Samantha glanced around the room filled with politicians, policymakers, and media her family had appealed to in trying to find her sister. "Yes . . . yes, I stayed." She no longer wanted to answer Janet Spears's questions.

"Your sister's disappearance became almost as big a story as the attack," Janet observed. "Is there any news of her? Did they establish ETA was responsible for the bombs? They're still denying a kidnapping?"

Samantha reached for the butter and spread it on the popover and took a bite. She didn't want to talk about Monte anymore. She'd come tonight hoping to gather further leads, but leads weren't coming from Janet Spears. "What do you do, Mimi?" she asked.

"Is there any new information?" Janet pressed. Samantha wondered if she were as rude when she was on a story.

"How nice you came over for the party," Mimi intervened. "How old is your grandmother anyway? I can't believe Uncle Bud is seventy-five."

They were gathered for a joint birthday party for Bud Tremont and her grandmother Marjorie, whose husband had mentored Bud. In late spring a smaller party would be given for her great-grandmother Lala, who, at one hundred two, was a national statistic.

"Marjorie is ninety-three." With Monte still missing, her grandmother hadn't wanted to come to this party, but her mother persuaded her that Bud's wife had gone to great effort, and Samantha had flown over from Cairo. While Samantha was here, she planned to discuss a transfer to the Washington bureau since Philip and the children were moving back. Everyone had been living in limbo for the past eleven months but were now attempting to go forward with their lives.

"Is your sister still with the State Department?" Janet asked.

Cooke looked at Samantha as if also awaiting the answer. "I'm sorry . . ." Samantha blinked. "I don't understand your question."

Janet had discreetly started taking notes on a pad of paper she'd slipped onto her lap. Samantha recognized the act. "I heard she'd been furloughed since there's been no news of her for almost a year."

"Maybe we can meet for lunch," Cooke rescued Samantha from answering. "But right now, I think you have a toast to give." He nodded to the head table where her mother was gesturing for her to come forward.

Bud's second wife, Ruya, from Morocco was introducing Samantha: "I've asked Samantha Waters, whom you all know, to start off the toasts. Granddaughter of Marjorie Simkins Abbot, our honoree, and great-granddaughter of Elaine 'Lala' Waters, our national treasure..."

Samantha hurried to the podium, pitching forward slightly on the balls of her feet as if she were about to break into a run. In black cocktail pants, black top, patterned turquoise and rust silk jacket, she claimed the room as she lifted the microphone from Ruya's hand. Cupping her long chestnut hair over her shoulder in a trademark move, she focused on the audience and assumed the role she'd maintained for almost two decades, reporting news no matter what was happening in her personal life. Maybe that was why she had so little personal life, she thought standing there.

"Good evening..." She slipped into her public voice. "I've been thinking about what I wanted to say on Marjorie's birthday, or Ma-jo as we've called her ever since Cal, the first grandchild, mangled her name. I looked up what was happening the year she was born—1915. I also looked up what was happening the year Lala was born..." She glanced over at her great-grandmother, who dismissed the date with a wave of her thin hand. "Among the reasons I'm proud to be related to these two women is that neither hides from their ages or from anything else. They have lived history, and they challenge the spin we journalists and politicians put on things..."

The audience clapped. Samantha offered an easy, I'm-just-like-your-own-daughter smile to a gathering who accepted her as such. But as she stood there, she felt removed and outside herself. She tried to focus. She began the toast she'd prepared:

"The year Marjorie was born, World War I was underway in Europe. President Wilson was agonizing over whether to commit U.S. troops. It was a time of European aspirations and empire.

Britain and France began secret discussions on what came to be known as the Sykes-Picot Agreement in which they bargained to divide between them the Middle East regions of the Ottoman Empire after the war. America laid the first stone of the Lincoln Memorial, and that same year, *Birth of a Nation,* the racially problematic film, premiered. And the U.S. Congress rejected women's right to vote though Denmark and Iceland extended women's suffrage that year. Rights of citizens were limited around the globe, but that was changing. Little did Congress know of the young girl who'd just been born in Boston or of her sidekick in Texas who would soon be stirring up Miss Hockaday's School for Girls and be one of the early women voters . . ."

As the audience applauded, Samantha searched above their heads for Cal, who was standing at the back, his round patient eyes watching her. He nodded to her as he waited his turn. Seated at his table were his two daughters in flowered dresses. The whole family was gathered tonight except for Monte and her children, and their absence suddenly unsettled Samantha. She took in air and a sip of water to steady herself. The audience quieted as if acknowledging the loss. Samantha offered a half smile and tried for a brighter tone.

"Marjorie and Lala are my ground zero, the two people who have always been there in my life . . ." She looked over at her mother and father sitting with the two grandmothers between them at the head table. "Mom and Dad, you were there too, but while you were traveling or setting up a house at a new posting, it was Marjorie and Lala who came to stay with us. You all know that Marjorie is an artist. She taught me to draw. She told me that the picture is waiting inside for me to see it. I never had her talent, but I think about her words as I try to understand a story. Marjorie encouraged me to go into communications though recently she told me I might be getting too old for television . . ."

A few people laughed, but Samantha felt the room stir as she veered off topic and Monte filled her thoughts. Cal stepped away from the wall and quickly wound his way through the tables toward the podium. At the head table he put his arm around his sister, hugging her as he deftly took the microphone from her hand. "To Marjorie and Elaine—Ma-jo and Lala," he said, reaching for two glasses. "We, the grandchildren, salute you!" He nodded to Ruya. "Sam as usual has said it for all of us ..."

Ruya took back the microphone, clapping as she did so. "Yes ... yes ... well said!"

Cal escorted Samantha from the head table, steadying her with his arm. "Too much?" she whispered, her eyes seeking his.

He squeezed her shoulders. "You were fine ... fine."

As he and Samantha aimed back to their tables, a woman sitting next to the Moroccan Ambassador stood and headed toward the powder room. She was wearing African dress, long golden floral skirt, scooped neck jacket with flared sleeves, and intricate headdress of the same fabric. Passing Samantha, she slipped a note into her hand. Samantha knew her from the Guinea Embassy here and in London. She had been covertly helping Samantha with information for a story on diamond and drug smuggling in West Africa.

Samantha opened the note. *Café Milano noon tomorrow?* Samantha glanced over her shoulder and noted the Moroccan Ambassador also watching. The upscale Georgetown restaurant was not a usual venue for African diplomats. The woman paused at the powder room and waited for her answer. Samantha nodded.

*   *   *

"You need a new teapot," Samantha told Cal as she settled at his kitchen table after the birthday dinner. She spooned tea into a chipped pink and white rose china pot left over from his marriage. She'd set her evening bag on the counter and took off her shoes.

"I need new everything, but who has time or money?"

"I'll buy you a new teapot."

From the refrigerator Cal took out a carton of milk and set it beside a large wedge of chocolate cake he'd brought home from the party. Cal was over six feet, lanky like Samantha and able to eat unlimited quantities of food, though now that he was over forty, he'd thickened a bit around his waist and face, which had a permanent five o'clock shadow. He took a forkful of cake and drank milk from the carton. Samantha rose and carried over two plates and a glass.

From a desk tucked into the kitchen wall, Cal pulled out a folder. "Here . . . I got you the list of diamond mines and dealers in Sierra Leone and Liberia and private cargo airlines flying into Guinea Bissau and Mali. You said you're also getting information from Guinea? What's your theory?"

"A retired CIA guy I know from West Africa says he's been hanging out at some of his old haunts and hears the region has become a regular rogues' bazaar of smugglers—cocaine, heroin, diamonds, arms. Private flights—big planes—are coming in from Latin America loaded with cocaine. Diamonds are still arriving from Sierra Leone in large quantities. He says members of Al Qaeda and others he doesn't know are showing up as customers. Diamonds, in particular, are a safe place to put money; they can't be frozen in banks or confiscated and are easy to move."

"You think the traffic links to those who've taken Monte?" Cal knew that behind Samantha's research was always a view to finding Monte.

"My friend says kidnappings are rising as a source of money. My producer wants me to pursue the story."

"It's a good story. You have other sources?"

"A State Department/military source verified and showed me some of the illicit trade routes through the desert and told me about recent kidnappings, mostly French citizens. He speculated that Monte could be among these, but no one has asked anything for her so he isn't sure."

"It's dangerous," Cal said. "Mom and Dad . . . and I can't afford another crisis. You want to do this one together?"

Once before they'd teamed up on a story that Samantha broke on her network and Cal broke in his magazine. It was an unorthodox partnership since neither Cal's editors nor her producers had signed off on it, but everyone was happy with the results.

"I'll let you know."

*   *   *

Samantha arrived a few minutes late at Café Milano with its outside tables and glassed-in front porch. The restaurant wasn't bustling as it would be on the weekend. Today the clientele was not the political power brokers of Washington who worked east of here during the week. Instead, the patrons were local and social.

The maître d', who knew or pretended to know everyone, greeted Samantha with familiarity though she rarely came here. As he led her to a table in the rear, a woman with clipped blonde hair and sunglasses waved from the main dining room. Samantha didn't recognize her but waved back.

He led Samantha to an area occupied only by the Moroccan Ambassador and Celeste Diallo, the attaché from Guinea who'd approached her last night.

"Mes excuses de mon retard," Samantha apologized.

The Ambassador stood. *"Ce n'est rien,"* he assured. "I'm glad you could join us." He pulled out her chair.

So this meeting was the Ambassador's. To confirm, she glanced at Celeste, dressed today in a navy pantsuit and powder-blue blouse. Samantha looked around the space with its hanging plants and potted shrubs. The patrons in the front were well out of hearing range.

The waiter brought over drinks, took food orders, then disappeared as he'd been instructed. When he left, the Ambassador leaned toward Samantha. In tailored Armani suit and silk tie, he was as urbane and Westernized as any in the diplomatic corps and spoke five languages—English, French, Arabic, Spanish, and Berber. He addressed Samantha in English in a quiet voice and, uncharacteristically, without preliminary flourishes.

"We have reason to believe your sister has escaped with one of our nationals," he said, "possibly the same man who abducted her."

"Monte?" Samantha sat forward. Instinctively she reached for the pencil she kept behind her ear.

The Ambassador held up his hand. "Please. I am approaching you as the sister of Anne Montgomery Waters, not as a reporter."

"I'm not reporting," Samantha countered, annoyed by the suggestion. Holding a pencil was her security. "Is she safe? Where are they? Do my parents know?" Samantha felt a heaviness shift inside her, a weight that she'd been carrying for so long that as it started to dislodge, she felt a sudden pain.

"I was told last night by some of our local contacts that a small caravan was spotted making its way toward the Algerian border. We have reason to believe your sister is among them, but they've disappeared again. We're hoping they've found shelter or transportation. We've suspected for a while that she was being held deep in the desert. We thought possibly in the Western Sahara or more likely in Algeria or Libya."

As the Ambassador talked, Samantha flipped her pencil back and forth between her fingers to absorb energy. She heard and felt a fan stirring the hot air. She slipped her brown cotton jacket onto the back of her chair. The waiter arrived with the meal. As he set down plates, she could barely sit still.

While the waiter was there, the Ambassador asked, "Did you know Morocco was the first country to recognize the United States of America when it declared independence?" The waiter arranged the cutlery and set out the first and second courses. "Your young nation's first foreign legation was not to France or Holland or any country in Europe, but to Morocco."

Samantha wanted to tell the waiter to leave. "I didn't know that," she answered, though, in fact, she did know.

"My country and your country have been friends for a long time." When the waiter finally withdrew, the Ambassador leaned toward her. "You are a friend to us too, I hope. You are one of the people your sister trusts."

Samantha didn't know if that was true. "Where is Monte?" she asked.

The Ambassador's fine features furrowed into a frown. "We don't have an exact location. We have reason to believe there is an attack being planned by those who held her."

"You know who held her? You knew where she was?" Monte had been missing for almost a year. The possibility that the Ambassador may have known where she was for any part of that time without telling their family disturbed her impending relief.

"We don't know for certain," he answered.

"Who is *we*? I assume you're working with the U.S. government? Why are you, and not they, telling me? Who is briefing my family?"

The Ambassador lifted his spoon as if batting back her barrage of questions. He looked down at the mushroom soup set before them. "Please begin."

Samantha turned to Celeste whose striking Fulani features concentrated as she ate. "How is Guinea involved?" Samantha asked.

"Morocco and Guinea have mutual interests," Celeste answered, picking up the bottle of sparkling water and refilling everyone's glasses.

"Celeste has been helping us in spite of the many troubles in her country right now," the Ambassador answered. "She is discreet. We know traffic in drugs and arms are making their way through Guinea and Guinea Bissau to groups camped deep in the desert. I understand she's shared some of this information with you. We believe one of those camps was where your sister was held."

Samantha leaned her head back on her chair. She looked up at a blur of white cubes on the ceiling. Monte was alive. She felt her eyes filling with tears. Was it possible Monte had escaped? Was it possible she was on her way home? She didn't dare hope. There'd been too many false hopes and false leads. She sat forward. "So, what do you want me to do?"

"We need your sister's cooperation to tell us if an attack is planned . . ."

"Of course she'll cooperate. You don't need me." She felt suddenly irritated that she was being sought as a back channel to Monte. "Some would find it inappropriate that you've approached me."

"Your friend Alex Serrano, who is also a friend of ours, suggested I contact you," the Ambassador said.

"Alex?" She hadn't seen Alex since her weeks investigating in Spain after Monte's disappearance. Her friendship with Alex went back to high school in Brussels. They'd stayed in better touch since the kidnapping. She knew he'd recently transferred to the Spanish Consulate in Casablanca. "How is Alex involved?"

"The Moroccan, Spanish, and U.S. governments have been work-ing together. Alex wanted you to know we may have located your sister, but he didn't feel at liberty to contact you directly on this. He thought you might be able to help. He knew you were coming to Washington, though he says you're living in Cairo with your sister's family."

"I'm living near Monte's family," Samantha corrected.

"We've lost track of your sister at the moment, but we think we know where they were. Alex said you may be the first one she calls."

"The Ambassador is in a difficult position," Celeste offered.

The Ambassador raised his hand, indicating he would speak for himself. "You are correct. Normally I would not go outside of chan-nels, but we are in a time-sensitive situation. We informed your gov-ernment yesterday. Your government didn't want to get your family's hopes up until we are certain."

"What is it you want from me?" Samantha repeated.

"You'll have access to your sister. It may take her a while even to realize what she knows. If you could be available . . ."

"Of course I'll be available. My whole family will be available. But Monte is a professional. I assure you she knows what is critical."

The Ambassador exchanged a glance with Celeste. "We can't share information with your whole family yet," he said. He set his plate aside and steadied his gaze on Samantha, who didn't know for certain if her sister was free or even alive, and yet already the Ambassador was asking her to spy on Monte, at least that's what she thought he was asking.

"My first priority is Monte's health and well-being," she said. "I'd like to know who your U.S. counterparts are. I'd like to speak with them directly. Will that be a problem?"

The Ambassador waved to the waiter who was standing discreetly by the bar. "Would you like coffee?" he asked. Samantha declined.

"The check," he said. When the waiter left, he answered, "That will not be a problem."

Samantha nodded. Before the check arrived, she stood, put on her jacket, and set $30 on the table. *"Merci, mais je paie toujours pour moi-même."*

CHAPTER THIRTEEN

MONTE DIDN'T WANT to cry. She didn't want to upset her children. She steeled herself for walking through the front door, reminded herself of the surroundings—the dark wood entry table with curved legs and cheetah's heads for feet, the worn brown leather sofa, the tooled leather ottoman, the toys . . . dolls, trucks, balls all tucked into the lower bookshelves. She would concentrate object by object, room by room so she wouldn't break down when she saw her children for the first time in eleven months.

The embassy staff met her at the airport in Cairo. She didn't want to reunite with her family in public with other people looking on. She didn't want the press to know when she was returning. An officer from the embassy in Rabat had escorted her on the night flight, and the Cairo staff whisked her away and drove her home. She'd talked to Philip from Rabat, and they agreed the children would take long afternoon naps so they would be awake when she arrived. He would tell them when they woke up that their mother was coming home.

She knocked at the front door; she didn't have a key. Philip instantly opened it, and her escort withdrew. The embassy in Rabat had offered her clothes, but she'd preferred to wear the white kaftan and sandals Safi had bought her. She'd tied her very long hair back with a blue ribbon given to her by an embassy secretary in Rabat. As she stepped across the threshold, she glimpsed herself in the mirror above the hall table. She looked wraithlike, her arms and legs so thin, but she was substantial at the core. She recognized the entry table but nothing beyond that. The house was filled with packing boxes.

For a moment Philip hesitated as if trying to remember her, then he stepped forward and awkwardly put his arms around her. She flinched, nodded, and stepped into the hall. Emma and Craig also hesitated as if unsure who she was. Did she look that different?

Only Samantha rushed forward, her arms out. "Oh, Monte . . . Monte . . . Monte . . ." And uncharacteristically, Samantha broke into tears.

"Sh-h-h," Monte soothed. "Sh-h-h. It's all right. I'm all right."

When Samantha cried, the children rushed forward and also started to cry. Monte sank to her knees and embraced them. She held back her own tears. "My loves . . . my loves . . ." If she let her tears fall, she wouldn't be able to contain them. "My loves . . . my loves . . ."

Philip stood ill at ease in the doorway. Monte saw him from the corner of her eye, but she didn't know how to reach out to him or build the bridge back, so she stayed on the floor with her children in her arms. Finally, Samantha helped lift her. Monte took Emma into her arms as Craig took her hand and led her toward the bedroom. Philip followed behind.

Over the living room doorway, a banner hung decorated with Emma and Craig's drawings of red and blue and yellow flowers and hearts they had made after their naps when they found out their mother was coming home. "WELCOME HOME!" the banner read in Philip's big block letters.

*   *   *

Monte waited now in the dark on Cal's glassed-in sunporch. Emma was curled asleep in her lap on the wicker glider. White lights twinkled in the bushes out back. Cal had strung up Christmas lights early this year, or more likely never taken them down from last year. The tiny lights lacing the bushes and trees made the backyard look enchanted. His daughters lived with him half time since his divorce; he wanted it to be the best half. Monte understood his need—his urgency—to hold onto normalcy for his children and for himself. Her own bearings were strung across continents.

Just two weeks ago she'd been in the desert with Safi and Tayri. Safi had come to their tent and told them it was time to go. They'd been waiting; they knew the time was near. Others were already breaking up camp.

"We leave tonight," Safi said. "I'm coming with you." He brought a saddle bag packed with food and water. "We'll take the two best camels." They couldn't take a car because the noise would wake the others, and they couldn't hide their tracks, and if they ran out of gas, they'd be doomed. Tayri knew the desert and the stars and said they needed eight to ten hours' head start. Safi didn't tell them the enforcers were due at the camp the following day. That was what he called the Elder's Russian partners. They were the only ones the Elder deferred to, according to Safi. He also didn't tell Monte, but she knew, that it was they who would kill her because she served no purpose and was a liability. They had no loyalty to Safi either. He feared they would kill him too if they found out he was writing a book about the Elder. The Elder had hidden this vanity from them.

At midnight with no moon, under a desert sky lit with stars, Safi and Tayri drained the cars of gas and released all the camels. Safi kept his eyes on the light coming from the Elder's tent. The Elder had trouble sleeping so was often awake. Monte rode with Safi. The two camels dragged sheets behind them to erase their tracks. If they could get to the dunes, they could hide until the next nightfall. If they could get beyond the dunes, they might get away. It wouldn't take long for the others to figure out who had released the camels and drained the cars. If they were caught, they would be killed, if they were lucky.

After four days traveling at night, they reached a small desert city where Tayri had a cousin who drove them in his taxi for the next two days to Rabat. There they found the American Embassy. Safi and Tayri stayed in the taxi at the bottom of the road as Monte walked alone up the palm-lined street to the barrier. She was wearing her kaftan and carrying a plastic bag that contained her other kaftan, her wallet, and a cell phone, which Safi had also managed to get her but wasn't charged. Out in front of her, she held her American passport, which Safi had managed to retrieve. Around her head was wrapped a long red cloth with braided tassels and birds embroidered in multicolored thread. It was the scarf Tayri had worked on during her captivity. Tayri said the birds were symbols of freedom.

At the embassy guardhouse, Monte presented her passport. As the barrier rose to let her in, Safi and Tayri drove away. They'd told her not to look back, and she didn't.

She asked to be flown directly to Cairo. She answered questions that day but asked there be no announcement or press conference until she got safely home to see her children. She refused a medical examination; she refused to let anyone touch her.

In Cairo, Monte found Philip already packing up the house to move back to Washington. Samantha had flown over as soon as she heard Monte might be coming home. Monte asked Samantha to handle the press. She didn't feel safe. She wanted to get everyone back to the U.S. as soon as possible. She was grateful Philip had already made the decision, though she wasn't sure she would feel safe even there.

That first night Monte told Samantha she couldn't move back into the bedroom with Philip and asked her to tell him. Philip hadn't protested. In Washington, Samantha arranged for the children and Monte to move into Cal's house in Cleveland Park, and Philip agreed to sleep at a club while he found them a place to live. Their own house in Northern Virginia was leased for the school year to another family. Philip was gentler and more solicitous of her than before, but she didn't know if they could find a way back to each other.

As Monte stared out at Cal's garden now, she wondered how she could guide her children when she was questioning the bonds of marriage and career that had always held her together. She'd been in Washington only a week. Counselors and colleagues told her that she needed time to recover, that she needed to open up and share what had happened, but she didn't want to share. She wanted to sit here holding her child and stare at the flickering white lights while she contemplated retribution and her future. It was at the threshold of the future that her thoughts stopped. She wondered if retribution canceled the future.

Emma twitched in her sleep. Monte covered her with the soft green afghan on the glider and rested her head on a yellow-flowered pillow. Was she having another bad dream? Ever since Monte had returned, Emma had clung to her. She wouldn't let Monte out of her sight. Monte also clung to Emma and to Craig. She stroked her daughter's strawberry blonde hair, the same color as her mother's, at least the color her mother maintained every other month at the hairdresser's. Of the three granddaughters, Emma looked the most like her grandmother. Monte thought Emma was her mother's favorite though she knew her mother would deny having favorites as she denied having favorites among her own children. But Monte had always believed Cal was the favored and only son and Samantha was the favorite daughter.

The front door opened, but Monte didn't get up. She didn't want to wake Emma. Monte hadn't been sleeping, but here, wrapped in a blanket with Emma's warm body against her, she could at least rest. The problem with being home was that her thoughts kept drifting backwards, circling the past instead of moving into the future. That Samantha and she were returning to Washington at the same time was one of life's calibrations.

"There you are." Samantha stepped onto the sunporch.

"How was the party?" Monte whispered. Monte had chosen not to go to the fundraiser tonight for the children's charity her mother presided over. Her mother had urged her to bring the children or leave them with Philip, but she hadn't wanted to leave her children, and the party would have been too much for all of them.

Samantha settled in the wicker rocker facing the magnolia tree. "Mom did a good job, but you were right not to come."

"I don't know if I can stay here in Washington where everyone wants to know your business," Monte said.

"No one wants to know your business unless you're connected to power or in the news cycle. The problem is you're still news, but that will pass. How does Philip feel?"

"He wants to stay. Lambent and Taylor have offered him a job lobbying for the defense and aerospace industry."

"That doesn't work for you, does it? Can he even do that with your job?"

"It's cynical. He doesn't see that, but it is so cynical. He says it's his turn. He's been following my career for the last decade and see where that's gotten us."

"That's harsh. Is he blaming you for getting abducted?"

"It was hard on him and the children."

"It was harder on you."

"He doesn't blame me, but . . ." Monte hesitated. "He questions why I followed Stephen." Samantha watched her. Her whole family had been watching her ever since she'd come home as if trying to recognize her. Some mornings she stood in front of the mirror and tried to recognize herself, so thin, her brown hair filled with gray, draping over her shoulders like a shroud. Her mother had offered to take her to the hairdresser, but she declined. She heard her mother tell Samantha: *She looks a decade older than you.*

"What did Philip mean?" Samantha asked.

"We don't talk about what he means. When I asked him what he meant, he retreated. 'I just wonder,' he said, 'with all you know, why would you go with him?'"

"You said he forced you, that he lifted you from your chair." Samantha repeated the story Monte had told her.

"I've asked myself. My debriefing team asks me every day. I'm no longer sure."

"It was a confusing time. I would have followed him too," Samantha said.

"I doubt it. At least you would have challenged his reading of events, asked how he knew what he said he knew. I am not without blame."

A light flashed in the front hall. "Monte . . . Sam . . . ?" Cal called.

Samantha stepped into the doorway. "Sh-h-h. We're out on the porch. Emma's sleeping."

Cal and his daughters fumbled with their jackets, hooking them on the rack by the door in the hall, which opened onto the dining room and kitchen on one side and the living room and the sunporch on the other. Cal's house was furnished in what their mother called Alexandria yard-sale antiques and with art from Cal's travels. On the Regency dining table spread a red and yellow Nepalese cloth. Wooden and stone-carved statues of tribesmen and animals perched on tables and shelves that were overflowing with books. Cal's wife had let him keep all the furnishings and decorations in the divorce settlement. Her lack of interest in any of their possessions made him more sorrowful than if they'd had to fight over ownership, he'd told Monte.

Cal lowered his voice. "I'll get the girls to bed then join you."

Samantha returned to her rocking chair, curling her feet under her. "Did you and Philip go to the counselor today?" she asked.

"We agreed the man had nothing to offer us."

"Mom seemed to think he was good."

"Another cause for disappointment. He's a friend of hers. That in itself doesn't work for me. His first question was, 'Do you want to stay married?'"

"What's wrong with that? What did you say?"

"It's a stupid question. Why were we there? No, we want a divorce; we want to break up our family and hate each other and screw up our kids' lives."

"Monte . . ." Samantha reached out and touched her arm. "How long did you give him?"

Monte withdrew her arm and folded it around her body. She didn't want Samantha touching her. She didn't want anyone except her children touching her. "We lasted fifteen minutes, then we both chose to leave. I'm tired of answering questions about myself."

Every day Monte reported to a debriefing team for her job. She'd already told them about the terrorist groups in the camp, about the illicit trafficking in drugs and arms and diamonds. She'd told them about the money laundering. She didn't have information on the impending attack they kept asking her about, but she confirmed their intelligence that one might be in the making. Safi had told her that he thought "something big" was in the works. He didn't give her any more information. Maybe he was protecting her, she told them. "She's unwinding slowly," she heard one of the agents report.

Cal stepped onto the porch and turned on a light then saw Emma curled like a sleeping cub under the blanket. "You want me to carry her upstairs?"

Monte hugged her daughter closer. She didn't want to let her go, but she didn't want her waking and hearing them. She handed her to Cal, who laid her on his shoulders and headed up the stairs.

Monte looked back into the garden. "Is that our old swing set?" she asked.

*   *   *

Cal dropped into the white wicker chair and flipped on the lamp on the glass-topped table.

"We were talking about Stephen Carlos Oroya," Samantha said, turning off the lamp, "and we were enjoying the lights in your garden."

"Are there any new leads?" Cal stretched his legs onto the footstool.

"He's made Interpol's list," Samantha offered.

"They won't find him," Monte said.

"I still don't understand what he was doing there," Samantha said.

Ever since Monte had come back, Samantha had been listening to her sister's version of events, but there were gaps. Something was left out. Part of the story hovered in the shadows. She knew when a story didn't cohere, when the linchpin was loose or missing altogether. She hadn't pressed Monte in spite of the urgings of others. She was trying to abide, to help with her return to the States, to listen when

Monte wanted to talk; but Monte didn't talk much. Fortunately, there had been no attacks, no cataclysmic events as the Ambassador had warned, but she worried at any moment the truck with no lights could veer around the corner and mow them down.

"I know you can only share so much. You're being debriefed, but can you at least tell us what Stephen wanted?" Samantha asked.

"He was pursuing a fortune."

"He kidnapped you for money? But no demands were made, no contact in all that time." The family's desperation had fed on the silence, which suffocated them. If there had been a demand, they could have mobilized, maybe even rescued Monte.

"You sound surprised. Philip is taking a new job, setting aside a career in public service, for money."

"Monte . . ." Samantha stopped her. "You can't compare the two."

"I can't compare anything. Clearly, I don't know Philip after twelve years of marriage."

"You said Stephen forced you . . ."

"He forced me only at the beginning. There were guards, but they didn't really guard me. We were in the middle of the desert. There was nowhere to go."

"Did you try to escape?" Cal asked.

"I tried once on my own, but that was a mistake I paid for. There was nothing but desert for hundreds of miles. There may have been oases, but I didn't know where they were. I've tried to locate the camp on a map, but there's no public data for the area. There must be data somewhere, on a satellite, on a map filed in a highly classified chamber at top-secret agencies—at the NSA or the CIA or the Pentagon, but when I tried to locate the camp on my GPS, I was told NO DATA."

"How did you get Stephen to let you go?" Cal asked.

"I remember him from the Festival," Samantha said. She remembered a man with white hair and dark eyes who spoke good English. "He seemed smart . . . and rather charming if I remember."

"He was very charming," Monte said. "He was also an impostor."

"When did you learn that?" Cal asked.

"I should have known when he seduced me."

"He did what?" Cal sat forward on the chair.

Monte began rocking slowly back and forth on the glider, the sun-yellow pillow hugged to her chest. She pulled the blanket around her shoulders. She was still wearing the kaftan she'd worn every day since her release. When Samantha had suggested she change clothes, Monte had given her such a withering look that Samantha hadn't persisted. Even their mother held back, though she suggested to Samantha that Monte at least wash the kaftan. Samantha explained that she had two of them and did wash and alternate wearing them.

Cal got up and sat beside Monte, putting his arm around her shoulders. "What did he do, Mont?" he asked quietly, but firmly. "You haven't told us."

Samantha watched Monte in her loose white dress with her gray-brown hair falling over her face. She appeared a shell of the sister she'd known. "What did he do?" Cal repeated gently, so gently that Samantha wanted to cry for how good Cal was and for what a self-absorbed major screwup she had been to let her sister slip off the earth, to have failed to take it seriously for seven hours that day that Monte was missing.

*   *   *

"You want whiskey?" Cal asked as they adjourned to the kitchen. From a top shelf he took down a bottle of Jack Daniels and set it on the large oak table. Samantha set a saucepan of water on a gas flame.

"I'll stick with tea," Monte said as Samantha extracted loose Darjeeling from a gold foil pouch, reading the unfamiliar package: Traditinal [sic] Tea, made in Rajistan [sic], India."

"Win gave it to me last time he was here," Cal said of the Burmese refugee their dad once helped who showed up from time to time unannounced. "He likes to bring a gift."

"Tea is a good gift," Monte said in a voice that came from far away.

Cal and Samantha exchanged glances. "I'll make you some." Samantha scooped the tea into the infuser and set it in the new blue-and-white teapot she'd bought for Cal.

"I think I'll go to bed and try to sleep." Monte stood from the table though she was the one who'd suggested they come into the kitchen after Cal and Samantha started asking her questions.

"You sure you don't want a drink?" Cal asked.

"What I want is sleep." Her eyes searched the room, then she went to the refrigerator and extracted from the top shelf a large rectangular container. In her billowing dress, with the Tupperware under her arm, she ascended the stairs.

"Is that what I think it is?" Samantha asked after she left.

Cal nodded. He returned the whiskey bottle to the top of the cabinet unopened.

"She told me a friend of a friend at work got it for her."

"She never even smoked pot," Samantha said. "She never took any drugs."

"She told me her guards felt sorry for her and shared their stash. What do you think happened to her in those months?"

"She hasn't told me much. I feel sorry for Philip. He's being patient, but he feels he's lost his wife, and he's not sure she wants to come back."

From somewhere in the house a brown-and-white mutt of a dog and two Persian cats appeared in the kitchen doorway. The cats hopped onto the table, and the pug-nosed dog pumped its stubby tail when he saw Samantha and Cal. Samantha reached down to pet him.

"How was she in Cairo?" Cal asked.

Samantha sipped the bitter Darjeeling. "The first sign something was wrong was when she told me she couldn't go back into the bedroom with Philip. Maybe that was understandable, I thought, given what she'd been through. She refused a medical exam. She wouldn't talk to the press. She'd talk mainly to Emma and Craig. They held to her, especially Emma. Whenever Monte retreated to the bathroom, Emma squatted outside and would break into whimpering sounds. Philip finally realized Emma's whimpers were echoes of Monte's own quiet sobbing, locked behind the bathroom door.

"When Philip or I tried to talk to her, she told us she was just exhausted and needed rest. She didn't eat, just picked at food. She told us, 'I've fought my whole life with weight. Let me enjoy being too thin.'

"One of the first things we both noticed was that she never changed her clothes, or rather wore the same two white kaftans. 'Safi gave them to me,' she told Philip. 'I'd think you'd want to burn them,' he said."

Samantha got up to let the dog out the back door. "One afternoon in Cairo, when Philip came home early from work, he found Monte behind their apartment building talking to a man he didn't recognize. He saw an exchange of money, then saw her receive a large bundle of plants, but when she came inside, she didn't have anything in her arms. Philip went back outside and found an ice chest in the garage and inside it, in plastic bags, was the plant. He took a stem and the next day showed it to a colleague who informed him it was khat. That afternoon he took a bundle inside and asked Monte what it was for.

"I came home and found them in the living room among packing boxes with a wad of khat on the table between them talking as rationally as if they were discussing a policy difference. 'Just give me time,' Monte said. Philip took one of the stems, bit off a leaf and began to chew, then he spit it out. 'That's god awful, Monte,' he said. She smiled and tucked a few leaves in her mouth. It was so strange to see my Harvard/Oxford-educated sister chewing khat. I remember once when Dad caught you smoking pot."

Cal pulled the cookie jar in front of him. "He told me if I didn't stop, he wouldn't pay for college, and he made me sign an oath.

"I remember: you at Dad's big desk in Brussels and Monte standing so serious beside you. Dad made it a ceremony, like signing a peace treaty. It was so like Dad to make everything bigger than it was, but it worked," Cal said. "When I was tempted later to light up, I could see Monte—what was she, thirteen, sober as a judge—and Mom, and thinking I'd given Dad my word. I didn't worry about you.

"In the long run the family meant more to me than a few joints. I think about that now as a father. Before the ceremony Dad told me about his own father who was an alcoholic; that ultimately killed him. He said he'd never really known his father, and he couldn't count on his father. He was so serious, and I don't know, vulnerable, that I didn't argue with him. Because of his father's addiction, he was worried about me."

"You never told me that."

"He asked me not to. He said it would hurt Lala. His father was her only son."

"I think we need to tell Dad about Monte," Samantha said, "but he seems so frail."

"I've been thinking we need to tell him and Mom."

"Mother knows something's wrong. You can't look at Monte and not see something is wrong," Samantha said. "Dad told me to give her time. He's had friends who were kidnapped. He's so relieved to have her back; he's not focused on anything else. But the security services are worried there's an attack being planned. They think Monte may have information, but she's not opening up. They've located the camp where they think she was held, but everyone's scattered, including a central figure known as the Elder. He hasn't turned up, but others have been spotted entering Morocco. Security services are on high alert."

CHAPTER FOURTEEN

MONTE SLIPPED INTO her children's room and sat in the wooden rocking chair by the window, covering herself with a quilt Cal's wife had made as a young mother and left behind. Monte had never connected to Cal's wife. She'd been home the summer he started dating her, the summer he moved back to Washington, having abandoned his New York law firm after only two years. She'd finished university and was about to embark on her own next step, studying for an MPhil at Oxford in International Relations. Samantha was already working in London.

"You barely gave law a try," their father had challenged at Cal's first dinner back. "You spent less time as a lawyer than you spent in law school."

"It's just not for me, Dad." Cal had smiled without taking offense. They were eating in the formal dining room of their Kalorama home, candles flickering on the mahogany table. "I should have quit law school, but I wanted to tough it out. I don't want to spend my life doing something I don't like."

"What will you do?" their mother had asked.

"I've got a job writing."

"Writing?" Their father repeated the word as if Cal had said "pimping." "What kind of writing?"

"Politics. I've been hired by *Newsweek*."

"*Newsweek*?" Even now she remembered her Republican father repeating the word *Newsweek* as though Cal had said *The Daily Worker*. Cal had since moved to *The Economist*, a worthier publication in their father's eyes, but he considered reporting a subordinate calling for those who couldn't serve on the front lines of the world. He'd accepted Sam's choice in television because she was a woman and was at least reporting from Europe, a more serious enterprise in his opinion.

Though their father had been in the Foreign Service and served as an Ambassador and Undersecretary of State, Monte knew he felt he hadn't achieved what he considered the pinnacle of his career— National Security Advisor or Ambassador at the United Nations— and he hadn't written the book that would secure his legacy. She knew he was looking to them, his children—mostly to her—to bring him to the top of that mountain he'd been climbing, to secure peace and security in the world, he would say, lest his ambition appear personal. He'd told her in high school she was the one who could follow in his footsteps and go into the Foreign Service and into the world to represent the country and its values. Samantha had made it clear government service wasn't where she was headed, and he must have suspected Cal was too much of a maverick and too prone to adventure to move from embassy to embassy, pushing and tugging at the bureaucracy to make it move; but she had accepted the mantle with pride and set her course. She'd met Philip her first year at the State Department and married him in a quiet Washington wedding before she shipped out to be a political officer in Tunis. Philip was six years older, an accountant, one of the experts in auditing government contracts, and was happy to follow the adventures of her life, pleased to have a wife and later children and to live around the world. She'd loved Philip because he loved her. He was the first man or boy ever to fall in love with her while Samantha had strings of men proclaiming love while she committed to none.

Monte opened the window beside the rocking chair so she could feel the night air. In spite of herself, her thoughts returned to the desert and what she'd left behind. She thought of Tayri, who had said she would help her, but Monte hadn't understood how. Her mind stirred. She hadn't known well the quiet woman who offered such profound kindness. She hadn't told her family all that had happened to her there, the multiple rapes and the consequences, because she feared it would so complicate the world she was trying to reenter that she might never find her way back.

She glanced over at Craig and Emma tucked in their beds. Between them two pygmy hedgehogs Philip had bought them slept in a cage on the nightstand. They had been so excited to introduce her to their new pets that she'd accepted the ridiculous furry creatures and agreed they should accompany them back to Washington in spite of the extravagant expense.

She looked out on the street at the shadows across the road. She worried someone would step out from the shadows and snatch her back. She'd managed to escape, but she still didn't feel safe. She knew too much. She didn't share her concern with those debriefing her because she didn't want a security detail inhibiting her when she finally decided to act.

The last day before they reached the desert town where Tayri's cousin lived, they'd stopped at a transit hotel in a no-name village on a road that barely existed. She and Safi had shared a room and lay on a hard double bed on a thin shred of a mattress. They didn't touch. They were fleeing a dream . . . or rather a nightmare, and they knew without saying so that they mustn't let anything hold them there as they shuttled between realities. They couldn't occupy both worlds. Like Lot in the Bible, Monte knew she mustn't look back lest she turn into a pillar of salt.

They lay with the bright sun filtering through the closed gauze curtain. Water of questionable origin stood on the nightstand in a clay pitcher with two paper cups. It was hard to sleep in the heat of the day, but it was more dangerous to travel. They had hardly slept in three days. They worried the Elder's men were tracking them. And they worried about what lay ahead.

"The Elder told me he will short the hell out of what is coming," Safi whispered. "He said it will be 'the deed of deeds.' 'What markets? When?' I asked. 'Not yet,' he said, 'but soon.'"

"When will he tell you?"

"He won't tell me now. He will hunt me down and kill me when he understands I've left and taken you. I told Kenneth and his wife to get out of Gibraltar. But we have to stop the Elder."

"We? I can't, Safi. I have to go home. But I can tell others."

"Others have no idea how to stop him. They'll send in their Special Forces and bombers and helicopters. He'll just burrow underground."

"I have to see my family," Monte said. "I have to recover."

Safi hadn't argued. Instead, he told her how to contact him if she ever needed. He gave her an email address. "But I may not be able to check email . . ." He took from his pocket an old phone. "Here is also a number. It's not registered to anyone. I never answer it. I keep the battery separate, but once a day I'll check for texts. Memorize the number, don't write it down."

She repeated the number. She has repeated the number over and over ever since like a mantra that briefly lulls her to sleep, but the sleep doesn't last.

"If we ever have to meet, the caves of Gibraltar are the safest place I know," he said, then a shadow passed over his face.

"What?" Monte asked.

"The Elder once asked me if I knew where hell began. 'In the caves of Gibraltar,' he said. The Greeks thought that was the entrance to Hades where the underworld began. Do you know the caves?"

"Yes, I've been there."

As the sun outside faded and the air, thick with dust, settled in the room, it finally grew cool enough to sleep for a few hours before they had to leave.

"Will you betray me?" Safi asked as they closed their eyes.

"I don't know," she said.

Monte stared now at the shadow outside the bedroom window at Cal's. Her gaze lifted to the lamppost casting the shadow and then up to the full moon, which lit the sky outside and the pink-flowered wallpaper within, the same moon she used to look at in the desert, the same moon her children looked at. In her waking and sleeping dreams, she'd returned to her children, though not to her husband. When she thought about Philip, she heard all his complaints—that she wasn't home enough, that she was on the phone or on her computer, that her body might be with him in the room, but her mind was elsewhere, that she didn't hear the children when they talked. But he was wrong. She was present; she heard everything.

Monte opened the Tupperware container in her lap and lifted out a bouquet of leaves, which she tucked one by one into her cheek and began to chew. The sour juice mixed with saliva. The leaves reminded her of where she'd been, and the rush they gave her kept her vigilant while she tried to figure out what came next. Soon she would give up the khat. Soon she would change her clothes and cut her hair and go on with her life, whatever that would be. But for the moment the khat and the clothes allowed her a mask to hide behind, protecting her while she planned her reckoning.

Shutting her eyes, she listened to the night. She heard Samantha and Cal talking in the kitchen below. She knew they were talking about her. Everyone expected her to be who she'd been or who they thought she was—the civil servant FS-2 with only one more notch to achieve the top of the Foreign Service ladder, one of the youngest at age thirty-seven, or was she now thirty-eight, to achieve this rank and salary, eligible in only six more years for a pension after twenty years of government service. Dad and Philip had pointed out that she could then start a whole new career if she wanted, with a pension to secure it. She didn't know what she wanted, but a pension at forty-four wasn't it.

She looked again at Emma and Craig in the twin beds under sky-blue blankets, small bundles of love and sleeping energy. They were the reasons she wanted to do anything. She stared out the window at the lights across the street as if waiting for Peter Pan or Tinker Bell to arrive and lead her away to Never-Never Land beyond the far side of the desert where she could restart the whole enterprise of her life. If Philip would come with her, then maybe they could survive together, but if he stayed and chose to plant himself in this province, they would separate; she would leave him behind. But . . . and here was the *but* she had yet to resolve . . . she couldn't leave her children behind, and she didn't know how to live with them without their father whom they loved and who loved them entirely.

As she chewed the bitter leaves, she felt on high alert. Her thoughts raced to a cool, high place in the desert where she needn't worry. The wilderness was where she left herself. In the distance she heard Sam telling Cal good night at the door. She heard Samantha gently shut the door of her car and drive away, considerate of those sleeping . . . able to sleep . . . in the house, in Cal's house on the quiet street with the twinkling lights in the bushes.

CHAPTER FIFTEEN

"I NEED TO GO TO Morocco tonight," Samantha told Colin, her producer in London.

"For your trafficking story?"

"That too."

"We need that story, Sam. You want someone with you?"

"Not yet. I'll let you know. Could you clear it here?" Samantha asked. She'd been working out of the Washington bureau for the past week with the hope she might eventually transfer.

"If news happens over there, we want to call on you," Colin said.

"Of course."

"You owe me, Sam."

"I always pay my debts."

Samantha phoned Cal next. "I'm going to Morocco. I met with the Ambassador again this morning. I think the key to what happened to Monte is there."

"What does Monte say?"

"I'm meeting her in half an hour at Ma-Jo and Lala's apartment."

Their grandmother and great-grandmother lived together. They weren't directly related except for sharing the last fifty years of their children's lives. They lived with a housekeeper half their age at the Watergate. On the way, Samantha stopped by the apartment she had on loan in the same complex to pick up a carry-on bag permanently packed with slacks, skirt, tops, blazer, underwear, nylon jacket, black shawl / head scarf, gold chain belt, toiletries, spare credit card, and $1,000 cash.

By the time she arrived at her grandmothers', Monte and her mother were already there. Her mother was trying to deflect Monte's complaint that she'd interfered by calling the counselor to see how Monte's session went yesterday.

"That's not your business, Mother. That's why we could never trust him—he's your friend!"

"He would never tell me anything personal, and I would never ask," insisted their mother, whose flowered skirt and cotton top hung wilted on her tall frame. "I merely asked how he enjoyed meeting you, but he said you walked out. He didn't seem nearly as upset as I was."

"It is not your business," Monte repeated.

Samantha went over and kissed her mother and gave her a gentle hug.

Their grandmother raised her hand. "Please . . . I thought you were here to see me."

"I am . . ." Monte glanced over her shoulder. "I'm sorry." She went to kiss Marjorie, her grandmother, who was sitting at the dining table, and then Lala, her great-grandmother, reclining on the sofa in velour sweatpants and top. As the housekeeper set a plate of cookies on the table and Emma and Craig came running in from the TV in the den, Samantha asked Monte if they could step outside on the balcony for a minute.

The terrace overlooked the Potomac River and the Kennedy Center. Lala had moved into this apartment when the Watergate first opened almost forty years ago, and Marjorie had joined her after her husband died. The break-in of the Democratic National headquarters in 1972 forever memorialized the complex. Today on the terrace the warm wind blew briskly, shaking the leaves on the trees along the riverbank below.

"So, what is it?" Monte asked, leaning against the balustrade.

"I'm going to Morocco tonight. I met this morning with the Moroccan Ambassador. He told me they've located Stephen Oroya in Rabat."

"They found Safi?" Monte began pulling at a thread on the sleeve of her kaftan. "What are they going to do?"

"The Ambassador said they need to find out what he's doing there and who he's contacting. If an attack is being planned, they're hoping he'll lead them to the others. The Ambassador thinks you may know something. I told him you were sharing all you knew, but he doesn't think you are."

Monte continued pulling at the loose thread. "So are you working for the Moroccan Ambassador now? That's not like you, Sam."

"I told him your health and welfare were my first priority, not the capture of Stephen Oroya."

"Is that true?" Monte looked over the railing and peered down at the river.

"Why do you ask that?"

"If it's true, why are you racing off to Morocco? You think there's going to be a big story, and you'll be on-site."

"That's not fair. I haven't reported a word of this story for the past year. But, yes, I am reporting another story. I have to work, Monte."

At the meeting that morning, Celeste Diallo had told her an arms shipment was making its way up the coast from Guinea Bissau to Morocco. "Do you know what Stephen Oroya—or whoever he is—is up to?" Samantha asked Monte. She watched her sister, who was staring beyond the river as if looking for her house in Virginia.

"He is not a terrorist if that's what you're asking. He doesn't know what's being planned, and neither do I. Most of those in the camp seemed to me your basic criminals, but I didn't see everyone. I was kept apart."

"Why did he set you free? You've never explained how you got to the Embassy in Rabat."

"Would it matter to you if I asked you not to go?" Monte turned. She sat down on a deck chair.

Samantha remained watching the river flowing slowly under the Memorial Bridge, winding around Roosevelt Island in the middle. The Potomac was not like the powerful rivers of other cities. No large ships and commercial barges floated down it the way they did the Hudson in New York or the Seine in Paris or the Thames in London. The muddy brown waters of the Potomac were benign and domestic, like the city itself, which was a smaller version of more powerful-looking capitals. No building here rose higher than the Washington Monument so the architecture didn't dominate its citizens. Power in Washington was hidden at first glance—cumulative, institutional, procedural, not historic and ceremonial.

"Yes, it would matter," Samantha said turning. She sat in a chair beside Monte. "But I'm going because I'm worried about you. And I am following a lead for another story. Maybe I can find answers that will help me understand what happened to you and help you. Maybe I can assemble facts, draw a picture—that's what I know how to do—gather the notes for that first draft of history, not even the draft itself."

"You think this is history?"

"You tell me. The ambassador is worried. Our government is worried about what may be unfolding. Should they be?"

"Yes." Monte looked over at her sister. "If you think you can help, then go. I don't know what Safi is doing in Rabat, but don't underestimate those around him."

"The Ambassador thinks he may be visiting his mother."

Monte smiled and for a moment was quiet. When she spoke, the edge had softened in her voice. "I'll give you a contact who can help you. Tell her you're my sister and that I sent you. Maybe you'll know what to do with what she tells you."

PART THREE

PART THREE

CHAPTER SIXTEEN

"SAM! SAMANTHA!" Samantha heard her name before she spotted the man waving and lumbering toward her. "Here you are!" He embraced her.

"Alex, I didn't expect you to meet me."

"Oh sure. You leave a message, 'I'm coming to Casablanca for a few hours . . . can we talk?'" Alex Serrano, now a diplomat like his parents, took her bag. "I've got you a room at the Hyatt where you can freshen up and get a bit of rest."

"I have to leave for Rabat tonight."

Alex's genial smile and curly black hair hadn't changed since their days when he was her sidekick and best friend, her news editor when she was the editor-in-chief of the school paper at the American School in Brussels. When she went off to university in the States, he returned to Spain for an additional baccalaureate year then university. He'd reached out to her several times, but they had lost touch until her visit last fall to the Festival. After Monte's disappearance he'd arranged for Cal and her to work out of a government office until she and Cal agreed the association could compromise them and they'd moved their base to their small hotel.

"I assume you're here because we've tracked Stephen Oroya to Rabat," Alex said as they settled into the back of his town car. He took off his jacket and dropped it on the seat. In this taller, slimmer adult, she still saw her slightly disheveled friend.

"How did you find him?" She glanced out the window at the jumble of buildings—red-roofed houses, office towers, palm trees, date trees. She hadn't been in Casablanca in years, not since suicide bombings rocked the city in 2003 just days after similar attacks in Riyadh, Saudi Arabia. The attacks had all been attributed to Al Qaeda. She hadn't covered the bombings in Casablanca last year. After Evan's death she didn't have the heart. A younger correspondent had gotten the story. Suddenly she felt weary and leaned her head back against the dark leather seat.

"I made inquiries among his school friends and found out where his mother lived," Alex answered. "We started watching her house." Samantha pulled a pad of paper from her purse. "Are you reporting on this?"

She offered a tired smile, pushing back her hair, which had pulled free from the ponytail at her neck and flared in a messy, fiery halo. "No. But taking notes keeps me awake."

"Why don't you go to the hotel, take a nap for an hour. Tell me what you want to know, who you want to see, and I'll set up some meetings for you. I'll make sure you get to Rabat tonight."

She let Alex drop her at the Hyatt, which backed onto the city's oldest market. His parents had access to a small suite for just such last-minute purposes. "Wake-up call at three thirty," he said. "I'll meet you refreshed in the lobby at four."

*   *   *

As they drove into the city center, Alex handed Samantha a typed-up fact sheet on Stephen Carlos Oroya:

—Born Nov. 12, 1968, Chicago, Illinois, USA
—Profession: Freelance Writer
—Financial Consultant/Advisor/Investor
—Education: IB, International College Spain, Madrid, 1988
    BA, Universidad de Sevilla, History and Business, 1995
    MA, SOAS, University of London, History 1996
    MBA, Universidad de Sevilla, 1997
—Military Service: U.S. Army 1988-1991
—Employment: Morgan Stanley, Madrid, 1997-1999
    SWG Financial, Gibraltar, 1999-2000
    El País, Financial reporter, 2000-2001
—Book Publication: *Chaos and Old Night: A Study in the
New Revolution,* C. Ashdown Publishers, London: 1998

"So, what do the facts tell you?" Samantha asked.

"That he's well educated, multilingual, and either can't keep a job or doesn't want to. We know his father is Spanish; his mother is Moroccan. And he was born in the U.S. His father was a professor in Chicago, but at seven his parents divorced, and he and his brother went to live with his mother in Morocco. His father remarried and moved back to Spain. Stephen was a whiz in math, according to schoolmates. After university he trained and then worked at a top investment bank, paid off his student debt, then left to work for a small investment firm in Gibraltar, left that, and joined a major newspaper in Madrid to write about finance. We were told other financial firms wanted to hire him, that he had talent, but he didn't like being trapped in an office. He turned freelance both in writing and investing. He liked being his own boss. When he was younger— around twelve—one of his uncles was killed in a raid on ETA in Spain so he has access there. His brother died in prison in the

Western Sahara. He started writing about insurgencies like ETA and Polisario. He has dual citizenship and served in the U.S. Army where he trained in munitions and was also a marksman on the firing range. He missed fighting in the first Gulf War by just a few weeks when it ended."

The town car pulled up to the bustling market in Habous Quarter. Before the driver could open Samantha's door, she did. "*Ce n'est pas nécessaire,*" she said.

"Still won't let anyone help you?" Alex asked.

"You can help, just don't wait on me."

"Noted."

Alex led them into the souk with its myriad stalls selling fruit, nuts, dates, flowers, tee shirts, blue jeans, hijabs, cameras, cell phones. The market smelled of mint and oranges and coffee in one section, slightly acrid butchered meat in another, and fried fritters and sweet almond pastries in another. The stalls backed onto each other in narrow alleyways where Alex greeted the sellers in Arabic, French, and Spanish. "*Salaam Alaikum! Bonjour . . . ca va? Hola, Diego, ¿Cómo estás?*"

As they moved through the noisy crowds, Samantha asked, "So what do *you* think Stephen is involved in? The Moroccan Ambassador is afraid he might be killed in the process of capturing him and what he knows will go with him."

"We don't know what he knows, but I agree, we have to be careful and try to take him alive."

Samantha pulled her camera from her satchel as they passed baskets of nuts and dates and grains—a bouquet of autumn colors— next to displays of orange blossoms, roses, orchids, and sunflowers. She panned slowly over the colorful stalls.

"You planning to broadcast?" Alex asked.

She turned off the camera. "Can I be honest, or do you have to report everything I tell you?"

"You can be honest. Put away your pad and paper, and I'll put away mine."

They moved past stalls with Berber carpets hanging from wires, into the copper and brass souk with trays and samovars and tea sets, tables with inlaid chess boards and cases of silver jewelry. "I want to meet him and talk with him."

"You want to interview Stephen Oroya?"

"Not for television . . . though that would be a coup." Samantha considered the possibility. "No . . . not for the record, though I'm researching a story on arms trafficking that keeps bumping into Monte's. But I want to understand what happened to Monte. She's not talking. She's deteriorated. I'm worried. Stephen must know what went on. I don't know if he'll talk to me or shoot me. Did you ever meet him? Why am I not surprised you know people who did?"

Alex smiled and took her hand. "Because I know everyone. But they knew him twenty years ago. They don't know the man who kidnaps people."

As they walked shoulder to shoulder through the small corridors between buildings and modest houses, Samantha wondered fleetingly what life might have opened if she'd ever encouraged Alex's attentions. But she dismissed the thought and removed her hand, reaching out to touch the fabric of a hijab at a sidewalk stall. Alex was married with three children; she didn't want any confusion between them.

"Whoever he is now, I'm fairly certain the health of your sister is not his priority," Alex added.

They emerged at a café and settled at an outside table where Alex leaned toward her and lowered his voice. "Our security tells me there's internet chatter about blowing up a major thoroughfare or market or monument to destabilize the government here. Perhaps also in my country. It's talk and rumor at the moment, but rumor can turn quickly to action."

"Who is *they*? Monte said Stephen is not a terrorist."

"The evidence is persuasive he's at least connected to terrorists. He kidnapped your sister. He didn't put her up at the Hyatt."

"No, he didn't. They hurt her. I'm not sure exactly how, but she says he's not a terrorist, at least in the conventional sense."

"I don't know how she distinguishes." Alex ordered them mint tea while they waited for his contacts.

"He's American, Moroccan, and Spanish?" Samantha confirmed.

"He's lived in all three countries. I don't know how many passports he has, at least American and Moroccan."

"Monte said he didn't use force with her, except at the beginning. She won his confidence somehow and her freedom, but I don't know what was required of her. I'd like to go to his mother's house."

Alex smiled. "This is a major security operation, Sam. We can't let you just go knock on the door."

"Who is *we*?"

"U.S., Spain, Morocco—no government is going to let you interfere. Surely you know that."

"Could I go if I were with you?" she asked. She sipped the sweet mint tea in a glass with gold filigree; the tea soothed her. She shouldn't have told Alex what she had in mind. She and Alex had known each other more than twenty years ago when they felt the first flush of adulthood, scouting out stories together. She took for granted that their friendship endured though Cal had reminded her that, as a diplomat, Alex represented the interests of the Spanish government just as Monte represented, or used to represent, the interests of the U.S. government.

*   *   *

Moha DeVere strode over to the table, a big man—6'3"/250 pounds—in a loose mustard-colored burnous and maroon fez, accompanied by a slighter man with dark brown hair, dressed in blue jeans and Adidas tee shirt and sneakers who introduced himself simply as Jim. His tee shirt was tucked in over a flat, hard stomach and his biceps strained at the short sleeves of his shirt.

"Do you have a last name, Jim?" Samantha asked as the two men settled at the table on either side of her. "I know it won't be your real last name, but just so I can think of you with two names." She smiled. "Are you the tourist and he's your guide?"

Jim and Moha exchanged glances, but Alex laughed. "All right, Sam. We know you know your territory. The Ambassador told us you wanted to meet a U.S. counterpart. Jim is at the U.S. Embassy. Today was his day off so we called him from home. Moha works in the security services here. Both have been involved for the last year on your sister's case. Moha was aware of Stephen when he lived here, though he called himself Safir Brahim. Brahim is his mother's name. I told them anything they share with you is on deep background. You won't use it without checking, and you won't quote them."

"Of course," Samantha agreed.

"Safir Brahim disappeared over a year ago," Jim began the briefing. "He told colleagues he was writing a book. No one paid notice since he operated freelance and was often gone for long periods. A few months ago the police arrested a young man who'd come to Casablanca to blow up the Hassan II Mosque. He was supposed to blow himself up too, but he had second thoughts. He didn't want to die so he tried to leave his backpack and run across the plaza before it detonated."

"The Hassan II Mosque?" Samantha knew it well. Spreading over twenty-two acres on the coastline of Casablanca, two-thirds built over the ocean, it was dwarfed only by the Grand Mosque in Mecca and the Prophet's Mosque in Medina. Its minaret, the tallest in the world, rose almost 700 feet. During Ramadan she'd seen over 100,000 worshippers gathered at the mosque and surrounding plaza, which also housed a library and museum. Constructed during the time of King Hassan II, father of the current king, it was a symbol of a regime both beloved and hated. The audacity of blowing it up—the heresy—surprised her. "That would violate religion and the state—an ultimate attack and blasphemy," she said. "Worse than the blowing up of the Golden Dome in Iraq. Who would do that? For what purpose?"

Moha seemed less impressed. He waved to the waiter and ordered a mezze platter for the table. "The young man was an amateur," he said. "That was clear from the start. His pack was loaded with low-quality explosives that would have killed him and maybe a few bystanders but would have done limited damage to the mosque. We think he wanted to be caught. He started talking right away. He was afraid he'd been given a mission that would send him to hell. Those who sent him were perhaps delivering a warning, not a death blow."

"You think Stephen . . . Safir was involved?" Samantha asked.

"We think he knew," Jim said. "The young man mentioned a Safir at the camp—that was the only name he gave. His description matches Stephen. He says Safir told him that he must have the conversation with Allah, and if he didn't hear Allah's voice in his actions, he shouldn't proceed."

"That must have been a radical concept for him," Samantha said.

"Certainly a confusing one," Jim agreed. "Safir was not the leader of the camp, he said, and was often away. From what we know, the camp was a way station for various radical groups—guerillas, separatists, Islamist extremists—not necessarily connected to each other, but connected to a man called the Elder. The Elder was an experienced fighter, trained in Libya, fought in Chad. In the first Gulf War he fought against Saddam. Along the way he connected up with smugglers in West Africa, Latin America, then Afghanistan and Russia who trade in heroin, cocaine, blood diamonds, and heavy arms."

"I wonder why Monte says Stephen isn't a terrorist," Samantha said.

"He's certainly consorting with those who are," Jim answered. "We have reason to believe he may want to get out but doesn't know how. We think that may be why he let your sister go and why he has so openly arrived at his mother's home. We'd like to help him and bring him in."

"I'd like to talk to him," Samantha said.

"That's not possible," Jim answered.

"Sam is a professional," Alex said. "She may be able to get him to talk, even turn himself in."

"I'm sorry, but you're not that kind of professional," Jim demurred. "No offense."

"No offense taken. If you have a professional, why don't you send him or her in?"

"The target is a flight risk. He may flee if he knows we're there."

"His name is Stephen or Safir," Samantha said, "not *the target*."

"Stephen . . ." Jim corrected, ". . . Safir."

"Why haven't you just gone in and arrested him?"

"We're concerned if the security forces rush the house, he could be killed, then we lose him as a source." Jim—or whoever he was; Samantha assumed he was CIA—added, "Moroccan security has the house under surveillance and listening devices honed in. We're hoping to hear who he contacts, but the quality isn't good, and he doesn't appear to be speaking to anyone but his mother. He may be communicating in other ways."

"He'll talk to me," Samantha said. "I've met him before. He'll remember me."

"You'll compromise the operation and put yourself in danger," Jim challenged. "He kidnapped your sister. We can't risk another hostage."

"I might be able to get you what you need," Samantha pressed.

Jim looked over at Moha, who opened his palm and lifted his hand as if to say, Why not? "If we agreed, would you be willing to wear a wire?" Jim asked.

"No," Samantha answered without considering the request. "If I talk with him, it's for personal reasons, and that's the only reason he would talk to me. I'll share information that would prevent an attack, of course, and I'll try to persuade him to give himself up, but the personal relates only to my sister. A listening device would compromise that."

Alex leaned forward and put his hand on Samantha's. "It would protect you. If anything goes wrong, we would be able to intervene."

Samantha picked up her glass of tea. "Can we order dinner? I'm starving."

Alex signaled the waiter.

"Would you be willing to wear a discreetly placed tracking device?" Jim asked. His intent brown eyes focused on her as though trying to read her.

"All right."

After the waiter took their order, Moha spoke. "Stephen Carlos Oroya . . . Safir Brahim may not be at the center, but we must assume he is dangerous. Are you sure you want to meet him?"

Samantha's instincts told her this man was central to understanding what happened to her sister. "Yes, I'm sure though I still don't understand why you don't just arrest him."

"We want to know who else is involved and what they're planning," Moha answered. "Friday prayers are celebrating an anniversary of the completion of the Hassan II Mosque. An incident could be timed then to maximize damage. Our security will be especially tight, but there will be tens of thousands of worshippers so it will be impossible to watch everyone."

"But we can watch you," Jim said as the lamb and chicken and vegetable tagines were set on the table, "though first we must get you in."

*   *   *

On the drive out of Casablanca to Rabat, Samantha asked to stop briefly at the Hassan II Mosque. She hadn't been there in years. If an attack did happen, she would have to report on it for her network. She wanted a visual memory and some personal footage just in case. They agreed to a fifteen-minute stop.

It was after sundown prayers, and the worshippers were leaving. Samantha wandered on the edge of the plaza in a long black skirt and headscarf while Moha and Jim and Alex watched nearby. The magnificent white-and-sea-green marble building rose above the Atlantic, its minaret towering like a lighthouse into the heavens. As she scanned skywards with her camera, laser beams flashed at the top, pulsing eastward toward Mecca.

Few women, but thousands of men, milled about. Samantha had reported regularly from the Middle East and also from North Africa. She understood the social and political nature of these evening prayers—the need for community, for tradition, for rituals—but did all these men in baggy trousers and blue jeans, djellabas and burnouses and prayer caps long for and achieve a spiritual connection? She envied them if they did and wondered what it was. Over the years she'd asked this question of all religions and of herself. Her own faith had dissipated though she wished she could reclaim it. She wanted to go inside the mosque, but these were not visiting hours for non-Muslims, and Alex and Jim were signaling her it was time to go.

Jim and Moha spent the hour-and-a-half drive to Rabat arranging clearance for Samantha to approach the house tomorrow. It was agreed she'd go alone carrying her cell phone and wearing a tracking device in her waistband and a small camera pinned to her clothes. It was also decided if Stephen made no outside contact by the following afternoon, they would move in and arrest him.

When they reached the hotel in Rabat, Samantha told the others she was retiring for the night and would see them for an early breakfast. Inside her room she used her mobile phone to call the number Monte had given her. In French she identified herself as Monte's sister to a woman—Tayri—who seemed to be expecting her call and to understand what was being asked of her even if Samantha did not. She suggested they meet in an hour at the entrance of the Kasbah Oudaia where she lived.

*   *   *

Samantha cautiously approached the thirty-foot gate in the red stone wall surrounding the Kasbah. On the wide steps and terrace, young boys kicked a soccer ball in the evening light. A petite, wiry woman swathed in a patterned skirt, blouse, and hand-woven hendira stood waiting, her dark eyes studying each passerby. Her gray-black hair hung in a long loose braid down her back. Her coffee-colored skin was dried and wrinkled.

"Tayri?" Samantha advanced toward her.

She greeted Samantha in French. *"Vous êtes la soeur de la femme enterrée dans le sable?"*

Samantha wondered if her French was up to the conversation she wanted to have. "The woman buried in the sand?"

Tayri took her hand. Her palms were hard and dry. *"Venez avec moi."* She led Samantha through the gate into the Kasbah. A high-walled narrow corridor opened onto a faintly lit street of broken cement and cobblestones, flanked by white stucco houses connected to each other. As they descended into the Kasbah, a car honked its way along the road sending pedestrians crowding to the walls. Samantha wondered where she was being taken and whether she should trust this woman. She looked quickly around to see if anyone was following them.

Tayri led her down the hill toward the bay where the moon darted in and out of clouds over the water. They arrived at a familiar café perched on the promontory above the ocean. The café was filled with people. Samantha had been here before. She saw the neighboring medina and the estuary and fortress, which for centuries protected these waters from pirates marauding the shipping lanes from Europe, North Africa, and the Middle East and from the plundering tribes and acquiring governments that threatened this city on the cheek of the Atlantic. Tayri gestured for her to sit at a table by the rail while she went to get them tea and pastries.

"Why do you say my sister was the woman buried in the sand?" Samantha asked in French when Tayri returned.

"That is what I called her." In French Tayri recounted for Samantha how Monte had dug a bunker in the sand under a tree and refused to go back into the tent where she'd been assaulted.

Tayri had finally persuaded her to return to the tent and promised to stay with her and helped Safir choose guards who would protect Monte.

"My sister was assaulted?" Samantha asked. "How?"

Tayri's eyes fixed on Samantha like a cat watching its prey or its predator. "I am a friend of Safir Brahim, who protected your sister."

"He is the one who kidnapped her," Samantha countered. She was struggling to fit the pieces of Tayri's story together. She studied her face—dark, almond-shaped eyes, small nose, full lips, handsome. Who was she? Monte had been in a desert camp with her, with guards hand-picked by her, guards who had given Monte khat. Yet Monte put her in touch with this woman who was friends with Monte's abductor. "Protect her from whom?" Samantha asked.

"*Les Guerriers de l'Enfer,*" Tayri said. Samantha raised her eyebrows. "That is what Safi calls them. They bet on the devil's fire." Tayri stood. "Come with me."

"Where?" Had she won this woman's confidence or was she about to be abducted herself?

"*Venez avec moi,*" Tayri repeated. Her sister had directed her to this woman so she must trust her. Samantha stood.

Tayri led them to a small stucco house attached to other houses in one long unit winding like a snake through the Kasbah. She unlocked a weathered blue door that had a metal handle and a plaque where the street number had fallen off. A small palm tree and a bright red hibiscus bush flanked the door. A neighbor's doorway showcased a potted lemon tree. Across the path a bougainvillea vine grew up the wall. Samantha tried to memorize the landmarks on this narrow lane in case she ever needed to find the house again in the Kasbah's maze of pathways. Tayri gestured for her to enter.

Inside, three small rooms opened onto each other. Rough woven carpets in oranges and browns covered the floors, and pillows in cotton prints were stacked in the corners. In the main room a TV with an old-fashioned rabbit-ear antenna rested on a table. Tayri locked the door. She set about lighting candles and wicks in bowls of incense. The candlelight flickered on the white walls.

On a hot plate in the main room Tayri heated water and insisted on serving her more tea. From under a cabinet covered by a printed cloth she brought out a dish of reddish-brown paste and another of a dark red powder into which she poured the strong tea. She began stirring until it also formed a paste. She set the bowls aside and took Samantha's hand between her own rough fingers. She studied her palm.

"*Pour la chance,*" she said. "*Pour l'enfant. Vous la retournez.*"

"Return whom?" Samantha asked.

"*L'enfant.*"

Samantha didn't know what she was talking about. "Whose baby?"

"*Votre soeur.*"

"My sister's?"

Tayri picked up a stylus and dipped it in the bowl with the newer mixture, stirring the paste. "It is not ready, but it is sufficient," she said in French, combining the two bowls and dipping the tool into the henna dye. She again took Samantha's hand and began to make marks on her palm, explaining the decoration would protect her from evil spirits. It would also signal that she could be trusted.

"The child of my sister? How?" Samantha pressed.

But Tayri concentrated on shaping a design in dashes and dots like an elaborate Western Union message. The room smelled of melted wax and jasmine incense. The candlelight danced with shadows on the walls. Samantha had little faith in the protection of a henna-painted hand, but if the art could provide some bridge, she accepted the help. Her mind rushed, ferreting through information in order to make sense of this conversation and put it in context as Tayri adorned her palm. Slowly and then with clarity Samantha grasped what must have happened. Monte had been gone eleven months. All at once Samantha's anger swelled like a river overflowing its banks, and she feared suddenly that it would undermine her whole mission to meet and interview Stephen Oroya.

CHAPTER SEVENTEEN

SAMANTHA SAT ON the edge of the hotel bed clicking through pictures from the day of the Festival. She'd looked through these dozens of times, but this morning she paused at a photo taken after the attack. She zoomed in on an image in the mirror behind the bar. For the first time she saw the face she'd been searching for—the reflected image of Stephen Carlos Oroya.

She had tried to remember him. Monte had since told her that his gray hair had been a wig. She wondered if she'd recognize this man with the dark Andalusian eyes and, she presumed, black hair. In the photo his skin was bronzed, his cheeks rosy. He was handsome even in a wig, and in the photo he was smiling, a dimple visible when she magnified the shot.

She'd called Monte last night immediately after meeting with Tayri. "Tayri says you have a child. Is that true?" Her question sounded more like an inquisition. Monte didn't answer. "Where is it?" Monte still didn't respond. "What do you want me to do? Did you put it up for adoption? Is it in an orphanage?"

"I don't know," Monte said finally.

"Don't you want to know?" Samantha sounded angry. She didn't want to be angry. But why hadn't Monte told her? "It could be hurt or in danger . . ."

"Bring her home," Monte said.

This was the first and only acknowledgement by her sister that there was a child and that the child was a girl.

"How?" she asked. "Will you and Philip adopt her?"

Again, Monte fell silent. Finally, she said, "I can't ask that of Philip. Safi and Tayri said they would find a place for her. You decide."

"Monte!" Samantha protested. "On what basis can I decide? Give me Cal . . ."

Samantha wondered now if Stephen was the father. As she prepared to meet this man, she hoped she could keep her poise. She needed to get him to talk, to find out if there was an impending attack, urge him to give himself up. She needed him to tell her what had happened to her sister.

*   *   *

Samantha walked slowly up the hill toward the row of white lime-washed stucco houses, which were painted royal blue at their base to repel mosquitoes. She'd never understood why the sky-blue paint repelled mosquitoes. Most of the houses needed repainting. Down the street she saw a man feigning sleep in a parked car and a woman examining mangos and oranges at a fruit stall. She assumed these were her security. She'd been assured she would be safe, that the house was surrounded, though she was as concerned about the intrusion of the police as she was about Stephen.

Inside the waistband of her loose black slacks, a tracking device had been sewn and deep in her pants pocket was her cell phone. She wore a white shirt covered by a hendira—a loose cloak of woven blue, white, black, and red stripes that Tayri had given her as a gift last night. Pinned to it was a broach in the shape of a star. The camera inside the star would film whatever she aimed at and transmit the photos to keep the police from making mistakes when they entered the house.

As she neared, she glanced at the palm of her right hand with its henna pattern of reddish dots and dashes and floral designs as if it held crib notes. Samantha knocked on the door. She remembered Stephen as educated and cultured, but she also knew violence could stir beneath the most sophisticated surface. She started to knock again when the door opened a crack. On the other side of a chain lock, aggressive brown eyes challenged her, questioning her even before she spoke.

"Bonjour," she said. *"Vous êtes Stephen Oroya?"* She found herself speaking French as if acknowledging the foreignness of this encounter. *"Je suis Samantha Waters, la soeur de Monte Waters."*

"I know who you are," he answered in perfect English. "I recognize your hair." It was an odd, personal comment, and instinctively she reached up and twisted the skein of hair over her shoulder.

"May I come in? I'm alone." She raised her hands, revealing the henna design. She thrust her purse through the crack in the door without being asked. "Here . . . you can check . . ." as if there might be someone tucked inside her bag.

He accepted the purse but didn't open it or the door. Instead, he looked down the street where the woman at the fruit stall had moved on and was now buying pastry.

"I want to talk with you about my sister," she said as she'd practiced.

"Don't say too much," Jim had warned her. *"Your goal is to get inside. Don't give him a reason to say no."*

He shut the door. Samantha didn't move. She heard the chain lifting; the door opened enough for her to slip in.

The house was small, no wider than twenty-five feet, but the abundant light and the water view opened up the vista. The interior was carefully decorated with a white cotton sofa, two white chairs with blue throw pillows the color of the Atlantic, royal blue shutters. Indigo blue bottles on the bookcase and hall table with yellow flowers—daisies and sunflowers. Samantha turned for the camera, surveying a living room, dining room with an adjoining kitchen, a stairway off the front hall, light wood furniture, tan matting on the floors. The space put her at ease in a way she hadn't anticipated.

"What do you want?" Stephen asked.

They were standing in the hallway when a short, gray-haired woman entered in loose white slacks and shirt with a cord belt. Samantha thought she looked as if she could sit next to her own mother and compare decorating and fashion tips. "Safi, aren't you going to ask your guest to sit?" she asked in perfect English.

Guest? Samantha wondered if she had any idea what her son was up to. Did she know the house was surrounded and shortly her son would be arrested for kidnapping and for conspiracies she couldn't imagine?

"She didn't come to sit," Stephen said.

"Please excuse him," the woman offered, gesturing to the sofa in the living room. "Can I make you tea?"

"No," Stephen answered even as she said, "Yes, thank you."

Samantha moved into the living room, accepting the mother's hospitality.

"Why are you here?" Stephen remained standing as she sat on the sofa. "Who is here with you?" He positioned himself in front of a cabinet near the back window where a small porch abutted the house.

"I'm alone."

"We both know that isn't true. Please don't insult me. Why have you come?"

Samantha wanted to examine the cabinet Stephen was blocking. "I need to know what happened to Monte when she was with you."

"Tea." Stephen's mother returned.

Samantha stood to assist with the tray and also to give the camera a view of the cabinet and the back porch.

Upstairs a baby cried. Stephen glanced at Samantha then at his mother. "Don't worry. I'll go," she said. "You talk to your company."

As his mother left, Stephen said, "It's hot in here, don't you think?" And without warning, he took her cloak from her shoulders and hung the hendira on the same hook as her bag with the broach facing the wall. He knew—of course he knew—the devices being used.

Samantha poured tea, acknowledging nothing. Matter-of-factly she began, "We don't have much time. You know they are coming for you." She got up and went to the coat hook where she turned the garment around so the broach camera faced the living room. She walked in front of it. Stephen turned on the radio, thwarting the listening devices aimed at the house. A lute, a clarinet, and drums accompanied a reedy voice singing a local version of "You Are My One and Only Love."

"I'm not wearing any listening device," Samantha said. "You have to trust me but let them see us. The picture may satisfy them and give us more time. I assume you have an escape plan."

"Your cell phone is a device," Stephen said. "Let me have it."

Samantha hesitated then reached into her pocket and handed him her BlackBerry phone, one like Monte and most U.S. government officials used. He opened the back and took out the battery and returned the phone to her.

"They can still track it," she said.

"Why are you here?" Stephen asked again.

"Monte's in bad shape. She's gotten worse since her release, at least it seems so to me. She isn't talking—not in a meaningful way— about what happened to her. The government is debriefing her each day so she must be saying something, but that process may be contributing to her decline. It's as if a central piece is missing, though I think I now understand what that is." Samantha spoke deliberately to keep her anger in check.

Stephen moved out of the sight line of the camera and opened the top drawer of the cabinet by the window. He pulled out a padded envelope. "I'm guessing we have only a few minutes," he said. "I hear footsteps on the roof."

Samantha didn't hear anything. Stephen lifted the hendira from the coat hook, aiming it away from the living room toward the front hall. He folded the envelope and placed it in Samantha's bag. "Please give this to your sister. I didn't anticipate events playing as long and hard as they did."

"Let me start at the end," Samantha said. "Is that child upstairs Monte's?"

Stephen returned to the cabinet and from the bottom drawer lifted out a large cloth bag, which he strapped around his waist. He was wearing jeans and a tee shirt. He was muscular like an athlete or soldier and surprisingly poised for someone about to be arrested. Without looking at her, he answered, "Yes."

"Is she also yours?"

He pulled a navy djellaba over his head, engulfing himself and the bag in the full-length robe with a hood. "No, but I told your sister I would make sure the child found a home. My mother will help."

"Whose child is it?" Samantha asked.

Stephen pulled sturdy leather sandals from underneath the sofa. Samantha sat down in the chair near him. "I didn't protect your sister in the first weeks," he said. "I didn't plan for that contingency.

But the truth is, the child saved her. When her purpose was served, others wanted to kill her." He said this matter-of-factly without looking at Samantha as he put on his sandals. "Because she was with child, I persuaded them to let her bring it to term. I brought in a woman to watch over her. No one would cross this woman." He looked up at Samantha, his eyes insistent as if seeking, or rather demanding, her approval.

Samantha wanted to shout at him, but there was no time for emotion. "Who wanted to kill her?"

"I argued that it was an abomination to kill a pregnant woman. I also persuaded them that the baby had a value—as much as $10,000 if it was a boy or a light-skinned girl, so they were willing to wait."

"What!" Samantha's voice leapt out. Who was this man? Samantha looked outside at the connecting porches of the houses, which interlocked like a beehive. She needed to stay calm, keep her distance. "You said Monte had served her purpose. What purpose was that?"

Stephen stood. He wouldn't look at her. She saw that he, too, was holding emotions in check. She rose to face him. They were almost the same height, eye to eye. She stood so close that she could breathe in his musky odor, like smoke from a fire. She wondered if Monte was attracted to him. According to Monte, she played him to win her release.

"What is the baby's name?" Samantha asked.

For the first time since she arrived, Stephen met her eyes. "Zahara." She heard a softening in his voice. He went over to the cabinet and began filling the pocket of his cloak from a drawer. She couldn't see what he was putting into it. The warm air settled heavily in the room.

In a flat voice she asked again, "What was Monte's purpose? You never asked for ransom. You never contacted the U.S. or any other government, so why did you take her?"

Stephen returned to the hall and aimed the camera toward the kitchen. "You should go into the kitchen for a glass of water," he said.

Samantha now also heard footsteps on the roof and shuffling outside the front door. They had told her they wouldn't make a move till afternoon. She wondered why they were accelerating the plan. Perhaps they saw Stephen getting ready to flee, but they weren't giving her enough time. "Is something being planned for tomorrow?" she pressed.

Stephen turned slightly toward her so that the sunlight illumined half his face. In the hooded robe, he looked like a medieval monk heading to prayers. "There is always something happening tomorrow."

"You won't tell me? I don't suppose you'd consider turning yourself in?" He offered a faint smile. "Then a final question . . ." Samantha walked in front of the camera toward the kitchen. "The day Monte was kidnapped . . . that same day three bombs went off at the Festival . . . How did the local financial markets open the next day?"

Nadia Brahim descended the stairs. In her arms she cradled a baby about two months old with curly black hair, honey brown skin, and green eyes. The infant was swathed in a yellow blanket. Nadia nodded to her son as though she understood what was about to happen. Stephen turned Samantha's cloak one last time so that the star broach focused on his mother, the child, and Samantha. He moved into the living room, where he slipped onto the back porch, and like a shadow passing, he leapt two porches over and disappeared.

The front door flew open. Nadia Brahim retreated farther into the kitchen with the baby in her arms. Men, guns drawn, hurried onto the porch; two men ran up the stairs, and the others fanned out in the downstairs rooms.

"He's gone," Samantha said to no one in particular. She backed into the kitchen, moving in front of the child to shield her.

Nadia asked if she could return the child to her neighbor's before she answered questions. Two policemen conferred then one accompanied her. Samantha didn't correct the deception.

*   *   *

Later that afternoon Samantha looked up the answer to her final question. The day after the bombs at the Festival and the kidnapping, the global stock markets remained on the ascendancy, but the Bolsas y Mercados Españoles (BME) and Bolsa de Madrid (IBEX) in particular, which were already in decline, fell precipitously and continued falling for the rest of the week, not necessarily prompted by the deaths at the Festival or the abduction of a senior U.S. State Department official, but the fall confirmed a loss of confidence and control. The decline assured that whoever bet against these regional markets would, depending on the size of the position, make a lot of money.

CHAPTER EIGHTEEN

"You sure you don't want to go to the Council on Foreign Relations dinner tonight?" Monte's mother asked as they waited together in the living room of their Kalorama home. "I'm sure Dad could get you in."

"I need to be with the children," Monte said. She was curled in a wing chair. She'd reluctantly agreed to this meeting with her parents after Samantha's call last night. Cal had persuaded her that she needed to let their parents know more than she'd told them.

"Cal's picking up your father at the office. You want to tell me what this is about?"

Monte set down *The Economist* on the cluttered antique coffee table. She was reading an article about Russia deploying missiles near Poland in response to U.S. missile defense plans. She stood and paced at the edge of the Persian carpet. She didn't like this room. It reminded her of an embassy with period furniture and gold-framed paintings. In high school she'd been embarrassed to bring friends home because the rooms were so formal, not that she had many friends.

"Let's wait till we're all together," she said. She made an effort to soften her tone. Cal had told her that their mother hadn't been well, that she'd worked tirelessly when Monte was missing, learned to use the internet to communicate with those who'd founded a "Free Anne Montgomery Waters" support group. "You need to make your peace with her," Cal insisted that morning. "You must." Monte didn't argue.

"How's Philip?" her mother asked. "You sure there isn't room for him at Cal's? You know you're all welcome to stay here. We have plenty of room."

"We're fine, Mother."

Lacey Waters reached for a sugar-coated almond in the candy dish, then passed the dish to Monte. "You know . . ." She began as if grasping at some image in her mind. "You know . . ." she repeated . . . "marriage, any marriage, is hard. Some are more difficult than others, but no one, at least no one I know, man or woman, hasn't wanted to flee at some point."

Monte set the white porcelain candy dish on the coffee table without taking any and returned to her chair. "Did you ever want to leave Dad?" she asked, meeting her mother's light lavender blue eyes.

Her mother laughed lightly. "At least half a dozen times, but only once . . . no . . . twice did I start packing my bags."

"I never knew that. How old were we? Where were we living?"

"Both times were after you'd grown and left. The other times . . . and there were others . . . I couldn't, wouldn't leave because of you and Sam and Cal. However angry I was with your father or he was with me, I couldn't have walked out on you. I assume he couldn't either, though we never talked about what brought us back from the brink. We always just returned to our routines and, over time, the bond between us reestablished, sometimes stronger than before. I think it was your father's career that kept him coming back in the door, though he would tell you it was because he loves me. I don't think he likes to consider much more than that."

"I always thought you and Dad had the perfect marriage," Monte said. "I knew you got angry, but I never thought it was serious."

"Anger is always serious," her mother said. Her strawberry blonde hair framed her face, which was wrinkled but still handsome. She'd resisted the facelifts so many of her friends had undergone so her age showed in a natural softening. "But in the end, the family was more important. Our marriage was more important. Because I know your father as well as I do, I stayed. I knew the boy who spent his adult life trying to prove he was worthy. Because he couldn't prove that to himself, I needed to be there because I knew he was worthy."

"Dad?" Monte sat forward on the chair. Her mother had never spoken with her this way before. "But he's been so successful."

Her mother sighed. "Your father can list his accomplishments, but in private he dwells on the failures—treaties he didn't get signed, positions he never achieved, personal slights, the investigation twenty years ago of his judgment. His failures wake him up at night. If you don't feel successful inside, no amount of acclaim can give it to you."

"What about you?" Monte asked. "You were a summa from Radcliffe, Mother. Why did you just live in his shadow?"

This was an old bromide—an excuse Monte had allowed over the years for the distance between her and her mother, but as soon as she spoke this time, she was sorry.

Her mother exhaled and leaned back against the pale-yellow wall as if she too was tired of swinging at this pitch. The top of her head grazed the gilded picture frame with the painting of a boat tossed on a Winslow Homer sea. "I want to help you, Monte, but I don't know how," she said with an exhaustion that gave Monte pause.

Monte leaned toward her. "I'm sorry. I don't know if I can stay here in Washington with Philip. It may not be as simple as your"— her mother's face tightened inadvertently—"or maybe yours wasn't simple." I know Dad can be self-absorbed, completely absorbed by his own world, so it can't have been easy for you. I think I'm more like Dad. Philip tries to figure out what I want and need, what everyone needs. I am the asshole in this, but . . ." Monte hesitated, saved from finishing her sentence by her father and brother coming through the front door.

Edgar Waters dropped his keys onto the mahogany hall table. The brass wall sconces flickered on in the late afternoon light and cast shadows on the maroon wallpapered entry.

"We're in here," her mother called as if also relieved to end a conversation she didn't know how to continue.

Her father stood in the doorway shoulder to shoulder with Cal, though his own shoulders were starting to stoop. Her father's white hair had thinned into a haze on his head. His sharp features and wiry frame were like their great-grandmother Lala's.

"Okay," her father said, stepping into the living room. "I'm here! What do you want to tell us?" He addressed Monte briskly. "Where's Philip? I've hardly seen him since you've been back."

"Philip is taking care of the children," Monte said.

Her father stared at her as if evaluating how she looked, then stepped over and kissed the top of her head, a gesture of affection unusual for him. "How are you settling in?" Monte reached up and touched his hand, but he took it away and went to sit beside her mother. "Now what is this all about?"

Cal sat in the wing chair beside Monte.

"Anyone want a drink?" Her father stood again as if he didn't want to hear whatever it was he was going to be told. Everyone declined so he sank back down on the sofa. "Where is Samantha again?" he asked. He pulled his phone from his pocket and set it on the table.

"Samantha's in Morocco, Edgar. I told you." Her mother reached out for his hand to quiet him.

"I persuaded Monte to come speak with you," Cal began. "She didn't want to at first because she didn't want to worry you."

"Worry us how?" Her father interrupted as if it was his responsibility to structure and lead the meeting.

"Dad . . ." Cal said firmly.

Monte kicked off her sandals and slipped her feet under her so that her kaftan covered her body and legs like a tent. She watched Cal, curious to see what he would say. Cal looked over at her, confirming that this meeting was in his hands.

"There are several difficulties . . . no, that's not the word . . . *outcomes . . . consequences* for Monte . . ." Uncharacteristically, he fumbled with words. "What we need to tell you . . . what Monte needs for you to know and perhaps advise on . . ."

At the word *advise*, Edgar Waters sat up straighter. Whatever it was, their father was ready to give advice.

Cal paused as if considering his course. He took the easier path first. "You see, while she was away, while she was held, Monte was given khat."

"Khat?" her mother looked over at her father.

"Khat is not addictive," her father said. "It is not a narcotic."

"It's a drug?" her mother asked.

"Yes, Lacey. Leaves, I believe. You chew it. Chester dealt with it in Yemen and Ethiopia . . . and also Somalia. People there spend a third of their income and time chewing it. It is a blight on their societies."

"Dad . . ." Cal interrupted. "We are talking about Monte, not Yemen."

"Then you must stop," her father said.

"Can you stop, sweetheart?" her mother asked, adding, "Do you want to stop?"

Monte picked up *The Economist*. "Sure. Okay, I'll stop." Turning to Cal and then her father, she asked, "What do you think about the Russians' move to deploy missiles near Poland?"

"Monte!" Cal admonished. "If she could stop or wanted to stop, perhaps she would, but that is the problem. It is one of the reasons you've gotten so thin," he told her. "All you eat is a few energy bars. The khat takes away your appetite. It's one of the reasons you're not sleeping. And it is slowly eroding your memory. That should worry you."

"It is also illegal," she added as if in a schoolroom, helping the teacher.

Her father studied her as though discerning what others were missing. "Monte, I'd like to speak with you in private," he said.

"How can I help?" her mother asked.

"There is an even more serious issue," Cal said. "One that Samantha is trying to help with on her end."

"Where did you say Samantha was?" their father asked.

"Feel free to step in here, Monte," Cal said.

But Monte grew silent. She couldn't bear what Cal was about to recount. Even now she couldn't talk about what had happened to her. She wanted to block out the rest of what he would say. She waved her hand in consent. "Go on."

"When Monte was captured . . ." Cal told her story as best he could with the information Samantha had provided and with occasional assenting nods from Monte. "She was assaulted in the first days in the camp. She became pregnant; she had a child . . ."

After Samantha's meeting with Tayri last night, she'd called, firing questions at Monte, who couldn't or wouldn't answer, questions that pushed at a boulder Monte had been unable to move. As Samantha talked, Monte peered out Cal's kitchen window into the backyard and tried to see the path ahead she'd been squinting at ever since she'd come home, but the path went only so far and then was obliterated as in a sandstorm when all paths were buried and the landscape emerged different. The dilemma this child posed confounded her.

"There is a child," Cal said, "around two months old. A girl . . . Monte's daughter. Samantha has a small window to find her and influence what happens to her." Cal stood behind Monte's chair then strode across the length of the room with its bay window at one end and the dining room at the other.

"Who is the father?" her father asked.

Monte hugged her knees under her dress.

"Edgar . . . it doesn't matter." Her mother came over and put her arms around her shoulders. "Have you told Philip?"

Monte didn't respond.

"I don't think he knows," Cal answered. "I don't think anyone knew until Samantha went over there."

"People knew," Monte spoke up. "Plenty of people knew . . . just no one here. Safi knew. Tayri knew . . . everyone in the camp knew."

"I meant you hadn't shared with anyone here," Cal said.

"People here don't know much. They don't want to know," Monte said. "They know what we tell them, stories you and Sam tell, stories I used to tell."

The phone vibrated on the table. Her father picked it up and looked at the incoming call. He glanced at Monte then at his wife and Cal. "I'm sorry . . . I have to take this." He stood and withdrew to the dining room.

Monte's eyes followed him even as her mother sat in the chair closer to her. "What is it we don't know?" she asked.

That her father had left at that moment . . . why was she surprised? How many times had an important call come in, some world emergency or just some person more important to him? No one else seemed surprised. That was who he was. Was that who she was?

"I don't know, Mother," she answered. "I'm looking for the burning bush and the blinding light . . . we don't know much."

Her father returned. "Tonight's speaker at the Council got called to Poland. They've asked me to step in." He gestured to Monte. "Will you come with me to my study so we can discuss this?"

Monte unfolded her legs and slipped on her sandals and followed her father. She wasn't sure if *this* was Russian missile deployment outside of Poland or her abandoned child.

*   *   *

Monte watched the morning sky turn from black to navy as the twinkling lights in the trees clicked off in Cal's backyard. The sun had not yet risen. She sat in front of her computer at the kitchen table before the children awoke. The dog slept at her feet. Her handlers had asked her to help bring Safi in. He was the link to the Elder. Her father was the only one who'd guessed what had been asked of her. That was why he took her into his study. He told her not to go.

"You're here. You're safe. You're still recovering," he said.

"I don't want to go," she answered, but she knew already that she would.

"It's unfair for them to ask you, though they wouldn't ask unless the stakes were high. Surely you can tell them what you know, and someone else can go."

But she couldn't tell anyone else what she knew. She watched her father from across his desk where she'd sat so many times in the past as they shared their views of the world. Her father gazed at her through his pale green eyes without really comprehending who she was or what she'd experienced. His wispy white hair made him look more vulnerable than she ever remembered. As they spoke, he fingered an old Roman coin that had been given to him by one of his favorite Foreign Service officers he'd sent on a mission that resulted in his death. She and Sam and Cal had been children at the time. There'd been an investigation; their father had been exonerated, but she knew he carried the mission's failure and this young officer's death with him.

Now she was being asked to travel back to the region she'd just escaped from to bring in the man who'd both captured and freed her. She wanted to put Safi behind her, but she knew she couldn't until the Elder was captured or killed. She didn't want Safi to be killed. When Samantha told her that he'd been located, she knew she would have to go. Yesterday she was told Safi had escaped the authorities who'd had him in their sights.

"Samantha can handle the child," her father had said as if trying to guess what she was thinking. "I can help." She nodded. She didn't argue. She needed to stay focused. When she didn't speak, her father said, "All right, do what you must. Bring your contact in, then come home."

Upstairs, Monte heard her children stirring as the sunlight eased through the windows of Cal's kitchen. She wanted time with them before she left. She should have told Samantha about Zahara, but she couldn't see a way forward. Now that Samantha had pulled back the veil and discovered the child, she felt more able to act.

Coming Friday to G. Alone. Confirm. She pressed SEND on the computer. She didn't know if Safi would get the email so she also texted the message to the phone number he'd given her. She hadn't told anyone of the phone's existence. She hadn't betrayed him yet. She closed her computer and went upstairs to her children.

*   *   *

Tucked in a back booth drinking black coffee, Monte watched Philip wrestle open the door of the 24-hour coffee shop on Wisconsin Ave. His face was flushed, his hair windblown across his pate. He stood awkwardly in his gray suit and striped tie under the fluorescent light that bounced off the lime green walls. He didn't recognize her at first in her new black tee shirt, black padded vest, and cap that hid her hair, which she'd clipped short that morning.

When he finally spotted her, he approached the booth cautiously, sliding his briefcase onto the cracked vinyl. Before he could comment on her appearance, she began, "I have to go away. Can you take care of the children? You can move into Cal's. That will be the easiest for them."

"When are you going? Where?"

"Today. I'll be back as soon as I can, but I may be away for a week or more."

"Have you asked Cal if I can stay?"

"He won't mind."

"So I just show up?"

"Craig gets out of school at three. Emma's done at two thirty. I told them you were picking them up today."

"You know I work today," Philip said. "Have you told them you're leaving?"

"I told them you would be picking them up from school and staying with them this week. They're happy about that." Monte passed him a key to Cal's house.

"You didn't say you were going away?"

"Craig suspected, but I didn't say it directly. It's too big an abstraction for Emma. She can't cope with it directly."

"It's going to be pretty direct when you don't show up tonight," Philip said.

"You'll be there. That will make it easier for them."

"Out of curiosity, did you consider asking me first?"

"Please, Philip, let's not do this. Yes, I considered, but I couldn't. I have to go. I knew you would be there for the children." She smiled and tried to offer a gesture, touching his hand on the table.

"Have you told Cal you're leaving?"

"I left him a note. I didn't want to face all his questions." She looked around for the waitress and waved her over. "You want breakfast? My treat." She smiled again, glancing around the run-down coffee shop with pictures of the specials behind the counter and a jukebox up front. "How are you anyway?"

"I've accepted the job with Lambent and Taylor. I start the first of the year."

She hesitated, but she didn't have the time or the standing anymore for this argument. "Well . . . if it's good for you."

"I'd like it to be good for all of us. For our family. It will mean a lot more money. You can take a break if you want."

Monte stared out the window onto the busy street with cars and red buses passing by. "I'd like it to be good for us too, but I'm not sure it can be. Will you stay on at the club?"

"I've contacted the tenants in our house. I found them an even better house and offered to pay their moving costs. They've agreed. I move back into our house the first of January. I've contacted the local school, and Craig and Emma can start in January. I'm hoping you will come too."

Monte leaned forward in the booth. "You did all this without asking me?" She felt both annoyed and relieved that Philip was taking action.

"You haven't exactly been available to consult with."

"I have to go." She couldn't allow herself to get distracted. She stood in her black jeans and heavy walking boots. She leaned down and kissed him on the top of his head. "What will you be lobbying for?" she asked.

"Missiles and fighter jets," he said almost defiantly.

"You'll make sure the bids and contracts are honest and accurate." She stated what she assumed was his job.

"That's what I do." As she turned toward the door, he said, "Take care of yourself."

She nodded and waved her hand over her shoulder.

CHAPTER NINETEEN

SAMANTHA PLACED the DO NOT DISTURB sign on her door and asked the hotel operator not to put through any calls. Dressing in her long skirt and headscarf, she slipped out the patio door and into the garden where a fountain spilled water over a blue-and-white-tiled basin. Earthen walls surrounded the courtyard filled with beds of blue delphiniums, pink and yellow roses, fuchsia bougainvillea, decorative grasses, and palm trees. She hurried past a filigree bird cage, home to a white cockatoo, and pushed at a heavy metal gate that opened only from the inside. She slipped into the bustling street where she hailed a taxi and headed to the Kasbah.

Moving along the narrow turquoise-and-white corridors of the Oudaia Kasbah, Samantha searched the lanes looking for Tayri's blue door with the missing numbers. She was hoping Tayri would know what happened to the child and tell her more about what happened to Monte. Now that she'd seen the baby, she wanted to know what was planned for her. With Stephen on the run, Tayri was her only connection, one she hadn't shared with others.

The muezzin's sunset call to prayer echoed from the local mosque where men were moving toward a large wooden portal; a few women entered by a smaller side door. Nearby she found the lane with the bougainvillea vines and the hibiscus bush beside the door whose numbers had fallen away. She knocked, but no one answered. She knocked again. She joined those descending to the tea shop where she and Tayri first met. She settled on a stool at one of the blue wooden tables above the bay. The sky shone a deep azure with pink-tinged clouds coasting out to sea.

She was dialing Tayri's number again when her phone rang. "Oui?" She expected Tayri.

"Samantha?" The voice traveled the ether and arrived as clearly as if Cal had just sat down at the table.

"Cal? Where are you?"

"In D.C. I wanted to let you know Monte is heading your way."

"Monte? When?"

"Apparently, she flew out today. Philip showed up this afternoon. Monte told him she needed to go away for a while but didn't tell him where. I talked with Dad. He implied her trip had something to do with Stephen Oroya and said she might be coming to Morocco. He said we needed to let her do what she had to do right now."

"What does that mean?"

"Honestly, I don't know. I'm just passing on information. Philip and I are taking care of the children. See if you can help our sister."

"I'm trying. I'll let you know." Samantha wondered why Monte hadn't contacted her. It wasn't a good sign that she was returning here. Monte was still frail both physically and emotionally. Samantha dialed Monte's phone, but no one answered. "Call me," she said, leaving a message, then she tried Tayri's phone a third time. She sent Tayri a text: *appelle moi* then pulled out a piece of paper and wrote a note: *Appelle moi. Dis à Monte que je peux aider. (44) 0793 273 3971 or 037 75 27 27.*

On the way back up the hill, Samantha knocked once again at Tayri's door then slipped her note under the threshold.

*   *   *

At the hotel Samantha showered and dressed for dinner in the same full-length black skirt, but she put on a top with a beaded neckline and draped a gold belt around her waist. She used her black scarf as a shawl. She was worried about Monte who got exhausted just climbing a flight of stairs or running after her children on the playground.

Before Samantha went downstairs, she reached into her purse for a notepad and instead pulled out the envelope Stephen had given her. In the rush of the security forces this morning, she'd forgotten about the envelope. Without hesitation she opened it and drew out a brown leather journal. Flipping to the back page, she saw an entry written this morning: *Who is this woman walking up the path as though it is just another day?*

She turned to the first page, dated February 5, and sank into the chair by the patio door. Several entries began with dollar figures and percentages. One entry had a summary: *MTD: + 1.01% +$5,757,000; YTD-+8.05%, +$46,343,850; Assets: $575,700,000; com+$17,904,770.* These appeared to be returns on investments and the commission earned. But then there was another list with negative numbers. She checked her watch. She was due at dinner with Moha and Jim and Alex, but she continued to read. Figures were sporadically recorded above the main entries in the journal. And then:

May 28: Born under a full moon in the middle of the night. A girl. Green eyes wet with tears, wrapped in Monte's old shirt, nursing. Tayri won't let anyone else in. The guards say they heard cries and ask if the baby has come. Tayri tells them it was false labor; the mother is in pain and must be left alone. Tayri and Monte understand once the child is born, we are all in danger.

When I see the child, her smooth caramel-colored skin, pursed lips, I know she isn't mine. Tayri tells me, "She is yours whoever the father. You brought her mother here. You are responsible." Monte assumes the father is Shar, not me or the Elder, but she doesn't know and says she doesn't care. Zahara—that is what Monte and Tayri have named her—her name means 'shining, luminous.' She nurses greedily. She doesn't cry. She clings to Monte, gripping Monte's fingers and suckling as if she will not let Monte escape. She watches me.

June 7: Ten days since Zahara's birth, three days since it is known . . . we have to leave. The enforcers arrive tomorrow. They will kill Monte.

As Samantha read these words, she shuddered. She flipped quickly through the rest of the pages. Near the end, on the eve of their leaving, Stephen recorded an account of his own brother's death in the Western Sahara. The entry concluded: *His single soul resisted.*

Samantha stared out at the evening light in the garden. Who was this man Stephen/Safir? If he only wanted money, he would have left Monte behind. He wouldn't have helped her escape and endangered himself. In scanning the entries, Samantha saw no mention of a plot to blow up the Hassan II Mosque. That was the main focus today of Alex, Moha, and Jim's questioning of Stephen's mother after the raid.

Early in Samantha's career one of her mentors had told her that a lie often hid within stories like a black snake coiled in the garden—sometimes harmless, sometimes deadly. From this lie other lies emerged. If you could find the truth, you could uncover the lie; but find only the lie, and you would keep peeling away its layers . . . lie upon lie until it possessed you. Samantha was searching for the truth about this man.

*   *   *

Moha paced between the lounging sofas in the hotel lobby, still dressed in his mustard-colored burnous and maroon fez, when Samantha came downstairs. She joined him under the beige silk that hung from the ceiling creating an illusion of a sultan's tent. Inside the folds of silk, hundreds of twinkling lights illumined the room. Jim perched on one of the sofas in this tent texting on his phone. He had changed from jeans and tee shirt into dark slacks and a loose embroidered Moroccan shirt. Both men carried black nylon travel bags.

Jim stood when Samantha appeared. He nodded to her, and his intense stare made her think he knew she'd been somewhere she wasn't sharing. The three of them joined Alex in the restaurant, settling on cushions around a low circular wood table.

"So what did we find out today?" Alex asked. They'd interviewed Nadia Brahim together and then separately at the police station. "You still think an attack is planned for tomorrow?"

Moha took a pinch of cumin seeds from a bowl in the center of the table and bit them between his teeth. "We will provide maximum security at the mosque," he said without answering the question. All day Samantha had studied Moha who waited for others to ask questions, listened to the answers, then added one or two questions that she suspected linked to information he already knew. There was limited translation so she had been dependent on Alex and Jim to fill her in when the discussion had accelerated in Arabic. If Moha anticipated an attack in Casablanca tomorrow, Samantha wondered why he was having dinner tonight in Rabat sixty miles away.

"Do you think an attack has been the goal all along?" Samantha asked.

"Are you covering this?" Alex asked as the waiter set down a basket of breads—khoubz, mufletas, and matlouhs.

Samantha took the khoubz. "If something happens, I can't ignore it. My network knows I'm here." Monte had once accused her of being addicted to the news. At the time she'd argued, but maybe it was true. For her, life was a story she was always pursuing; she wanted to be the first to tell it and to get it right. That instinct made her competitive and good, but it hadn't won her many friends and had upturned more than one relationship. Her mother once asked, "Are you chasing news so no one will catch you? What are you afraid of?" Samantha had laughed and hugged her mother. She didn't answer that she was afraid of living an under-loved and under-valued life, of missing the huge varieties of life.

Leaning forward on the table now, she tried for a less urgent tone. "Stephen said nothing to me about an attack. Maybe he's not involved. What would be the motive?"

"Chaos," Moha answered. "Disruption."

"Anyone who wants to overthrow this government could hardly choose a more dramatic target," Jim added.

"Would they be Muslims, outsiders, citizens?" Samantha recalled reports of the attack on the Grand Mosque in Mecca in 1979 when Islamic dissidents took hostages and declared one of their own as the Mahdi—the redeemer of Islam—and called on Muslims to obey him. Hundreds of pilgrims there for the annual hajj were held at gunpoint. In the battle to regain control over a two-week period, 250 people—troops, pilgrims, and insurgents—were killed and hundreds more injured. The false Mahdi was killed, and ultimately the insurgents were captured and beheaded in public squares in Saudi cities. Afterwards the Ayatollah in Iran speculated that the event was really a U.S./Zionist plot. That lie seeped through the air like poison gas, fueling riots and assaults on U.S. embassies.

"Who says they are Muslims?" Moha challenged. "There are those who claim to be Muslims who are no better than criminals. They wrap themselves in religious words the way your Ku Klux Klan claimed to be Christians as they hung innocent men."

That was as much passion as she'd heard from Moha all day. A bear of a man in his mid-fifties, he'd spent his life in the service of his country's kings.

"Where is your sister?" Alex asked as the waiter set down the first course. "Can we call her?"

Samantha took portions of hummus and carrot salad on her plate. She didn't want to tell Alex that Monte was flying over. She considered telling him about Monte's child, but she wanted to talk with Monte first. She pulled out her cell phone. "I'll try." Monte hadn't answered her last three calls so she thought it was safe to phone, but to her surprise, Monte answered. "Samantha?"

"Monte, where are you?"

"Madrid."

In the background she heard the gate announcements from Madrid's Barajas Airport. She looked at the three men and hoped they couldn't hear. "Mont, I'm here with Alex Serrano . . . remember him? Alex and the Moroccan security chief and Jim Leon from the American Embassy—they were asking me where you are . . ." She hoped her voice communicated caution. "Would you speak with Alex? He has a few questions . . ." She smiled at the men.

"I can't do that," Monte said. "You deal with them. I have a date with Hercules." She hung up.

"Monte? Monte?" Samantha frowned. "We were disconnected. Let me try again." She dialed, but this time Monte didn't pick up. She dialed one more time. "We'll have to try later."

During the main course of chicken and lamb tagines and bisteeya, Jim said, "A recent caravan passed the camp where we think your sister was held. It confirmed everyone has moved out."

"Whose caravan?"

"Local traders we work with. This was the first time they've actually gone into the camp," Moha added.

"How long did you know Monte was there? Was she in Morocco?"

"It wasn't in Morocco, and we weren't certain your sister was there," Moha said. "She rarely came outside. Our contacts never saw her, but there were rumors that an American woman was in the camp and that she was pregnant."

"Pregnant?" Alex glanced at Samantha.

"Yes," Samantha confirmed. She picked at the chicken and vegetables on her plate. The restaurant was dimly lit with candles on the low tables and lights like torches in the aisles between the enclosed eating areas. There were few patrons yet.

"Whose child was that at the house today?" Alex asked.

Samantha washed down her dinner with half a glass of sparkling water and feigned listening to the Andalusian music playing on guitars, drums, and tambourines so she didn't have to answer. She didn't want to lie. "So where did those in the camp go?" she asked Moha.

"That's our concern," he answered. The existence of a child was not his concern. "Most of the men made their way to the nearest villages then fanned out. Last night three of them landed in Casablanca. We think more are driving in or coming in private planes and landing undocumented."

The possibility of something happening at the Mosque suddenly took on a heightened urgency.

"There may be multiple targets," Alex said. "I'm flying back to Madrid."

Samantha assumed Monte was in Madrid en route to Morocco, which meant she could be arriving in either Casablanca or Tangiers tonight. "Where was the camp?" she asked. "How did you find it?"

"Deep in the Sahara, in a barren and unapproachable stretch of earth," Jim answered. "A Tuareg tribesman Moha and I have worked with spotted it and told us."

"He said there were heavily armed men so he never went too close," Moha added.

"What have you found in the camp?" Samantha asked.

"Can't tell you everything, Sam," Alex said.

"How long have you known?"

"I just found out a few days ago," Alex answered.

"I assure you, if you help us, you'll be helping your sister," Jim said. In jeans and baseball cap, Jim could pass for a young Peace Corps volunteer, but tonight in the candlelight, in local dress with a shadow of a beard on his tan skin and his wavy black-brown hair slicked back, he looked like the experienced professional he was. "Your sister's been briefed by the Agency. She may be on her way over here."

So Jim also knew she was coming. "Do you know where and when?" Samantha asked.

"I was hoping you could tell us—whether she's coming straight to Casablanca or here?" Jim didn't mention Tangiers. "She left without reporting in."

"What can Monte do?" Samantha asked as the waiter filled their glasses.

Jim held off answering until the waiter left. "She knows Stephen better than anyone. Stephen can identify the men we're looking for.

We're hoping we can strike a deal with him. We think your sister is the one to accomplish that."

Moha glanced at his watch; it was after nine p.m. He scanned the dining room where patrons were starting to arrive. "We need to leave," he said.

"Will you come with us to Casablanca?" Jim asked Samantha as if he wanted her to come. "We can wait for you."

Samantha's instinct was to go to Tangiers where she thought Monte might be headed. Monte said she had a date with Hercules. Was that a clue? She and Monte had read Greek myths together as children and knew them well, including the story of Hercules smashing through the isthmus between Tangiers and Gibraltar to create the continents of Europe and Africa. If Monte was going there, Stephen and the child might be headed there too. Yet if Samantha wanted to pursue the story, she should return to Casablanca where major news might happen tomorrow.

Jim and Moha stood. Moha indicated with a slight tilt of his head a table in the rear where two men dressed in black jackets had sat down and were watching them.

Jim's eyes darted to and from the table almost imperceptibly. "You should come with us," he said to Samantha.

"I'll get a ride in the morning," she answered. "I'm tired."

Alex's eyes also darted to the table in the rear. "You go on," he told Jim. "I'll stay here with Sam."

"You want to tell me who those men are?" Samantha asked.

"I'm not sure," Jim said, "but I don't want you to be the one to find out."

"I have a car," Alex said. "We'll leave early."

As Jim and Moha picked up their overnight bags, the two men at the back table signaled for their check. Jim fished a card from his pocket that said he was a regional specialist at the embassy and gave it to Samantha, then he pulled out his phone. "What's your number?" he asked Samantha. He dialed it, and a brief bar of Gershwin's *American in Paris* sounded from Samantha's purse. "Now you have my number, and I have yours if anything happens."

"So we'll find out who they're here to watch," Alex said as Moha and Jim left the restaurant.

The two men in the corner hesitated then the burlier one with dark hair and moustache stood and left. He wore a black leather jacket and looked like an aging wrestler. The slighter man wearing a tailored black jacket sat looking through credit cards.

"I guess we're all of interest," Alex said.

"Of interest to whom?"

"By the look of them, I'd say the Russian or Chechen mafia. If I'm right, we shouldn't stay around to find out."

"Why would they be following us? You think they're connected to Monte?"

"From what we know, the camp where Monte was kept was financed by drug and weapons trade. "Those guys"—he nodded toward the booth—"don't care about religion or politics. They're probably also looking for Stephen. Maybe they spotted us at his mother's house today."

Alex moved around the table and sat next to Samantha so they both had a view of the man in the rear without appearing to look. He was fair-skinned with white-blond hair, tall and rail thin. The dim lights made it difficult to see his face. "I think we're all right as long as we sit here talking, so let's take advantage. Tell me why you're really here," Alex asked quietly.

"I told you."

"I didn't want to press with Moha and Jim around, but I know you well enough, even after twenty years, to know that Stephen told you more than you're telling us. The child . . . is it Monte's? Is it also his? If these people . . ." he again cocked his head slightly toward the rear table, "know about the child . . . and surely they must . . . they won't think twice about using it for their own means, at the very least to get from Stephen what they want."

"She's not Stephen's child."

"But she is Monte's?" Alex asked.

Samantha nodded. "Though Monte didn't tell me till I got here."

"Why not?"

"I think she planned to leave the child with others and didn't want everyone second-guessing her or judging her. Or maybe she was protecting her other children or protecting the child. I don't know what she was thinking."

"I always pictured you with children, though I confess I couldn't imagine when you'd slow down enough to have them. I imagined you with teenage sons. I read about you and Evan Brady. I'm sorry about his death."

Samantha nodded. "Thank you." She reached for her water. She waved to the waiter. "Shall we order tea?" The man in the corner was on the telephone but was watching them.

Alex leaned toward Samantha and touched her hand. "You remember in high school when we hid out in front of that Minister's house because we thought Ivan Molinsky's father was a Russian spy, and we followed him?"

Samantha smiled. "I still think he was a spy, but we couldn't prove it."

"We couldn't . . . at least that's what your father said. Maybe your father was protecting him."

"My father took our meager dossier to check it out, but then we graduated, and life moved on."

"I learned a lot from you, Sam."

"And I from you." She removed her hand and cupped both palms around the glass of tea. "You're lucky, Alex. You have a family and a loving wife." Alex raised his eyebrows questioning the latter assumption. "Well, that's yours to figure. Let's keep it simple between us."

Alex touched the side of her cheek. "You're the boss. You always have been."

"So, let's focus on logistics and lose this guy."

"I suggest you get up and make your way toward the ladies' room, then slip off to your room and pack. I'm already packed. I'll keep his attention here. We'll have to find a way to get out of the hotel so he doesn't see us."

"Is your room on the garden level?" Samantha asked. "There's a gate in the garden that opens to the street on the northwest wall, near the bird cage."

"Perfect. I'll get the car to meet us there. Fifteen minutes enough time?"

Samantha stood and asked the waitress in a projected voice, *"Où sont les toilettes?"*

*   *   *

Back in her room Samantha changed into her slacks and hendira and threw her skirt, sleeping tee shirt, and toiletries into her suitcase. She'd never fully unpacked. When she went to unplug her computer, she noted it had been moved. She also noticed the curtain over the door to the garden was half opened. Perhaps housekeeping had come in. She tested the patio door. It was locked. She tried to keep in check the paranoia she felt rising. Over the years she'd felt the trembling in the atmosphere before a story broke. Tonight, the air was vibrating.

She dialed Tayri's cell, but Tayri still didn't answer. She texted Monte: MEET U IN TANGIERS? WHERE? AM ALONE. SAM.

She needed to get away from Alex. She had decided not to return to Casablanca, but she didn't want Alex following her to Tangiers. She didn't want to dance through the emotional and diplomatic minefields he had laid around her.

She dropped a note for him at the front desk, then she headed out the front door and into a taxi to the Sofitel. She looked through the rear window to see if anyone was following. At the 5-star hotel with security guards, she went inside, waited until her taxi driver left, then took another taxi. Pulling her scarf around her head, covering her hair and part of her face, she handed the new driver a slip of paper. When they arrived at the address, she gave him a large tip and asked him to carry her suitcase to the door and wait for her on the street.

She wasn't sure how long she had until surveillance notified Alex and Moha and Jim that she was there. Her plan was risky, but when Alex told her tonight that others might find and threaten the child and use the child as leverage, she knew what she had to do. She had figured out where the child was. Stephen had gone onto the porch just moments before the security forces entered the front door today. The house and street were surrounded and later searched by surveillance teams. It occurred to her that he hadn't escaped at all. He'd simply disappeared into a neighbor's house. When Nadia Brahim delivered the child to her neighbor, she was in fact handing it back to her son, who was either in disguise or hiding there.

Alex had given her the clue when he reminded her of their stakeout of the Russian minister's home all those years ago. Her father had pointed out that the easiest way to hide was to hide in plain sight. "If you want to exchange important ideas or secret information, call a press conference," he said. "Tell the press and your adversaries what you're doing, just don't tell them everything. If you try to hide everything, they'll search out a story."

*   *   *

Nadia Brahim appeared to be expecting Samantha, who pulled out a pad and wrote rather than spoke: "I have come for my sister's child."

Nadia nodded and let Samantha in. She also didn't speak but took Samantha up the stairs to her bedroom, which looked out on the harbor. Inside her closet she led Samantha up another flight of narrow stairs that ended on the roof where the lights of Rabat twinkled below. Nadia locked the doors behind them and slipped the key into her pocket.

Samantha followed her, moving deftly across the rooftops to a small greenhouse tucked at the back of an adjacent building. Nadia unlatched the door. Potted fruit trees—orange, lemon, lime, and apricot—lined the walls, along with small planters of herbs. The room was lit by a flashlight hanging from the ceiling. Under the light in a sagging brown chair sat Stephen. Beside him a bassinet, improvised from a laundry basket, rested on the concrete floor. The space looked like a tiny Garden of Eden with a crèche. In the basket a wide-eyed child observed Samantha's arrival. Her small legs began to kick.

Stephen didn't look surprised to see Samantha. He set the basket onto a cot strewn with clothes. He lifted out the baby, dressed in an oversized green sweater and pink tights, and handed her to Samantha. "Zahara," he introduced.

Awkwardly Samantha accepted the small bundle. The child's large green eyes peered up at her. Her skin was like coffee-colored silk; a full head of curling black hair framed her oval face. She grasped Samantha's finger with one hand and reached toward her hair with the other. She put Samantha's finger into her mouth.

"Ah . . ." Samantha gasped. "She's so alert and . . . so beautiful."

"Yes," Stephen said. Stripped down to a tee shirt and jeans, he quickly began picking up the clothes from the cot and attaching the pouch he'd belted earlier around his waist. He looked around the greenhouse floor and located a zipped cloth bag, which he handed to Samantha. "Here are a few supplies. Take her home."

"*Home?* Where are *you* going?" Samantha kept her eyes on the child, who was staring back at her. "I can't just walk out of the country with her."

Stephen dug into the bag and pulled out a blue American passport. "You'll need this."

Samantha opened the passport, which was in the name of Zahara Waters. "How did you get this?"

"It will get her into the U.S., then you can sort out the rest."

"I can't use a fake passport," Samantha protested as Zahara reached up toward her face.

"It's legitimate," Stephen said.

"But how?"

Stephen pulled a loose shirt over his head then sat on the cot and took off his sandals. "Your father arranged it. My mother picked it up this afternoon."

"My father?" Samantha looked over at Nadia Brahim, who was packing towels into the diaper bag. "How do you know my father?"

"I don't," Stephen said. He dropped the sandals into his backpack. From behind a plant, he pulled out heavy desert boots. "Monte texted me to send my mother to the U.S. Embassy with a photo. I assumed she or your father got in touch with you."

Samantha reached into her pocket for her phone and saw that her father had called twice. There was also a text from Monte. *Don't come. Go home. Take Zahara. M*

Monte must have told their father about the child when they met yesterday, and in spite of what Samantha imagined were his and her mother's considerable reservations, he must have contacted the American Ambassador here. She wondered if he'd given the full story or just vouched for the baby of a U.S. citizen, who happened to be his daughter. American passports were hard to get, but a newborn baby, the granddaughter of a U.S. diplomat, was perhaps above suspicion. At what age, she wondered, did suspicion take root?

"It was waiting at the embassy," Stephen said.

"Have you talked to Monte?"

Stephen attached his pack then pulled the navy djellaba over his blue jeans and shirt, shrouding his whole body. "I researched you the night we first met," he answered instead. "One article said you were dangerous." He leveled his gaze on her, his dark eyes searching hers. He hadn't answered her question about Monte. "It said you exposed the hearts of the people in your stories."

Samantha held the baby to her chest. She could feel the small heart beating. She couldn't remember when she'd held a child this small. She wasn't around when Monte's children were born—where was she? Covering what . . . the aftermath of 9/11, the invasion of Afghanistan? She had no memory of Cal's children as babies. Zahara held tightly to her blouse with one fist. With the other she gripped Samantha's finger, which she returned to her mouth.

"She may be teething early," Nadia Brahim offered. It seemed a non sequitur in the face of what was happening and about to happen, but what did this child know about the world swirling around her? She knew that a soft finger in her mouth to suck on was soothing, and she held onto Samantha as if she sensed Samantha's importance to her. The world both shrank and opened for Samantha.

"I would feed her now," Nadia suggested. "You have a journey ahead of you." Nadia opened a can of formula powder and measured it in a bottle then poured in water, screwed on a nipple, shook the bottle, and handed it to Samantha, who observed the simple procedure. Nadia motioned for her to sit in the chair and adjusted the baby in her arms.

"I read about you too," Samantha said as she held the bottle for the baby and watched Stephen dress. Was he going to see Monte? "I read your journal." She glanced over at Nadia Brahim, who was still packing the diaper bag. "Is your brother why you joined the Elder and *Les Guerriers de l'Enfer?*"

At the mention of his brother and the *nom de guerre* he'd given those around the Elder, Stephen looked up. "I didn't join them."

"You kidnapped Monte," she said carefully. She wondered how much his mother knew, how complicit she was, or perhaps she was just supporting her son, whatever he did.

"That was a mistake."

"You kept her for eleven months. If I read your journal correctly, you invest and make money for them . . . and for yourself."

"Another mistake," he said. "Giving you the journal. I didn't calculate you would read it." His voice was hard.

"Monte is my sister."

"And you are a journalist. When you see her, I hope you'll still give it to her."

"She'll have to turn it over, you know?"

"I leave that to her."

"I assume you're meeting up with her?" Stephen didn't answer. He laced up his boots then glanced at his mother, who looked at neither of them as she fussed with the child's bag. "How old were you when you found out your brother had died?" Samantha asked.

Nadia touched the top of her son's head with her fingertips, like small feathers alighting then flying away. Stephen sat up and leaned toward Samantha. "I was twenty-eight."

Samantha had read his account and also read about his guilt that he didn't work harder to find his brother and his shame that his parents didn't do more because they were afraid for him and his own anger that the United States military he'd served also trained Moroccan soldiers who imprisoned his brother.

"Monte told me you wouldn't let her just disappear," he said.

"And yet we couldn't find her," Samantha answered. During the months Monte was missing, panic and fear had lodged under all her routines. In the end Monte had saved herself with the help of this man, her captor, who had himself lost a brother. She glanced down at the baby whose warm body comforted her. She wanted to ask Stephen how he could inflict the same fate on someone else, but first she asked, "Is there an attack planned for tomorrow at the Hassan II Mosque?"

Before he could answer, her phone rang. "What are you doing there?" the voice asked.

"Who is this . . . Jim?"

"Don't talk. Just listen. If you're with Stephen, keep him there. Police are on the way."

"How do you know . . . ?"

Nadia Brahim had locked all the doors as they disappeared up the attic stairs. She assumed crossing the roofs to another building would buy them time.

"You're still wearing your tracking device. We've got your location . . ."

"I've got a child here," she pleaded. "Please . . ." She looked up, alarmed at Stephen and his mother, who were watching her.

Stephen didn't wait for an explanation. He grabbed his backpack from the cot and bolted behind the citrus trees. She heard a door open in the rear.

"Stay low," Jim said.

CHAPTER TWENTY

MONTE LEANED HER HEAD against the window and shut her eyes as the plane banked to the left then dropped into the clouds from the clear night sky. She needed sleep, but her mind was racing. She was running through the desert looking for shade and a place to hide . . . she was studying ancient Greek by flashlight . . . her father was telling her to learn languages so she could communicate when others could not. She was speaking her languages . . . French, Spanish, English, German from high school, Arabic from college, but it was the ancient Greeks she loved. The Greeks slayed monsters and saw beauty where others saw terror in the world. The Greeks imagined Hercules to clear the earth of monsters. She wanted the courage of Hercules and the imagination to see beauty so she could prevail over terrors.

The plane emerged from the clouds into the lights along the coastline of Tangiers. On the opposite shore, the twinkling city of Gibraltar and the glow from Algeciras, Spain, lit up the corridor where the Mediterranean met the Atlantic at the doorway to Africa. Rising into the dark sky were the two Pillars of Hercules—the Rock of Gibraltar in Europe erupting from the sea like a giant's thumb and the gentler Monte Hacho in Ceuta on the coast of Africa, one of the places Greeks and Romans thought the world ended, now a city in Spanish Morocco. The Romans believed Hercules created the Straits by pulling apart the landmasses, using these two pillars, then he wrote on the rocks: "Non Plus Ultra": *There is nothing beyond.* When Columbus "discovered" America, the Spanish Royal Coat of Arms had been amended to include, "Plus Ultra," acknowledging something did exist beyond.

As the plane followed the coastline, Monte reread the reply she'd received from Safi before she left: HEADING TO THE INTERIOR. He hadn't signed the message, but she thought she knew where he was going. She answered him before she flew out of Washington: MEET U THERE FRI PM. She wanted to persuade him to come in before he was killed by those he'd betrayed or by the security forces of the three countries hunting him.

She tried to sleep. When she landed, there would be little chance for rest. She would take a taxi and make her way down the coast to a marina where Tayri was waiting for her. From there she would cross the channel in a private boat to avoid a record. At the airports in Washington and Madrid she'd watched each passenger to assure she was traveling unobserved, but she didn't underestimate surveillance.

Two days before, in Washington, she had ducked out of Cal's after the children had gone to school and shopped for the jeans and tee shirt and boots she now wore. Fitting her new body into a size 4, she'd felt oddly reborn. She'd never worn a size 4 in her life. She stared at herself in the mirror, trying to recognize the petite person who looked more like a cheerleader than the debate team captain. She stuffed the other new clothes she'd bought into a small duffel. Yesterday, after everyone left the house, she had cut her hair in the bathroom and flushed it down the toilet. She put on her cap and went to meet Philip to tell him she was leaving for a while and tell him he needed to care for the children, then she hailed a taxi to the airport. She told no one where she was headed.

As the plane lined up with the lights of the runway, Monte reviewed her plan ... if it could be called a plan. Cal was right; her thinking had blurred. Her mother used to say, "Monte is my smartest child." It was a harmful thing to say, she realized now as a parent, comparing and classifying one's children. "Cal is my adventurer and writer. Samantha is my beauty and personality. And Monte is my smartest child." Samantha and Cal had lived beyond their mother's definitions. They possessed a confidence she'd never felt.

In the desert where no one knew her or her family, she'd stood alone with only the universe looking on. She'd stared back at it, awestruck by its immensity, diminished by her need to put herself at the center. She wished now she could step out of her life and live on a berm in the desert under the night sky like a wolf watching her borders and protecting her cubs. Only there were no wolves in the desert where she'd been, only a few diminutive foxes. The wolves couldn't survive, though there were human wolves.

In her job at the State Department, she'd studied those who could threaten the U.S. and the larger world. Many were surprisingly banal and local in their ambitions. They wanted the patch of earth where they stood. But the Elder wanted more. Maybe Safi was right. Maybe the Elder was a kind of Azazel teaching war and distributing weapons and demanding that he be recognized after he had been cast out. She didn't know the Elder nor want to know him, but she feared him. She wondered what good it did to bring Safi in if the Elder remained at large.

The plane hit roughly on the tarmac at Tangiers International Airport. She retrieved her backpack from under the seat and pulled her duffel from the overhead rack. She was trembling.

*   *   *

The moon bled onto the water as the motorboat churned across the Straits of Gibraltar. Monte sat in the front of the skiff. The Rock towered above with glimmering lights clustered at its base and a thread of lights winding up its dark face. The boat veered north to avoid a security perimeter where naval vessels protected the Rock. Oil tankers, commercial ships, and cruise liners anchored in the bay. A cool breeze blew across the bow. On the wooden bench beside her rested her backpack and red cloth bag. On the facing bench sat Tayri in a long skirt, hendira, and headscarf tied tightly against the wind. Tayri peered into the dark toward the land. Next to her slept an elderly man with skin like leather, muttering in his sleep. He was Tayri's grandfather and fishing buddy of her nephew who was guiding the boat.

The small skiff maneuvered the fifteen miles through the open bay, a lantern attached to its stern. It kept its distance from the cruise liners and tankers asleep in the water. If one of these should start up its engines, the movement could capsize the boat. They watched for the huge ferry that crossed the Strait each hour. Monte studied these looming giants then shifted her gaze to the hills along the shore where rows of windmills spun in the moonlight like colossal white birds flapping their wings. The wind was picking up. She hunkered down and shut her eyes as the boat navigated the open water and the wind.

The wind . . . the wind . . . she remembered the wind in the desert unsettling the sand and the sand enveloping her like a shroud . . . She and Safi wrapped in a sheet, their hearts beating, accelerating, unhinged, holding each other, breathing the same air until there was little air to breathe. How many moments was one allowed in life for

such abandon? She had used up hers, she was sure. Was it only abandon or a desperate reaching for something that in the end they
couldn't give each other? But they had survived. Now she was moving through dark water to bring back this man who had derailed her
life, before the men he'd betrayed could kill him.

And what about Philip? She'd loved Philip once, but they had lost
the oxygen between them, only their loss didn't lead to ecstasy but
to suffocation. Philip hadn't argued or even complained when she
returned and wouldn't share a bed with him. She wondered if there
was someone else in his life, but she didn't ask the question because
she didn't want to answer the question herself.

The wind died down as the boat neared land. She sat up and
watched the shapes on the shore coming clearer. The coast was
patrolled for just such boats as theirs trying to slip into Europe carrying contraband. But Tayri's nephew knew the coastline well. For
Tayri and for a fee, he'd agreed to transport her into a cove and wait
there until she was ready to return or sent word for him to go back
on his own.

Monte checked her phone, but there was still no message from
Samantha or Safi. She considered calling Sam, but she worried someone could track her location. She wondered if Samantha had Zahara.
She'd counted on Safi to find a place for her, but he was on the run.
What would happen to this child? Zahara had shown surprising
endurance given the wretched conditions of her birth and the harsh
journey across the desert. In the weeks Monte spent with her, Zahara
fed without complaint and slept. She was far more tranquil than
either Craig or Emma who were needy babies and hadn't slept
through the night and demanded food and attention, often demanding more than Monte thought she had to give. But Monte couldn't
think about the child right now. She sat silent and still as the boat

sliced through the dark water at low speed. Soon the skipper would shift to the oars so no sound would betray their approach.

When the motor switched off, the only sound came from Tayri's grandfather snoring and from the distant hum of a large engine turning over somewhere. As the boat neared land, the skipper pushed away from the rocks with his oars, steering toward the mouth of a small cove where waves picked up the skiff and with a gentle hand lifted its flat bottom and swept it into shore, depositing it on a narrow strip of sand.

Quickly the skipper disembarked. Monte followed, her pack on her back, her duffel slung across her chest. She helped pull the boat onto a small extension of land while Tayri roused her grandfather. No one spoke. The skipper pointed to where he would hide the boat, under bent cypress trees. He spread a rough blanket on the tiny beach and pulled out two fishing poles. He and the old man settled on the blanket to sleep until the sun rose. If anyone found them, he would explain they were fishing for mackerel.

Tayri led Monte quickly up the embankment to the highway, where they set off on the road to Gibraltar. Tayri also carried a cloth bag slung across her shoulders. They would either walk or hitch a ride to the border. To any passerby, they looked like local women up early on the way to market to sell their wares. At the border Tayri would leave Monte and spend her day in the Spanish markets nearby, while Monte, passport in hand, would get onto the Rock.

Safi had told her that it was from Gibraltar he and his partner ran the Elder's money. He'd urged his partner to leave with his wife right away, but his partner had offered to meet Monte there. She hadn't shared his name with anyone.

* * *

Monte sipped espresso at an outside café in the Old Town. The sun shone in a clear blue sky. The air was crisp. She stared across the narrow cobblestone street as this British city of 30,000 residents awakened. Proprietors rolled up their protective metal screens and unlocked their doors at the clothing stores, souvenir stalls, and Cambio/Change shop. A woman dropped a letter into a red GR post box like those found on London streets. Farther down Main Street, a Marks & Spencer department store was coming to life.

Monte spread out the local Gibraltar paper, glancing briefly at the headlines. She had sent her message to Kenneth at the Gmail address Safi had given her on their last night together. She knew only Kenneth's first name. Kenneth diversified his and Safi's holdings into banks and institutions in Gibraltar, Monaco, England, France, the U.S., Singapore, and Hong Kong to protect the investments and their identities, Safi had told her. He and Kenneth had set up accounts and shell companies for the Elder in Cyprus, Dubai, Switzerland, the Isle of Man, the Cayman Islands, the Bahamas, and the British Virgin Islands. As long as they showed profits, Rainer, the Elder's Austrian partner, left Safi alone, he said. She'd only once seen Rainer, on the day the Elder came to lock her up. Safi told her only that he and Kenneth knew all the institutions and banks that held the funds around the world. Rainer only knew some of these.

Over their last weeks in the desert Safi had shared with her his plan for taking down the Elder. Eventually she would share what she knew with others, but so far she had told those debriefing her only that Safi invested money for the Elder. She hadn't told them that he ran two sets of books, the true books Kenneth kept and the books they showed Rainer. Safi had told her that he planned to turn over whatever accumulation of funds they had to charities when the time came, though he would keep a commission. She had tried to persuade him to turn over everything.

"To whom?" he'd asked. "Who should be the recipient of illicit global funds, not the governments that allowed the transactions in the first place or looked the other way?"

"To the U.S. government."

He laughed. "Half the arms traded are U.S. issue. The U.S. is the biggest arms merchant in the world. The drugs come from fields the U.S. has allowed to flourish in Afghanistan and elsewhere. The Elder parks funds in U.S. banks—Florida, Delaware, Nevada, and Wyoming where secrecy laws protect accounts. The same in Britain, which gives cover not only in London but all over its former empire. Some of the best havens are former British colonies. Don't even consider the French. They've been hand in glove, profiting from illicit funds for decades."

"Then to the UN," she'd suggested. Safi smiled grimly without responding.

"Charities can also be corrupt or corrupted," Monte said.

"Yes," he agreed.

At the time, their debate in the desert night had seemed theoretical and the hundreds of millions of dollars, a fantasy. What did Safi expect the Elder and others to do when they discovered he'd taken their money, she asked.

"They'll kill me. But first they have to find me."

When she emailed Kenneth, she said simply that she was a friend of Stephen Carlos Oroya/Safir Brahim; she wasn't sure which name Kenneth knew. She said she hoped they could meet. He replied immediately, suggesting this café in Gibraltar.

The sun climbed in the sky, shining on the pink-and-white building behind her with the Gibraltar flag fluttering on its roof. She ordered another espresso, then changed her order to decaffeinated coffee. She couldn't afford to get any edgier. She'd quit chewing khat only two days ago and still felt its kick. She checked her watch. She'd been early, but now Kenneth was late. She checked her phone. Still no messages. As a precaution she'd bought a disposable cell before she came to the café this morning. On the new phone she texted Samantha: *WHERE R YOU? DO U HAVE ZAHARA? M.* As she pressed Send, a black-haired man with a neat gray-black peppered beard sat down across from her. His dark eyes peered at her, and his mouth hardened into a frown.

"Anne Waters?" he asked.

"Kenneth . . . ?"

"Kenneth Shawcross." He extended his hand, set a ledger on the table, ordered coffee, orange juice, and a full English breakfast, then handed the ledger to the proprietor, who came to the table. "You're good to date," he said to the man, who tucked the notebook under his arm. When the proprietor left, he explained, "I do a quarterly check on his accounts as a favor."

"You're an accountant?" Monte was under the impression he was a major financial trader.

"*No account too big; no account too small.* That was the founder's motto when he started the firm." He reached across the table for cream. "How is it you know Stephen?" His voice was gruff with a European accent. "Or what did you call him . . . Safir?"

She wondered if he really didn't know who she was. Who exactly was he? She hadn't expected an accountant helping a local business-man. She glanced quickly around the patio. Two men had just sat down a few tables away, a thin, blond-haired man in a tailored suit, along with a muscular balding man with a brush moustache.

"Have you heard from Stephen?" she asked quietly. "I was hoping I might see him here."

"Is he expected?" The man was smiling a narrow smile as his eyes also darted to the two men at the edge of the café. He seemed distracted. He lifted his brow as if signaling something . . . what? Was he cautioning her or signaling them? With her foot, she drew her bag and backpack closer to her under the table so she might pick them up at a moment's notice. "Do you know where Stephen is?" he asked. "I've been trying to reach him too."

She wondered if she'd made a mistake contacting this man. Safi said Kenneth was his old friend. She assumed the role of the innocent. "I haven't seen him for months, but I told him I might be coming to Gibraltar for . . . you know . . ."—she glanced across the street—"for shopping," as if the small tourist shops and chain stores in this corner of the British Empire were worth a transatlantic trip. "I thought we might catch up."

Kenneth continued a forced smile. "Yes, I'd like to catch up too." She saw the two men from the edge of the patio rise. She reached under the table and curled her fist around her backpack and bag. When the men split up to approach from either side, she suddenly bolted from the table.

Without looking back, she plunged down a side street beside the café and ran into a clothing shop where she hurried around poles of children's clothes to the rear. She ducked into a storeroom, then out the back door into the alley. She moved faster than she had in a year. Training from years before on diversion and escape took over. She ran downhill toward the harbor, where a blue city bus was just pulling up to the stop. Jumping on the bus, she moved quickly to the rear and slunk down on the seat so she couldn't be seen from the outside. No one appeared in pursuit. She was barely breathing, her heart racing. She'd assumed the men moving toward the table wished her harm, but she wondered now if she was paranoid—all nerves and caffeine and lack of sleep. Perhaps the two men were tourists seeking a better table. She hadn't waited to find out. She knew that to wait could be fatal.

She realized how unprofessional she'd become in her year away . . . that she would sit in the open with a stranger and expect him to answer her questions and hand her information in a neatly typed ledger. *Oh, yes, Ms. Waters, here are the accounts of all the criminals you're seeking. I've been waiting to give them to you.* What was she thinking?

At the bus stop by the town's funicular, she again peered up and down the street then got off the bus. She hurried into the building where she surveyed the small crowd in line for tickets. No one entered after she did. She bought a ticket then waited anxiously for the ride to open. She scanned the brochures and posters on the wall. Finally, she boarded the cable car with the other tourists to ride to the caves at the top. She again checked but saw no one in pursuit. She pulled out her new phone and texted Safi: *WHERE R U? M.* Resting her head against the car's window, she peered out at the blue expanse of the Mediterranean below. She was wary of heights so she didn't look down, just out at the sea and the continent of Africa. On her honeymoon she and Philip had ridden the funicular in Monaco overlooking the Mediterranean. Afterwards they took up their post in Tunis, across the water. Their lives were in front of them then. She'd felt triumphant, marrying before her sister, marrying a shy, handsome, responsible man who, as an auditor/accountant with the State Department, wanted to follow her career. Cal had married two years earlier and was soon to be a father, but seemed unprepared; whereas, she, the responsible younger sister, was prepared for life.

Before they married, Philip had asked her what she was afraid of. They'd been dating only a month. Without thinking, she answered, "Failure." Then she added, "Suffocation." They were having dinner . . . where? . . . there was a fireplace; Philip would remember the restaurant.

"What does that mean?" he'd asked and listened to her answer.

"I come from a family bred for success, measured by education and public service. *To whom much is given, much is expected.* That's my father's motto."

"What's wrong with that?" he asked.

"It's a burden, though my brother and sister don't feel it. They tell me the burden is in my own head, but they're not in the family business."

"Who's measuring you?"

She laughed. "My mother for one, though she would deny it. And my father, who doesn't miss a chance to tell me how proud he is of me, and because he says it so often, it makes me think he really isn't or maybe is compensating for not knowing me; he only knows what I do. Does that make sense?"

Philip had smiled and taken her hand on the table. "No, not really." She'd felt easy with him, sharing feelings she hadn't shared with anyone.

"Why suffocation?" he asked.

"If I don't fulfill expectations, I suffocate and disappear, and if I do, the expectations just grow until they suffocate me."

"Wow!" Philip had laughed. "You've thought your way into a real corner. Are you sure it's that bad?"

Philip hadn't meant to be unkind, but his laughter had made her retreat. How could anyone understand? As she rode up the chair lift, she considered that she'd never asked Philip what he was afraid of. She hadn't reciprocated. Even now she wasn't sure of Philip's fears, except his fear of living alone. Most of their conversations were about her and her activities. Had he ceded the space to her because her life was more interesting or because her need was more compelling?

She was thinking about Philip even as she was heading to Safi who demanded everything of her, who'd taken away her freedom and imposed his own complicated view of the world, who needed argument and debate and moral guidance, who demanded body and soul. Safi operated alone. He had little family, no group or political party, no church, no business to which he belonged. No single nation he called his own. He sought a higher power and then wrestled with its existence. Yet in the flickering in his eyes and the gentleness of his touch, she felt his vulnerability and need, which embraced her own.

The cable car drew to a stop at the summit. Outside, a cluster of monkeys waited, anticipating peanuts and bits of food even though signs warned: DO NOT FEED THE MONKEYS. These tailless Barbary macaques had inhabited the Upper Rock for centuries, ever since the time when the Moors occupied southern Spain in the 8th century, the signs said. No matter what politics or wars played out in the world and on this Rock, the Barbary macaques endured, fed and taken care of now by the government. Legend was that they came to Gibraltar via underground tunnels and caves that ran beneath the sea connecting Europe and Africa over 1000 years ago.

It was to these caves she was hurrying. She'd texted Safi again from Madrid telling him: *MEET FRI. ST. M*, which was St. Michael's, the main cave inside the Rock, a thousand feet above the Mediterranean and the Atlantic. Here she'd make her case for him to come in. If he agreed, she'd get him safely and secretly off the Rock.

Her cell phone beeped. The message was from Samantha: *S GONE. I HAVE Z. MEET u WHERE?* She texted back on her new phone repeating: *GO HOME. TAKE Z.* She didn't want Samantha showing up, though she doubted her sister knew where she was. She also doubted Samantha would take instructions from her. As she walked down the path toward the caves, she decided to risk a one-minute call on the new phone.

"When did Safi leave? Where are you? You can't come here. Get the child to safety." She spewed her message before Samantha could even identify who was calling.

"Monte?" she asked.

"Do me a favor . . . at your hotel go on the internet and search for a photo of a Kenneth Shawcross, SWG Financial . . . send it to this phone," Monte said.

"At the moment I'm being questioned by the police," Samantha answered.

"Where are you?"

"In the Rabat police station."

"Shit!" She hung up. She quickly took the batteries out of both phones.

Monkeys scurried along the fence beside her and on the rocks watching for signs of food. She kept her hands out of her pockets lest the monkeys jump on her shoulders. They weren't vicious, but they were entirely self-interested.

She looked out at the Atlantic Ocean spread before her in the sunlight with the Bay of Gibraltar at her back, Spain to her right, and Africa in front of her. On the water below, power boats sliced through the waves, navigating around the tankers and cruise liners, their white wakes leaving patterns on the water. Above, sea gulls coasted on the air currents and called to each other . . . *cha! cha! cha!*

Monte rested for a moment, leaning against the rocky cliff and watching the gulls gliding on the wind. She wished she could be as free and unencumbered, coasting from current to current above the power and politics below. She felt exhausted and too young to be this exhausted. Inside the Rock were miles of tunnels where soldiers and ammunition had been hidden and from which battles had been staged through a thousand years of history. Even today, NATO stored ammunition here. This morning's paper reported Spain, a NATO ally, still protested the sovereignty of Gibraltar and enforced a no-fly zone for military planes going in and out of Gibraltar. Spain had lost the Rock in the 1700s when the Spanish king accorded it to Britain "Forever."

Monte was no longer sure she wanted to engage the world. Samantha was engaged. Samantha should take Zahara, but she couldn't ask her sister yet. Safi also sought release from the world's struggles, but he was using the very tools—money, crime, power—of those from whom he sought release.

A large group of tourists speaking Spanish, French, Arabic, and English overtook her on the path. She stepped aside, pressing against the rock to let them pass. She stared up at a purple wildflower hugging the cliff. In a light breeze a pine shaped like an acacia tree waved in the sun. Everywhere she looked she saw blue sky and ocean and sea gulls. She walked slowly on.

At the opening of the cave, she sat on a bench and listened to the men in the entry house talking in Spanish about their wives and what they'd eaten for dinner last night. She'd never lived with such everyday talk. Her family talked about politics and foreign affairs at dinner. Perhaps she'd take cooking lessons. This fleeting thought was interrupted by the arrival of another white van full of tourists. Before these new visitors walked up to the cave, they stopped in front of a tree whose limbs had been chopped off where monkeys now posed. One of the younger monkeys hopped onto the back of Monte's bench. From her backpack, Monte had pulled out an energy bar and a bottle of water. She took a bite of the bar then set a small piece on the bench for the baby monkey who grabbed it before the larger monkeys saw him.

As the tourists moved past her into the cave, Monte again looked out at the endless blue. She wanted to sit there and enjoy the sky and the sea with no problems to solve, no puzzles to untangle, just thoughts drifting in and out of her head. The funicular would have gone up and down by now, bringing more tourists. She wanted to be a tourist, wandering through her life, observing what life showed her, but not responsible for it. Another white van made its way down the path.

She briefly put her battery back in her original phone to check for messages. The phone vibrated. *WHERE R U?* The message was unsigned, the phone number blocked. She'd called Sam on the disposable cell. This text must be from Safi. Did she dare answer? She typed: *AT THE TOP, ABOUT TO GO UNDER.* The message was cryptic enough. If it was Safi, he would know where she was.

On the back of the bench the baby monkey edged toward her, his hand out. The tourist bus stopped and opened its doors. She shouldn't assume she was safe here. She stood, paid her fee. As she entered the cave, the funicular arrived again at the top of the Rock.

CHAPTER TWENTY-ONE

ZAHARA HAD WAILED as the police crashed through the small greenhouse. Samantha held her close, rocking her, soothing her. *"S'il vous plait!"* she addressed the police. *"Attention pour l'enfant!"* She stayed seated, reached out a hand to Nadia Brahim, who sank onto the cot as the officers overturned the plants as if a man might be hiding beneath the miniature lemon trees or under orchids.

Finally, the police insisted Samantha and Nadia accompany them back to the station where they held them in an office until the captain arrived. Samantha carried Zahara in the laundry basket, laying one of her sweaters over the top to hold in the warmth and block out the light. She telephoned Alex, who talked to the captain and arranged for a car to pick her up after the questioning and drive her and Zahara to Casablanca.

Alex had organized food for them in the car and also had an infant's car seat installed. Samantha was touched by Alex's thoughtfulness. She wished she'd known him better over the years. At the hotel in Casablanca, he was waiting for her with more baby formula and a bag of diapers. He'd arranged a flight back to the United States for her and Zahara that afternoon, though first he said they needed to get a few items for the baby.

"I'm sorry I skipped out on you in Rabat," Samantha apologized.
"Why was I not surprised?"

"Because you still know me." She settled Zahara into the blue
cloth carrier on her chest that Nadia had shown her how to use.

Alex put his arm around her shoulders. "Let's get to the market.
Your flight is in a few hours."

She didn't know what was going to happen to this child, but she
understood she was now the one who must get her to safety and
eventually to Monte though the possibility that a major news story
might be breaking stirred her. She wanted to stay. As they wandered
through the market stalls looking for children's supplies, Zahara
slept bound to her chest, breathing in unison. Samantha was still
wearing her clothes from the evening before, though she'd pulled
out the tracking device from her waistband, and she'd draped her
black shawl over her head in the market.

"You need at least a stroller and an infant seat." Alex walked
beside her as she checked her phone.

"You think there'll be an attack tonight?" she asked. "I'm not convinced I need to leave . . ."

"If there is an attack, the airports will close. You won't be able to
get out. Jim and Moha are concerned you've been identified and
could be a target. Your niece as well." Alex looked over at the baby.
"Your plane leaves at six; mine's out of here at three. Jim will meet
us back at the hotel and take you."

Samantha texted as she walked. "I'm telling my editor to get
someone to Casablanca right away."

"Don't say more than that. We're hoping this will be a story that
doesn't happen, one we're able to prevent. The last thing we need is
the press on top of us."

As her thumbs flew over the keypad, Zahara shifted in the sling
and leaned her head back looking up at Samantha as if to say, *What's*

up? Samantha stroked her soft black hair. They moved among stalls of blue jeans and tee shirts and hijabs, toiletries and kitchen implements. How could she protect this child and do her job? It was a new and disconcerting dilemma for her.

Alex stopped at a shop with children's clothing hanging from a pole out front and led her inside where he pulled an umbrella stroller from a bottom shelf. "Here . . . this will at least get you from here to there." With his foot he pushed the lever between the wheels, and the stroller snapped open. "You want to put her in it?"

Samantha was enjoying the small body close to hers, the tiny hands holding onto her shirt. "Not just yet. Let's get the other things you say I need first." Alex had three children so she deferred to him.

"You need something to put her in on the plane." He waved to a woman in the back of the store and addressed her in Arabic. She led them to a modest offering of two infant chairs and a navy cloth basket with handles.

Samantha chose the basket, though she was having trouble focusing on baby gear when she knew security forces were mobilizing for an attack. As the saleswoman, dressed in long skirt and headscarf, headed toward the cash register with their purchases, Samantha and Alex lagged behind. "Tell me what you know," Samantha said.

"I know you're making the right decision. If we aren't able to stop what we think is planned tonight, you'll be trapped for days. I've been told to return. I've done what I can here, and now I need to get back to Madrid to coordinate with authorities there."

Zahara wriggled her legs and reached up for Samantha's hair spilling out from her scarf. From a shelf Samantha took a tiny rubber camel and slid it into Zahara's fist. The camel went straight to Zahara's mouth. Samantha also selected a baby rattle and a child's abacus with colored beads. At the front a man rang up the purchases.

With Alex's help, Samantha untied the harness and lowered Zahara into the stroller.

"You have a beautiful daughter," the woman said to both of them.

*   *   *

Alex handed off Samantha, Zahara, and the equipment to Jim in the hotel lobby. "Come to Madrid sometime," he said to Samantha. "Take care of her," he said to Jim.

"My impression is she takes care of herself," Jim answered.

A message beeped on Samantha's phone. "My editor is asking what's happening in Casablanca and why I have to leave."

"Tell him your friend at the Spanish Embassy insisted." Alex kissed Samantha on the cheek and left.

"We have two hours before we have to go to the airport," Jim said. "You want to get something to eat?"

They settled at a table in the corner of the lounge where Samantha measured out formula as she'd been shown and asked for bottled water. "I'm getting good at this." She offered a self-deprecating smile as she shed her headscarf. Her hair cascaded onto her shoulders and into her eyes, which were tired, but she felt animated. She shook the bottle. Jim reached down and picked up the rattle Zahara had dropped to the floor and wiped it off.

"Do you have children?" Samantha asked.

"I did. I mean I do . . . I have a son, sixteen. He lives with his mother in Virginia. I can barely remember him at this age. My biggest regret is missing so much of his childhood." Jim met Samantha's question with a direct gaze. "What about you? Any regrets?"

"I don't think we have time or know each other well enough for that conversation." Samantha smiled as she held the bottle for Zahara.

"How did you answer your editor?"

"I haven't yet. I understand why Zahara should leave, but I don't have all the facts behind the reasons why I should leave."

"What do you want to know?" Jim stretched out his legs clad in blue jeans.

"Are you sure there'll be an attack tonight? Why don't they close the mosque? Who's responsible? Are they the same people who held Monte? Is Stephen involved? Finally, exactly what do *you* do? I assume CIA?" Samantha asked this last quietly.

"Is that all?" Jim's hazel eyes were set off by his pale blue shirt; his brown hair peppered with a few flecks of gray curled on his neck.

"No, but it's a start."

Jim pulled his chair closer to hers. They sat in a dim corner on green velvet chairs with palm trees and potted plants shielding them. Few people were in the lounge. Samantha wanted to go upstairs and bathe and change. She'd been in the same clothes since yesterday, and they felt sticky on her skin, but she also wanted time with Jim. She looked down at Zahara in the stroller. Her eyes were closing as she sucked the bottle. Jim waved to the waiter, and they ordered kebobs and hummus and flat bread and mint tea. He pulled a pad and pencil from his satchel and began to sketch.

"I can't tell you everything, but here's what I can share." He drew a map of Spain and part of Northern Africa—Morocco, Algeria, Tunisia, and Libya, then beneath these countries he sketched Mauritania, Mali, Niger, Chad, and the Sudan. "This northern region I've been focusing on is where the flow of drugs, weapons, diamonds, and women move into and from Europe and into the rest of Africa and the Middle East. Money from trafficking funds terrorists. There are training camps in the eastern part of the Western Sahara, also in Algeria and Libya. We've also picked up activity in Chad and Mali and the Sudan. Others are monitoring Mauritania.

The Sahara is so vast it's almost impossible to capture those who know how to move around it. That's why it was so difficult to find your sister. Some converge around a man known as the Elder."

Samantha wondered if Jim knew about the rape of Monte. He'd surely concluded something by the fact that there was a child. She wondered if Zahara could be the child of the Elder. "What does the Elder look like?" she asked.

"I've only seen pictures from his student days. He's fair-skinned with curly reddish, almost rust-colored, hair, an odd combination in this part of the world. Some say he's ugly, though in old school pictures I couldn't make out his features very well. I don't know what he looks like today. He travels with a Sudanese man, striking by contrast, over six feet, dark-skinned, muscular, and handsome from all reports. We don't know too much about him except that the Elder is said to have saved his life once."

Jim took a wedge of pita bread and dipped it in the hummus. "The Elder also associates with an Austrian man who was his classmate at the London School of Economics. How does this fit with what you've learned?"

"I ran the names Stephen Oroya and Safir Brahim by friends in the Spanish and Arabic press. For a while he worked at an investment firm, then wrote for the financial press, then a few years ago started writing about insurgencies. Some say the shift had to do with his brother who died in prison. I assume you've received Monte's intelligence debriefings?"

"Some of them. We're still trying to connect the dots."

Zahara's eyes were closed now. She still wore the pink leggings and green sweater from the night before. Samantha had forgotten to buy baby clothes in the market and had only a spare sleep suit Nadia had packed, but there would be time enough for clothes. She imagined her mother shopping at the children's boutiques in Georgetown, though she wondered how her mother would relate to this child of unconventional origin. Her father had at least connected enough to get Zahara a passport.

"Do you know where Stephen might be now?" Jim asked.

Samantha pushed the stroller with her foot to rock Zahara and keep her sleeping as a noisy party entered the lounge and sat nearby. "No. I'm surprised he got away. The police arrived right after your call. I didn't tell him they were coming, but he was watching me as I talked to you, and he bolted."

"You think he's gone to see your sister?"

"Possibly."

"Do you know where she is?"

Samantha drank the tea that had been steeping and ate one of the kebobs. She assumed Jim knew Monte was flying over because Alex knew, but she didn't want to expose Monte. "Honestly, I don't know where she is right now."

"Have you spoken to her?"

She considered dissimulating, but her phone might be monitored and besides, she didn't want to lie. "I've spoken with her briefly, but she didn't say where she was going."

"Where did she call from?"

"She was using her cell." In fact, Monte's name hadn't shown on her phone when the most recent call came in.

"Could you check?"

Samantha looked at her phone, remembering now that Monte had asked her to send a picture of someone . . . who? She'd written down the name. She looked at Monte's incoming call.

"What?" Jim asked.

"It's not her regular number."

Jim put out his hand, reaching for the phone.

"I'd rather not. If you know her, I'm sure you have ways to be in touch."

"She probably bought a disposable phone. I'm worried about her safety. We think the Elder's mafia contacts are looking for Stephen, or who they identify as Safir Brahim. If she's heading to see him . . ."

"Would you mind watching the baby for a few minutes?" Jim raised his eyebrows, but Samantha didn't offer an explanation.

Samantha took her satchel and headed to the business center where she checked her notepad for the name Monte had given her. Kenneth Shawcross. Two entries on the opening page of a Google search caught her attention. One was the Queen's honors list, which included a Kenneth Robert Shawcross of Gibraltar honored for charitable work. The other was an obituary dated two days ago for Kenneth Robert Shawcross of Gibraltar. The obituary ran as a small story in the *Financial Times* with a photo of a man with glasses and receding hair.

> *Kenneth Robert Shawcross, 42, Chief Executive Officer of SMG Financial, Gibraltar, was found dead in his hilltop home yesterday, shot in the head. His wife discovered the body when she returned from shopping. Police are investigating. Kenneth Shawcross is survived by his wife, Irene Whitman Shawcross, and two sons, Michael (18) and James (19) and a younger brother Roland Shawcross of Perth, Australia. Funeral services are private.*

Samantha printed the obituary and tucked it in her bag then forwarded to Monte and herself the link to the story and the photo. Is THIS THE MAN? she texted Monte. Jim's warning of the forces at work suddenly took on a more sinister and palpable threat. If this was the man Monte knew or was looking for, she was in more danger than she realized. Samantha phoned Monte, but no one answered. She tried the second number, which had a U.K. area code, but again just ringing, no answering voice. Once more, she tried Monte's regular cell and left a message: CALL ME. THE MAN YOU ASKED ABOUT IS DEAD . . . MURDERED. CALL ME.

Samantha felt the same panic rising she'd felt a year ago when she'd realized Monte was missing. Why had Monte left the safety of the U.S.? For the first time in her life, Samantha wanted the protection of oceans and the distance America offered from the chaos and meanness in the rest of the world. She knew the feeling was irrational. She'd spent her career outside U.S. borders, and she knew there was plenty of chaos and meanness within its shores. She prayed Monte would be safe. Only then could she be safe. She couldn't leave without her sister.

When she returned to the lounge, Zahara was sitting in Jim's lap. For a moment she watched in the doorway until a woman in a gold lamé top and black pants exclaimed, "You're Samantha Waters!" with the excitement of recognizing someone from television.

Samantha turned. "Yes . . . yes, I am. Have a good day." She moved toward Jim.

"Another reason to get you out of here," Jim said as she sat down. "It's hard to blend in when you're famous."

"I'm hardly famous," she said. "Slightly recognizable to people in fancy hotels who have access to INN on their TV." She lifted Zahara from his lap. "I need your help, but first I need to change her diapers and clothes."

"You want me to change her so you can go upstairs and change yourself before the flight?"

"There's a living room upstairs. Why don't we all go? There's something I want to show you."

Jim checked his watch. "We have forty-five minutes." He waved for the waiter.

"Please, this is mine." Samantha paid the bill.

*   *   *

As they waited at the elevator, Jim asked, "Did you reach your sister?"

She looked over at him, and for a moment they watched each other, their gaze steady. How did he know that's what she'd tried to do? He read her in a way she wasn't used to, but then that was his job, she told herself. He was a spy. He watched, collected details, analyzed and read people. That was also what she did, but it was disconcerting to have the mirror turned on herself; it was also seductive.

He added, "If you talk to her, tell her to beware of anyone offering to take her to Stephen. She knows this ruse of course . . ." He hesitated. In his hesitation Samantha saw the failure Monte must feel among colleagues for allowing herself to be kidnapped. "Her defenses and instincts may be down. If someone offers, she should get out of wherever she is as quickly as possible."

"What do you know?" Samantha asked as she wheeled Zahara into the suite and over to a corner where she could be shaded from the sun streaming in but still able to look out the window.

"We've intercepted communications that indicate the Elder's Russian partners are looking for both of them."

Samantha decided to trust Jim. She needed help, and she had to trust someone. From the outer pocket of her suitcase, she extracted Stephen's journal. "Stephen gave me this to give to Monte. I can't let you keep it, but you may find some of what you're looking for in it while I go change." Samantha opened to the pages with the financial accountings at the top of the entries and handed him the book.

She took her suitcase into the mirrored bathroom where she turned on the shower, and for a full ten minutes she stood in the glassed-in stall letting the hot water rush over her as she searched in her mind through facts, people, plots, trying to sort out what she knew and what she needed to know.

—She knew Monte was on her way.

—She knew Stephen had financial connections to the Elder.

—She knew or suspected Stephen was not the father of Monte's child.

—She was fairly certain Monte and Stephen had a relationship, were even lovers.

—She knew she was in charge of Zahara until she found Monte.

—She feared Monte was in grave danger.

—She knew, or thought she knew, that she could trust Jim, both as a colleague and a possible friend, and she hadn't felt that for a long time.

—She knew what she had to do.

Samantha emerged from the bathroom, hair towel dried, without makeup, wearing clean clothes. Jim was sitting at the table with a pad of paper reading Stephen's journal.

"You finding what you need?"

"Have you read this?"

"Yes. I think it confirms Stephen had a role in the finances."

"And more. I need to keep this."

"We can get it copied in the business center, but I need to deliver the original to Monte."

"We don't have time to copy it." Jim checked his watch. "We have to go."

Samantha lifted Zahara from the stroller. She changed her diaper and put her in clean powder-blue pajamas then returned her to the stroller. She took out the baby bottle from the diaper bag and washed it in the sink at the bar and again filled it with formula and bottled water. "I'm not going," she said.

"What do you mean? I'll watch out for Monte. I promise. You and the baby need to get out of here."

"There's more." She pulled the obituary from her bag. "Monte asked me to check on a man. That's what I did when I left you. The man was found dead two days ago in Gibraltar. If you're right and Monte is heading to Stephen, and Stephen is in Gibraltar, then she's in more danger than she may realize. I can't leave her again."

"There's little you can do, and you'll get in the way," Jim insisted. Zahara, who was starting to get restless, began swinging her legs in the stroller. "For the child's sake, you need to go."

"I've thought about that. I don't know what this child's future will hold, but I suspect it won't be conventional. We might as well start here by not abandoning her mother. I have a plan."

CHAPTER TWENTY-TWO

BEFORE STEPHEN COULD DISAPPEAR, he and Kenneth needed to meet one last time. Kenneth told him that he and his wife were coming back to Gibraltar to pack up the rest of their things then they planned to move to England near their sons. Kenneth had made enough money on the recent commissions to allow them options for the future. When Rainer had tried to reach him, Kenneth's office told him that Kenneth was away on vacation.

It was to Kenneth's office Stephen was headed when he disembarked from the ferry at Algeciras, Spain, and boarded the bus to Gibraltar. He knew there was risk, but he calculated he could slip onto the Rock for a few hours then get away. On the ferry he stood on the upper deck in the early morning light watching the rolling whitecaps in the channel between Morocco and Spain. His face was shrouded by the hood of his djellaba. Alert for anyone watching, he periodically glanced around at other passengers. A mother and her daughter stood near him. He found himself looking at the little girl and thinking about Zahara whom he'd promised Monte to place. In the meantime, his mother and Monte's sister would take care of her.

He and Monte had agreed if they ever needed to meet, they'd come to Gibraltar. He knew it well, but few people knew him there. He'd received Monte's text, but he wasn't certain he would meet her.

He knew Monte wanted him to turn himself in and hand over the funds, but he had no intention of doing that. He planned to disappear, and he could disappear only if he was alone. He looked for Monte among the early morning ferry passengers. Maybe he would hand over to Monte the codes to the Elder's accounts and let her sort out the consequences. Let her be the hero. What did he care where the Elder's illicit money went?

In Gibraltar he passed through passport control with a Moroccan passport. He'd shed his djellaba on the ferry and stuffed it in his pack. Outside the small wooden passport building on Winston Churchill Avenue, a red British telephone box marked the entrance to the peninsula. The day was dawning clear with a slight breeze. As he started down the road past the airport, he looked up at sea gulls gliding in the air.

He again glanced around to see if he was being followed. No one was behind him, but he failed to notice the two men already waiting at the bus stop into the city. He saw them just as they stepped out and wedged him between them. It was too late to bolt and run. They each took an arm in a hold that would break his arms if he resisted. They shoved him into a silver Citroën at the curb, tied his hands, belted him in, then sped away without speaking, up to the Rock Hotel on the cliffs near the casino as the sun lit the morning sky.

* * *

"So you thought you could get away?" The Elder sat on a white leather chair in a room with closed curtains. His nose, shaped like a shovel, anchored his face, and his thin lips smiled. His eyes, piercing and menacing, fixed on Safir. "You have named your book about me *Goliath of the Sahara,* but you are no David. I have been fighting since I could walk. My father was a rich man and had four wives while your father was a teacher and couldn't even protect your one brother. And your mother is a whore."

Safir, his hands cuffed behind him, shifted on his chair. He stared directly into the Elder's eyes without flinching. He'd watched the Elder over the last months and knew the provocations he used to gain control. "My mother is your cousin," Safir answered. The improvisation had the desired effect, for a moment returning to him the initiative. "You went to London to study economics. My mother went to London to study economics. You failed out of university. My mother earned her degree. Your mother died when you were eight. My mother is still alive. If you met my mother, she would invite you to dinner. She would tell you that you have chosen the wrong path. But if you threatened her or her son, she would kill you."

For a moment the Elder remained silent, then he laughed. "I remember why I let you in. You are a storyteller. You have been telling me a story for months. But now I will tell you a story."

He stood and went to the minibar and took out a Cadbury bar of chocolate. "I miss nothing in England but this." He held up the purple-wrapped chocolate bar. "Far better to grow cacao for chocolate than coca for cocaine, but the rich and the poor of the West want their cocaine even more than they want their chocolate so we oblige them and make our profits. We will defeat your corrupt and hypocritical governments. I am sorry you won't be able to tell the world about the Goliath of the Sahara, but soon they will find out themselves. Others will write my story."

The Elder signaled to a man Safir hadn't noticed sitting in the shadows. The man stepped behind the Elder's chair and placed a cloth around his neck and drew out a pair of scissors. He began to clip the Elder's hair, which hung past his shoulders. As the reddish locks fell to the floor, another man collected them as if they were artifacts, like a Catholic collecting holy relics, Safir thought.

"Some claim a man is not religious unless his hair is long and he wears a beard," the Elder said, "but I hold no such beliefs. I say a man is not wise to set himself apart when he is attacking from the inside."

The barber combed out the Elder's gray-rust-colored hair, which now grazed the top of his ears. He cut off the Elder's long beard. He ran a towel under the hot water faucet of the sink with the minibar and set it on the Elder's face and gave him a shave. The beard remaining was only a tidy and punctilious covering.

"I don't have the accounts with me if that is what you want," Safir said. "I need to go to the office." He needed time. He felt his heartbeat accelerating. He'd miscalculated slipping back onto the Rock. He hoped Kenneth had left and stayed in England with his wife and sons. He hoped Monte wouldn't come for him.

The Elder's head was tilted back so that he answered to the ceiling. "Then we will go with you. You will either hand over the real codes or die a slow, painful death."

Safir knew the Elder would order him killed in any case, but he needed to buy time if such a commodity still had a price and a currency.

The Elder sat upright and fixed Safir with an amused and malevolent gaze. "The story I will tell you today is the story of Goliath slaying David and all his cowardly band, the story of the lions making a meal of Daniel, and those boys Nebuchadnezzar threw into the furnace burning up as they deserved. In my story Joseph's pretty coat is shredded, and he is left at the bottom of the pit so no one is there to tell the duplicitous Egyptians to save for years of drought. Instead, the people rise up and overthrow Pharaoh for his failure of leadership so that when Moses flees, the Egyptians with righteous leadership prevail, and the Red Sea wipes out Moses and all his people." After his rendition of the Old Testament, the Elder ate his chocolate bar.

"You are mistaken." Safir tried for a pedagogical voice to conceal his panic. He looked about for an exit. Was it still possible to wrest control from the Elder? "Moses preceded Joseph."

The Elder finished his chocolate then raised his hand. "No, it is you who are mistaken. Now take him. But first empty his pockets."

The flaxen-haired enforcer lifted Safir to his feet and stripped him of his papers, passport, wallet, everything including a card he'd written Monte on the bus from Algeciras to Gibraltar. He'd borrowed an index card from a student sitting beside him and written a short message. He put her name on the back. A memento, he thought, perhaps the only one she would keep from him.

When they left the hotel, the Elder with short graying hair, wearing blue jeans, a Nike tee shirt, and sneakers looked like a fit, aging tourist rather than one of the world's most wanted men. When they arrived at SWG Financial in the Old Town, the office was closed for the day, but a middle-aged man with a salt-and-pepper beard let them in. "Stephen . . ." he said, surprised. Stephen recognized him as Kenneth's chief operating officer.

At a computer Stephen feigned searching through the files for codes until finally the Elder barked, "Kill him! Slowly!" And he left.

CHAPTER TWENTY-THREE

MONTE SAT ON a stone inside the labyrinth of caves that funneled downwards into the Rock of Gibraltar. The dim lights along the path reflected off the limestone walls and cast shadows around her. Water dripped from above, sliding down the rocks, pooling on the path, occasionally landing on her head and shoulders. From her earlier visit she knew St. Michael's cave was one of the largest in the upper rock, created by rainwater seeping through the earth and dissolving the stone over thousands of years, tiny cracks grown into passageways and large caverns whose giant stalactites and stalagmites hung like daggers overhead and rose like swords from the earth. Inside the caves, relics had been found from prehistoric times.

Monte leaned her head on the ancient stone and wondered where Safi was. She was tired but felt restless. She got up and roamed, pausing to read illuminated plaques describing the history of these caves believed to be used by Berbers in the Moors' conquest of Spain in AD 711 and as hiding places for soldiers in later conflicts. When the British governed Gibraltar in Victorian times, the caves had been destinations for picnics and parties and even duels. British soldiers guarding the Rock had explored the caves until one day two officers got lost and never returned. Monte remembered that story. Expeditions went to look for them, but no remains were ever found. Mystery lurked at the bottom.

Monte had come to Gibraltar for a NATO conference years ago and climbed to the top of the Rock with fellow staffers. That was before she'd married. The cave had seemed as exotic as the life ahead of her then, like a hole in history burrowed into the limestone, preserving layers of geologic as well as human history. But now the accumulation of history and its conflicts seemed more like a sediment of plots and schemes that imperiled those in the present. She moved along reading the plaques to keep herself awake and occupied:

—World War II St. Michael's cave was an emergency military hospital never used.
—A system of lower caves was discovered, including a clear-water lake.
—Cathedral Cave was the largest and now an auditorium.
—Some said the caves were bottomless, the end of a subterranean tunnel stretching under the Straits of Gibraltar all the way to Africa.
—Greeks believed the Gates of Hades, the entrance to the underworld, was located here.

Monte returned to the smooth rock near the entrance bridge and tucked herself into its cleft. Music of flutes and violins rose through the sound system as lights danced on the dark, wet walls. The air was cool and damp. Visitors moved past her. In the pale light, few paid attention to her. It was already after noon. She wondered how long she should wait for Safi. She didn't know how she would get him to turn himself in. She wasn't even sure she wanted him to except that she thought he'd be safer in U.S. custody. He'd never confirmed he would meet her here. She pulled out her phone and replaced the battery. There was a message, but she couldn't retrieve the text. She considered stepping back outside, but she didn't want to risk running into anyone. If Safi had left Casablanca last night as Sam said, he should be here soon. She leaned her head against her backpack. She was sitting just on the other side of the bridge. He would have to pass this spot and would see her. She was exhausted. She shut her eyes . . .

". . . Excuse me . . . Excuse me . . ."

She startled awake. She didn't know how long she'd been dozing, but sleep had pulled her deep. A gray-haired woman stood in front of her in a bulky white sweater, a camera around her neck. Beside her stood a man, also with a camera. It took her a moment to orient herself.

"A man asked me to give you this." The woman held out a note card. "He said to give it to the woman sleeping on the rock."

She took the card. "Thank you." In the distance she heard a rushing sound of water over rocks and harps from the sound system. She surveyed the corridor beneath the earth. Three paths descended into the caves. The woman waited on one of them. She read the card.

"Who gave you this?"

"He said we should show you where he was . . . over there." The woman pointed to the path on the right, but no one was in sight.

Monte checked the exits. Omitting the path where the woman pointed, there was the narrow steep trail down on the left and the middle path that led farther into the caves or back up to the entrance. On the card were Safi's words in his handwriting, yet in a flash that balanced between intuition and training, she judged that he wouldn't have used these strangers to communicate with her.

"Tell him I'll come in a minute . . ." She uncurled from the rock and, without explaining, she started back over the bridge to the entrance, carrying her backpack and canvas bag. She walked quickly, tucking the note card in her pocket. But when she reached the top of the path, she saw the two men from the restaurant in the ticket line outside. She glanced over her shoulder. At the foot of the bridge stood the woman and her husband waiting for her. Behind them, she saw another man, no longer with a beard, but even in the muted light and even in Western clothes with his rust-colored hair cropped close, she recognized him. She stood in a blind spot and had perhaps thirty seconds to decide what to do. She remembered a steep stairway down to the theater and to the cave's exit. It was a less used path and had places to hide, but to get there she would have to go back into the cave. If Safi was there, he was either in danger or he had betrayed her.

As a group of tourists started over the bridge, Monte slipped into the middle of them, engaging the man beside her in Spanish. She turned her head and managed to pass unnoticed by the woman at the foot of the bridge. The man she'd seen behind them who she thought was the Elder was now nowhere to be seen. When the tour turned off to the chamber of history, she hurried down the steep stairway where tiny red lights marked each step. Ethereal music swelled, a chant accompanied by flutes and violins and harps in this perfect acoustical space. Other tourists speaking German appeared on the stairs. She turned her back and unwrapped the remainder of her energy bar so that she would look occupied. When the wrapper slipped from her hands, she left it rather than face the tourists. She stared out over the railing into the dark cavern. As soon as they moved on, she lifted herself above the rail and climbed onto a rock hidden from view. She would hide here for a while and hope somehow to connect with Safi.

There were no lights in this part of the cave. There were no steps here, no iron railing to hold onto. The walls and ground were wet and slick, and she began to slip. She was wearing thick rubber-soled walking boots, but even these offered little traction. Her backpack and duffel weighed on her so she slid her arms out of them to set them down, but they fell over the edge and hit the ground far below.

As the incline steepened, her fingers scraped along the rough rock trying to get a hold to stop herself. She was sliding into the interior. How would she ever be able to get back up to the surface even if she could stop? She was stumbling faster and faster on the wet rocks when she heard in her head Samantha's voice telling her to sit down. In a flash of memory, she saw herself on a ski slope as a child. Everyone else knew how to ski. She was at the top, out of control, pummeling down the mountain, panicked. Behind her Samantha shouted: "Sit! Sit!" She had sat just before she would have fallen head over heels down the mountain. So now as she was about to pitch into the abyss, or slide pell-mell into the tunnel that ran under the sea all the way to Africa, or blast through the gates of the under-world, Monte heard her sister's voice: "Sit down!" And she did.

Landing on her bottom, she threw her feet in front of her, pressing one foot against the side of the wall and the other onto a boulder to arrest her descent. She used her hands as brakes. Looking down, she tried to see her bags, but she couldn't see the bottom. She looked up. The path was at least thirty feet above. She took a breath and steadied herself. Steady. Steady, she told herself.

Was it possible Safi was in the cave? When she left him that glistening morning in Rabat and approached the guardhouse at the American Embassy, she thought she'd never see him again. She'd wanted to bury the past year in a cavern deep in her being and not visit it until she was an old lady remembering her life. Safi didn't fit into her life, but her government handlers wouldn't let her forget as they debriefed her. They wanted to know every detail. Resisting them was exhausting. She and Safi had agreed to meet in Gibraltar only in an emergency. Had he betrayed her? Would she betray him? It would have been an interesting debate between them, one he would have enjoyed. His last words to her that day were: "See you in hell."

But Safi didn't believe in hell and neither did she, though he wrestled without comfort to find grace. If there were no answers, he told her, then he might as well be rich. She asked why he hadn't taken a traditional route and stayed working in finance or gone into business with his friend?

"Because I don't want to live a boring life. And I'm arrogant. I will bring an end to Les Guerriers de l'Enfer *then go find the sunrise."*

"You can't operate in both worlds," she'd said.

"Why not?"

"Even you're not that smart."

"Then help me."

"I'm not smart enough either. But I can bring you in and others can help."

"I don't trust others," he'd said.

CHAPTER TWENTY-FOUR

SAMANTHA AND JIM were traveling as a family, speaking simple Arabic between them as they waited on the Tangiers dock for the ferry to Algeciras, Spain. The sun had set. The moon had risen, spilling light into the harbor. Samantha's hair was hidden under her scarf. Jim in a light tan jacket and jeans stood next to her shoulder to shoulder. They pushed Zahara, wrapped in a yellow blanket, in her umbrella stroller.

Jim had resisted Samantha's plan, but he finally accepted that she wasn't leaving without Monte. They agreed Monte was most likely in Gibraltar, not Tangiers. Monte's text: *AT THE TOP, ABOUT TO GO UNDER*, didn't make much sense. Samantha assumed it was an answer to her question *WHERE R U?* She had no way of knowing Monte had made a mistake and texted her instead of Stephen. She speculated "at the top" could refer to the Rock of Gibraltar. The news clipping about Kenneth Shawcross in Gibraltar and the country code on Monte's phone, which could have been purchased in Gibraltar, but not in Tangiers, supported this judgment.

On the way out of Casablanca, they had stopped by Jim's apartment so he could pick up his jacket, rugged shoes rather than sandals, and the small bag he kept packed in his closet just as Samantha did—a duffel with two changes of clothes, toiletries, a tool kit, a nylon rope, and an extra gun. His apartment was in a small, white-washed complex near the ocean—two bedrooms furnished with Berber carpets, books, multicolored pillows, coffee table and low dining table—a hybrid of East and West, easily disassembled. On his bookshelves and desk were photos of his son at different ages, the most recent of an open-faced teen, taller than Jim with wavy brown hair like his dad's and a smile on his face as he shot a basketball into a hoop.

"He's a much better athlete than I was," Jim said. "His coach thinks he can get a scholarship to college with his grades and basketball."

Samantha picked up the photo from the desk. "He looks like you. How often do you see him?"

"He spends summers and some holidays here, along with my mother."

Jim went into the other room to finish packing. While Samantha waited for him, she'd used his computer to check the internet for information about SWG Financial, founded by Roland John Shawcross, Kenneth Shawcross's grandfather, as "a full-service financial firm with custodial accounts all over the world." She wondered how wide a net "custodial" encompassed, but she didn't have time to research. She also checked the newswires to see if an attack had occurred in Casablanca. Nothing yet.

Jim had called Moha to let him know where they were going. Moha reported that so far all was quiet. He told Jim that Morocco's U.S. Ambassador had alerted the Security Services about a major arms shipment due to arrive disguised as timber or another commodity from Guinea Bissau, probably at the port of Agadir though it could be farther north. It wasn't yet clear who the shipment was for. That afternoon a ship from Bissau unloading petroleum in the port had been discovered with crates of arms hidden in the hold.

These had been confiscated and the captain and crew, detained. Samantha assumed this was the shipment Celeste Diallo had told her about.

"Do you trust Moha?" Samantha had asked as they'd turned onto the highway north to Tangiers.

"Moha, yes, but not everyone. He's always been honest with me. We worked together after 9/11. We uncovered a plot to blow up NATO ships in the Straits of Gibraltar. The men were Saudis living in Morocco, married to Moroccan women who gave them easy entry and a big family to blend in with."

"Where are those men now?"

"Still in prison, but they come out soon. The wives were given short sentences and have been out for a while."

"Why do you think Monte is headed to Gibraltar?'"

"That's where the money is," Jim said.

"Stephen's money?"

"Most likely everyone's. Stephen is just the beginning of the trail."

"Why haven't I heard more about the Elder?"

"How good a reporter are you?"

"Pretty good." Zahara had started to fuss so Samantha reached into the bag at her feet and pulled out a bottle then undid her seat belt and leaned over to hold it for her.

Jim pulled to the side of the road. "Get in back, strap in."

"You always so cautious?" Samantha had moved to the back seat.

"I've had colleagues in war zones who've taken risks you can't imagine then come home and die driving intoxicated or jaywalking on a street in Kansas. I avoid risks I can control." Jim sped up again on the highway.

"Maybe you'll tell me where you've been someday."

"Right now we've got to catch the ferry so I want you belted in as I speed." He downshifted and pulled in front of the cars ahead of them.

"Why haven't I heard of the Elder?" Samantha repeated her question.

"Not many people know him. Until recently he avoided publicity. Whatever political or revolutionary fervor he may once have had, he's been corrupted by the criminal means he's used to fund it. At least that's my opinion. The mafias he's in league with don't care about revolutions. They have their own code. In a recent intercept he talked about 'the deed of deeds' he's planning."

"That sounds melodramatic."

"He's a serious threat, and I am fairly certain making money is involved in the threat."

"You think that's what the attack on the Hassan II Mosque is about?"

"If that's the target. The failed bomber in the mosque may have been a warning or a ploy. The Elder usually stays out of sight, moving around the wasteland of the Sahara, which is why we know so little about him. But your sister must have stirred things up, and her escape must have set off a panic. Whatever was being planned has been accelerated. We're suddenly seeing a flurry of activity. But afterwards they'll retreat and try to get lost again. We can't let that happen."

"There was another woman in the camp who helped Monte," Samantha said. "Maybe she can help us. Can you hand me my phone?" Jim unplugged the phone charging on the cigarette lighter and passed it to Samantha, who held a bottle for Zahara with one hand and dialed Tayri's number with the other.

"Monte?" Tayri answered on the first ring.

Samantha shifted to French. "It's Samantha. Do you know where Monte is?"

Tayri explained she left Monte that morning heading to Gibraltar and was waiting for her in the border town of La Linea. Monte was supposed to have called by now. Tayri said she'd wait another hour but then had to go back to her grandfather.

"Is my phone being monitored?" Samantha asked Jim after she hung up.

"Not by us."

"Good." She believed him. "Otherwise, I need to get a new phone."

*   *   *

It was almost eight when Samantha and Jim guided the stroller up the ramp to the ferry in Tangiers. It had been Samantha's idea for them to travel and blend in as a family, speaking Arabic and French, but not English. Jim's Arabic was fluent; hers was serviceable. They both spoke Spanish, useful in transit and in Gibraltar, which sat as the last mile on the tip of the Iberian Peninsula, though when they went through passport control, they would enter the Commonwealth of Great Britain and the last outpost in Europe of the former British Empire.

As the ferry pulled away, Samantha and Jim stood on the deck looking across the Strait trying to see the imposing Rock, which rose 1,400 feet above the Mediterranean, a symbol of security, but they couldn't see it from where they were. As the ferry set out on the dark waters, they moved inside the cabin. Jim again phoned Moha, who told him the Friday evening prayers had proceeded without incident. Police from other regions had been called in and posted around the plaza. Everyone had been ordered to stay through the night.

"So the bomb threat was a false alarm?" Samantha asked, settling in a corner where they could talk in private. Zahara had fallen asleep as soon as she took in the sea air, and she now breathed softly, curled in her stroller beside them.

"That or a first act," Jim said.

*   *   *

White windmills spun against the night sky, hundreds of them, their three-pronged blades converting the ocean winds into energy hundreds of miles away. They worked soundlessly on the coastal hills between Algeciras and Gibraltar, ghostly in the full moon. As Jim sped along the winding road, Samantha watched the windmills and the lights in the bay. Ships from the British and U.S. navies anchored in the harbor. Samantha didn't know what she was rushing toward. She wondered how she would care for Zahara if events escalated. She had a friend in Gibraltar who had two children. Maybe she could help if necessary.

Jim accelerated down the dark, open highway. "We need to get onto the Rock in case it closes access for the night. How tired are you?"

"Bushed."

"I'm in better shape. I can drive while you sleep."

Samantha shut her eyes as they drove in silence. She was at ease with Jim behind the wheel and dozed off.

On the access road to the Rock, Jim touched her shoulder and said quietly, "We're here. The border's still open. Do you have her passport?" Samantha dug through her purse and pulled out both their passports.

Once on the Rock, they drove onto Winston Churchill Avenue past a red British phone box and a red double-decker bus down a palm-lined avenue to the harbor front where office buildings ringed the water, then up the hill into the Old Town. Jim looked over at Samantha and smiled. She smiled back. Neither of them spoke. Zahara was asleep.

Jim located the office of SWG Financial on a cobblestone street in a peach-colored colonial building with tan shutters. The building was set just off Main Street. Most of the financial service businesses were in the glass towers downtown, but SWG occupied its original building, according to a sign on the front, with an antique shop on the ground floor advertising "Historic Antiques, Furnishings and Memorabilia from the British Empire."

"Do you mind if I stop for a minute?" Jim pulled the car to the curb. The streets were quiet with no traffic at this time of night and only a few parked cars. "I'll be right back." He touched Samantha's shoulder again as he locked the doors. The clock on the dashboard read 11:30. Streetlights cast shadows. Samantha watched him wander down the road looking into shop windows like a wayward tourist, scoping out the landscape, measuring distances and angles. He stopped by a pub at the end of the block that shared an alley with SWG Financial. Patrons were coming out. He disappeared into the corridor between the buildings then he returned quickly, pacing to the car where he started up the motor and pulled away.

"What did you find?"

"Let me get you and Zahara settled, then I'll come back."

"What did you see?"

His eyes were alert, his expression animated. She recognized the look; it's how she looked when she had spotted a story. "There was a light on in the rear of the building and a car parked at the back door."

"You want to check it out now?"

"I want you safe first."

At a small pensione, they registered as a family. From the front desk Jim took the free local newspaper and glanced through the pages while Samantha signed the registry. They settled into a room with faded flowered wallpaper, double bed, small sofa, desk, and window to the front.

"Here's the obituary." He handed Samantha the paper with a picture of Kenneth Shawcross and his wife, Irene, proprietor of Shawcross Antiques and Fine Furnishings. "You and Zahara get some sleep. I'll wake you early." He tucked the rest of the paper into his back pocket.

"Be careful," Samantha said.

He nodded. "I'll sleep on the couch."

CHAPTER TWENTY-FIVE

MONTE HEARD DIGGING above her. The lights had turned off in St. Michael's cave hours ago. She'd been afraid to shout for help after she slid down the rocks. She wasn't sure who was up there. She'd carefully wedged herself in an indentation of stones. The darkness was complete. She opened her eyes wider as a creature scurried across her arm. She shivered. She couldn't see her hand in front of her face. Everywhere the ground was wet. The air smelled dank and musty. She reviewed her options. She could try to climb back up to the marked path, but without light or help or something to hold onto, she feared she'd fall and pitch over the edge. She could continue downwards into the cave, sliding carefully in the hope that at the bottom she could retrieve her bags and find a path out or at least a path to somewhere. Or she could wait and stay where she was and hope that in the morning when they turned on the lights, someone would see her. By then her pursuers should have left, and she could call out. She had chosen this last option and settled in for the night. She should have called Tayri before she entered the cave, but Tayri would know to return without her. That was their agreement if Tayri hadn't heard from Monte.

The dripping and trickling of water from the earth above had been the only sound, but now there was digging and voices. The acoustics here were clear so she could hear the voices like a distant stage play in rehearsal. They must be near the theater in the Cathedral Cave, she thought. She was probably below the theater, which itself was several hundred feet into the rock. They were speaking Spanish and talking about their families. One said his sister wanted to have a baby, but her husband was never home. They talked about their mother . . . were they brothers? As they talked, Monte realized one was the brother and the other the brother-in-law, the husband of the sister who wanted a baby. What were they doing? Did they also get trapped in the cave when it closed?

"Place it deeper and set the timer to noon," the huskier voice said in Spanish.

"*Iré primero?*"

"Don't worry. When it blows, no one will know who was first. We'll all be gone. Hold open the golden door for me if you get there first."

"No!" Monte exhaled out loud, then caught herself. Were they planting explosives, discussing their deaths tomorrow—or was it today—as casually as the weather? Monte felt a chill of memory. "You and others will not soon forget me!" the Elder had bragged when he'd chained her to the tent pole. In that moment she'd glimpsed the man/child capable of great destruction in order to be recognized. But she couldn't allow herself to think about him as a person. She had to stay focused to fight him. He'd raped her, hurt her; he would kill her if he had the chance. What would she do if she had the chance?

"Is anyone there?" a voice called out in Spanish.

Monte held still. She had to get out of here. She couldn't climb back up so she began sliding quietly down the stone in the hope of finding a subterranean exit. There were miles of tunnels inside the Rock. Maybe she could find one of these. The two officers who'd explored the caves at the turn of the century had never returned and were never found. Maybe they found the passageway under the sea.

"No one is there," the other man answered.

"How much longer?" called a third voice farther away.

She recognized that voice, the guttural tone and rasping *r*'s. She slipped quickly down the rough rock toward the bottom, scraping her hands and elbows. She wondered what the gates of Hades looked like. Wet limestone with stalactites hanging from above? As she slid in the dark, deeper into the unknown, she imagined this must be a version of hell, not fiery and burning, but dark and cold with sharp edges. She was afraid, but she was also determined to survive. She'd endured far worse—the burning desert, the nothingness of captivity, rape. She had to find an exit. She had to get out, to get home to her children. She thought suddenly of her mother. "Give Mom a break," Samantha had told her. "She's doing the best she knows how." Why was Samantha always giving everyone a break? And why couldn't she?

Monte inched her way more carefully as the incline steepened; she kept her feet thrust out in front of her, her hands behind her, grasping any outcropping of rock to control her speed. Her clothes were soaked. A dim light from somewhere above created shadows so she could just make out the shape of her red canvas bag in a shallow pool of water below. Finally, her toes landed on a hard platform of rock. She couldn't see where she was, but her feet told her the ground no longer descended. She'd reached the bottom, at least of this cave. She peered around as best she could in the dark. There was no mystery at the bottom, no gold, no gates of Hades, no secret grail. There was dirt, cold water, sharp rocks, and death if she couldn't find a way out.

CHAPTER TWENTY-SIX

JIM PARKED ON the street near the alley behind SWG Financial. He turned off the motor. Streetlights cast shadows across the road, empty now of people. He slipped out of the car and into the narrow corridor between the pub and the SWG building. A silver Citroën was parked in the alley. He jotted down the license plate.

A light glowed from the back of the antique shop. Peering through a window, Jim saw the profile of a heavyset man, along with a thin, fair-haired man holding a gun. A woman sat at a desk. He recognized her from her picture in the paper as the widow of Kenneth Shawcross. In the shadows he could make out a silencer on the gun and pulled out his own gun. Every nerve in his body came awake as he leveled his gun and approached.

Then, without warning—*pff-oot*—the man shot Irene Shawcross in the head. The other man scooped out the contents from the desk and emptied drawers on the floor as if to make the killing look like a robbery. He nodded to his partner who was rifling through a safe behind the desk. The two men pitched over a file cabinet and opened the back door. Jim recognized them as the men in the restaurant in Casablanca the night before. As Jim aimed his gun, the burly, balding man threw a torch into the office, and the whole room exploded, knocking Jim backwards onto the ground. The men jumped into their car and sped off.

Staggering to his feet, Jim called the police. He told them to send an ambulance and a fire truck, and he gave them the car's license number, then he plunged into the shop where he confirmed Irene Shawcross was dead. He grabbed a jacket from a coat hook and held it over his head, using its sleeve to cover his nose and mouth as smoke filled his lungs. As flames stirred through the papers on the floor of the antique shop, he raced up the stairs. Why had they killed her? Why had they set fire to the building? When he reached the second floor, he called out to see if anyone else was in the building, but the doors were locked. What files might still be upstairs? He ran to the third, then the fourth floor, where he found large, secured filing cabinets that he assumed were fireproof. In the corner he heard a muffled thud from a closet. The flames were already spinning up the stairs faster than he would have imagined because of kerosene poured on the floor.

He shouldered open the closet door where a man was tied like an animal on a spit about to be roasted. Jim had left his tools in the car and looked around for some way to free the man. Inside the man's mouth was taped a rag, which Jim pulled away.

"Pocket . . ." the man gasped, choking. "Wire in my pocket."

Jim fumbled, pulled out a thin sharp wire he used to slice through the ropes as the flames, licking the kerosene and devouring papers strewn over the floor, moved near the door. Smoke thickened with the fumes of burnt paper and kerosene. It was more and more difficult to breathe.

"Quick!" The man stumbled to the other side of the room. His muscles had gone numb, and he was having trouble standing. From behind a photograph, he opened a safe and scooped out flash drives and envelopes.

By now the heat had started breaking windows, and the flames were full force threatening the neighboring buildings. Jim heard sirens in the distance, still a way off.

"Come," the man shouted. "Back stair."

Jim supported him with his arm. "Who the hell are you?" he challenged.

"I'm who you're looking for," the man answered, "whoever the hell you are." With Jim's help they made their way down the back stairs shielded by fire doors and plunged into the deserted street.

* * *

Together Jim and Stephen Oroya went to awaken Samantha. In the car Stephen had acknowledged, "You can turn me in and be a hero for a few hours, but you're going to need my help."

"What do you know?" Jim had decided not to cuff this man.

"I know the Elder is on the Rock, and an operation is underway. Torching SWG is just a distraction. They've already killed my friend who was in charge there."

"They also killed his widow tonight."

"Shit." Stephen frowned. "The police will investigate the murders and the fire and miss what's going on under their noses."

"What's that?"

They pulled up to the pensione. The lobby was dark. No one attended the front desk. Inside, Jim and Stephen hurried down the rose-wallpapered hallway to Samantha's room.

Samantha was awake, sitting on the faded blue velvet loveseat with a floor lamp over her shoulder reading through notes. On the flowered bedspread in her basket, Zahara lay sleeping. "I couldn't sleep after all . . ." she said turning toward the opening door. When she saw Stephen, she stood. His face was bloodied and streaked with dirt, his shirt torn. He smelled of kerosene and smoke. "What's happened?" she asked. "Where's Monte?"

"She's not with us," Jim said.

"We don't have much time," Stephen pressed. "I'm soaked with kerosene. I need a shower." He looked over at the bassinet and lowered his voice. "Please."

Jim stepped into the bathroom and confirmed there was no exit, no window he might escape through. "All right but be quick." He opened his duffel and handed Stephen a change of clothes. They were about the same size.

"What happened?" Samantha repeated when Stephen disappeared into the bathroom.

Sitting on a chair beside her, Jim took a bottle of water from the desk and drank it in one long gulp, then he narrated the encounter.

"Where's Monte?" Samantha repeated.

"I don't know. She wasn't there."

Emerging in clean jeans and a hooded navy sweatshirt, Stephen dropped onto the edge of the bed near Zahara, his black hair slicked back, his dark eyes intent, his tanned skin scrubbed but with a stubble of beard over his face.

"Where's Monte?" Samantha asked for a third time.

"I don't know," Stephen answered.

"Do you know what this means?" Samantha handed him her phone with Monte's message: AT THE TOP, ABOUT TO GO UNDER. "Was she texting me or you?"

"She's probably at St. Michael's cave. I ran into the Elder's goons before I could get there."

"Did you know them?" Jim asked.

"The big one, Gregor, works for one of the powerful syndicates of the Russian mafia; Batir, his cousin, works for a German affiliate, an unholy alliance that enforces for the drug and arms cartels that finance the Elder. Sometimes the Elder plans operations for their bosses. He also gives them safe haven when someone needs to drop out of sight. He's stored weapons, even nuclear components, for them. I was following the movement of their funds. I'd tracked payments to a separate account here I'd never heard of. My friend Kenneth and I were going to shut down all the accounts we ran, but I arrived too late."

Stephen stood and began to pace. He stared out the window onto the dark city street. "I'd like to send Kenneth's funds to his sons . . ." he began, but he cut himself short. He turned to Jim. "Right now, while everyone is sleeping, men are burrowing into the caves and tunnels, planting explosives. From what I overheard, explosions will blast from the belly of the Rock tomorrow, or I guess it's today. They're also attaching explosives to ships in the harbor. The Elder is supervising, but he'll leave before the bombs go off and watch from across the Strait, then disappear into the desert."

"You're sure?" Samantha asked.

"I heard them. The Elder let me hear. He was showing off, taunting me. He thought I'd be dead by now."

"Why Gibraltar?"

"Gibraltar guards the mouth of the Mediterranean. It's long been a launching point for invasions into Europe."

"NATO stores ammunition inside the tunnels of the Rock," Jim added.

"The Elder's finances are orchestrated from here," Stephen said. "He wanted to destroy evidence, another reason for the fire at SWG. He killed my friend who had the evidence."

"They were going to kill you," Jim pointed out.

"Can they access the money without you?" Samantha asked.

"I assume they got the account numbers from the vice president, who I imagine will turn up dead. They've sold short into the markets.

After the explosions, certain stocks will plunge as they have in the past after a major attack, and the Elder will reap huge gains. Part of the Elder's hubris is playing the West at its own game. The more he destroys, and the more markets fall, the more money he makes."

"Who executes the trades if you and your friend are dead?" Samantha asked.

"There are plenty of willing bankers and lawyers. If we can stop what they've planned, we can bankrupt the Elder and those betting with him. But if we lose him, he'll win then head underground."

"Where do we start looking?" Samantha asked.

"At the top of the Rock, but we need help. We can't do this by ourselves."

"I'll make some calls." Jim turned to Samantha. "You need to stay with Zahara."

"I'm going with you. I have a friend here who can look after her."

Jim reached out and touched Samantha's hand, meeting her eyes with a steady gaze. "If something happens to you, who will take care of her? We don't know where Monte is or if she'll survive."

Samantha's mind raced over all the times she'd chosen the story over the personal. And now with this child . . . but it wasn't her child. It was Monte's child. Monte had to survive. She wasn't going for the story; she was going for Monte. She couldn't accept that Monte might not survive. She might not have the physical skills of Jim or Stephen, but she knew Monte as neither of them did.

"I'll be fine. I'll call my friend."

While Jim and Samantha made calls, Stephen stood over the basket and watched Zahara sleeping. He stared down at the tiny child with soft brown skin and wavy black hair. He swept his fingers lightly over her forehead. "For you," he said.

CHAPTER TWENTY-SEVEN

MONTE HEARD SINGING and a flute. Light filtered in from above. Was she hallucinating? She was curled up at the bottom of the cave, leaning against the wall in the driest spot, her arms wrapped around herself, her hendira over her shoulders like a blanket. It took her a moment to remember where she was. Last night she'd lost track of the voices as she wandered the stone floor in the pitch dark looking for a way out, but eventually she settled in for the night.

In the blackness at the bottom of the cave, fears stirred all the way back to childhood—an amorphous face pressing at the window by her bed. No one else saw the face, but she awakened screaming that fall when she was five years old until Samantha, who at first tried to comfort her, finally threatened to move out of their room if she didn't quit screaming every night. So she slept with a pillow over her head until the dawn chased the face away. Only later did her mother, who'd been away on her last assignment before she resigned her job, figure out that the face was the reflection of Halloween masks her father had hung on the mirror in their room. Her mother removed the masks and gave her a flashlight to shine into the eyes of any further intruders at her window.

Last night Monte wrestled with imaginings and the real fear that a blast could shatter all the faces in her life. She'd awakened with a start that morning. She shouldn't have fallen asleep. She'd intended only to shut her eyes. In the morning light she saw bits of litter tossed over the edge—candy wrappers, cigarette butts—who smoked in a cave?

She no longer heard the men. She heard only distant music piped through the sound system. If she called out, would the Elder, instead of the guards, come for her? But if she didn't call for help, they would all be blown up. What time was it? They said the detonation was set for noon. She'd lost her edge. *Think . . . think . . .* she told herself. She couldn't let fear trap her. She had children waiting at home, and Philip waiting . . . was he still waiting? He'd loved her once, and she'd loved him before they discovered their limitations, her limitations.

"Hello-o-o!" she called. "Hello! . . . *Hola! . . . Hola!* Help! I'm here. *Estoy aquí!*" But her words ricocheted off the walls, seemed not to rise, but to be absorbed by the rocks and echoed back at her. "Help!"

CHAPTER TWENTY-EIGHT

SAMANTHA RODE THE funicular with Jim and Stephen to the top of the Rock, reviewing in her mind the story she would tell if she were reporting this story:

> *WHO*—A major, yet little known, criminal who goes by the rubric of "the Elder" and operates in the service of the world's despots and terrorists.
> *WHAT*—Almost succeeded in blowing up the Rock of Gibraltar.
> *WHEN*—Today.
> *WHERE*—Planting explosives on ships in the harbor and in the caves and tunnels inside the historic and strategic location.
> *WHY*—The Elder and his *Les Guerriers de l'Enfer* sought to disrupt the traffic of the Mediterranean port, undermine security in the region, and reap millions of dollars.
> *How*—By selling short into the stock market in anticipation of the cataclysmic events.

Even as she crafted the story, Samantha realized it could turn out dramatically different if they didn't intercept the Elder and his men in time. Jim had called his local contacts and the commander of the military base in Gibraltar who was in touch with the British and American ships in the harbor. As the sun rose, the local authorities were gathering, bringing in bomb-sniffing dogs to enter the tunnels. Jim told Samantha they would also patrol the waters, warning smaller ships to get out of the harbor, but the likelihood of finding all the explosives was problematic. No one knew how many detonations had been set, though Stephen said the Elder kept his organization and operations small. They agreed the best strategy to abort the attack was to find the Elder, but he might already have fled the peninsula. Samantha still didn't know where Monte was.

As the funicular climbed, Jim stood on one side making phone calls, a small backpack slung over his shoulder. He had reached Moha last night and briefed him. Moha had arrived this morning and was already working with the local authorities. Only Jim, Stephen, and Samantha rode up in the cable car. The operator was taking them early. He hadn't yet been told to suspend service so a few tourists were queuing at the base, and others were already walking up.

Samantha and Stephen stood on the other side of the cable car looking out at the shimmering blue water and azure sky rolling into Spain and Morocco and at the sea gulls riding the air currents. Stephen's dark eyes, framed by thick black lashes and brows, searched the horizon. His hair fell loosely over his forehead and grew over his ears covering the collar of the sweatshirt Jim had given him.

"We talked about this place," he said quietly.

Samantha assumed the *we* was Monte. He spoke with familiarity, like a friend or lover. But Monte hadn't talked to Samantha or her family about him. Samantha wanted to despise him, but she didn't. She wondered if Jim had reported that Stephen Carlos Oroya/Safir Brahim, who was on Interpol's Most Wanted List, was riding with them.

"Tell me what the Elder is like," Samantha asked. It was the kind of open-ended question she usually avoided, but she wanted to see where he took it.

"He plans operations, but he leaves others to execute. He's a coward in his older years. He's afraid of loud noises, dogs, and beautiful women. I've seen him shoot a dog that got too close."

"Does he also shoot beautiful women?" Samantha asked. Stephen didn't answer. "How old is he?"

"He's only sixty-six, but in his business, that's old. He's fit, but he's starting to falter, and that frightens him. Though I've seen him shoot a dog; at the same time, I've seen him take a small fox into his tent—one of those desert foxes with huge ears. Someone found the kit abandoned. The Elder set up a nest for it among his pillows and started carrying it around in the sleeve of his robe."

"Why are you associated with him?"

"I had a chance to do a major book. No one has ever gotten close. He also paid me a lot of money." Samantha suspected Stephen's motives were more complex, but she didn't press. He asked, "If I got you an interview with him, would you take it?"

She hesitated then answered, "Yes."

"So, you, too, would bite the apple?"

"I might not broadcast it."

"Of course you would. I thought I could withdraw when the time came, but then I took your sister to him."

"Did you plan that all along?"

Stephen didn't answer the question. They arrived at the top of the funicular and disembarked. They moved quickly down the path toward the cave where Jim instructed Stephen: "I'll go with Samantha to the main entrance. You go to the exit. Work your way into the theater and stay there. Whoever's in the cave will have to leave that way."

"What about Monte?" Samantha asked.

"We'll look for her," Jim said. "And for the Elder and his men." He turned to Stephen. "You're the only one who knows what the Elder looks like. Sit at the top, out of sight. Read a paper." He handed Stephen a section of the newspaper in his pocket.

"Will you really stay?" Samantha met his heavy-lidded eyes directly. "Will you look out for Monte?"

"I know what to do," he answered.

"There shouldn't be people in the cave yet so we may get lucky," Jim said.

"He's probably left already," Stephen answered.

"You're our fixed point. Samantha and I will move toward you." Jim set his backpack with the rope and tools on the ground. From it he pulled out his second gun. "We want him alive, but we also want you alive." He handed the Beretta to Stephen. "I hope I'm not making a mistake giving this to you. I know you know how to use it."

Stephen checked the chamber to see if it was loaded then checked the safety and tucked the pistol under his sweatshirt, into his jeans. "Don't worry, I won't shoot you." As he started up the path to the cave's exit, he turned back to Samantha. "Your sister was my ticket in." He answered her question then disappeared around the rocks.

"Do you trust him?" Samantha asked Jim.

"No, but he's the only one who knows the Elder, and it's in his interest that we kill or capture him."

CHAPTER TWENTY-NINE

ON THE STAIRS ABOVE, Monte saw a shadow. Did she dare call out again? Had she really seen the Elder yesterday or just imagined him as she imagined insurgents taking over the hotel that fateful day she followed Safi? She'd perceived danger that day, but the wrong danger. Yet if she hadn't followed Safi, she would never have encountered the Elder, a career-changing encounter, according to her colleagues who pointed out that she might yet pull off a major triumph by capturing or killing this most wanted man. They talked as if nothing else mattered. That she'd spent the last year of her life in the heart of her own darkness was not their concern.

She stepped back into the light. "Hello!" she called out. "Hello? Help! I need help!"

She squinted into the darkness. There was no exit down here, no tunnel to Africa, no gates to the underworld, no boatman on a river. There was just herself and her ability to think. *Think . . . think . . .* she told herself as she peered into the light. *A sound mind . . . a sound mind . . .* she repeated the words from Safi's note.

"'God hath not given us the spirit of fear, but of power and of love and of a sound mind.'–True or false?" he wrote.

She stared upwards. She estimated the distance to the steps was sixty feet. She began unpacking her red canvas bag. She knotted the arms of two sweaters together, then tied those to two long-sleeve shirts; she looped the shirtsleeves through the arm of her hendira and tied that to two pairs of slacks. She unpacked a thin blue silk sheet from a tiny silk sack, which Samantha once gave her for her travels. She'd fantasized about this sheet when she was sleeping on the rough desert floor last year, wishing she had the soft fabric around her at night. She tied the sheet to her clothes rope and tightened all the knots. She didn't know how well the rope would hold her 105 pounds. That is what she'd weighed on a scale in Cal's bathroom when she'd returned. She hadn't weighed 105 pounds since junior high school.

She made a loop at the end of her rope of clothes and tossed it at an outcropping of rock ten feet above. It took half a dozen tries before the loop slipped over the rock. She pulled hard to secure it. If the rope held, it would help her climb up the steep incline, then she could climb the next ten feet the same way and then the next. The final ten feet she could negotiate by throwing the rope around the railing of the stairs and pulling herself back onto the platform. She had to leave everything else behind. She tucked her wallet and passport and phone into her jeans pocket. On the floor of the cave, she left her computer and backpack and bag. She quit calling for help. She kept looking up, not down. She thought only about the end of the journey.

CHAPTER THIRTY

SAMANTHA SPOTTED AN orange candy wrapper discarded on the steps in the cave. She bent down and picked it up. It was from an energy bar, the kind Monte ate. She looked over the railing into the cavern, but she couldn't see past the lights, which glowed upward from the side of the stairs. She and Jim had split up to cover the two main paths to the theater and the exit. She'd assured Jim that she would be all right. "Even if the Elder is here, he doesn't know me," she said.

"You're a public face."

"We don't have affiliates in the Sahara. I'm just a tourist, reading my guidebook." She'd picked up a book and a map from the gift shop.

"At the moment we're the only tourists here," Jim pointed out.

"What do you want me to do if I see him?"

"Put me in your phone and hit the number. Even if I can't answer, I'll see someone is trying to reach me. Just keep hitting my number. I'll find you." They checked their watches; it was 9:20 a.m.

Samantha picked up the wrapper and read the fine print . . . manufactured in Pittsburgh, PA. She wondered if Monte had dropped it on purpose like Gretel dropping breadcrumbs in the forest. She peered again over the railing. "Monte?" she called in a whisper. She worried about who else might hear her. "Monte? Monte . . ." she called again. As she peered into the dark cavern, she remembered their vacation in Pompeii when Monte disappeared into one of the excavated houses. They'd just moved to Europe as their father took up a post at the American Embassy in Madrid. Cal was eleven; she was nine, and Monte, six. Their mother had been away much of the previous year on her last assignment before she retired from the State Department. She didn't discuss her work; she said it was confidential. Now she was back with them. Over the summer, she'd arranged a Spanish tutor for them, and by the end of summer, Monte spoke Spanish better than everyone except their father. Monte hadn't wanted to move, and when they arrived in Madrid, she clung to Samantha even as she translated for her. That day in Pompeii their parents had asked Cal and her to watch Monte while they talked to someone, but she and Cal started racing each other up the steps of the ruins, and when they turned around, Monte was gone. They looked everywhere for her, shouted and whistled. Samantha felt frantic, yet also annoyed at Monte for not following her as she was supposed to. It was their mother who spotted Monte sitting on a stone bench at the bottom of one of the houses talking with an old woman who was speaking Italian.

"How could you understand what she said?" their father asked.

"I understood what the sounds wanted to say," Monte answered.

The family memory of Pompeii was not the city buried by the volcano at the height of the Roman Empire, but Monte talking with a stranger in a strange language. That was the day their father first set his sights on Monte as the one who might carry forward his legacy. "She has a gift," he said.

"Let her find her own path," their mother urged, but Monte aligned with her father, pleased finally to get his attention, and she spent the next thirty years trying to fulfill his vision with her talent.

As Samantha stood peering into the dark, she felt a chill . . . an air current spinning down into the cave or a flash of memory of what losing Monte again would do to their family. Her parents had aged so over the year while Monte was missing, but they'd finally gotten her back. From what Cal told her, their father understood why Monte had come here, but their mother, who never really understood Monte, seemed the most vulnerable, as if Monte represented her own failure. As Samantha stared over the railing, she wondered if she was fantasizing that the paper wrapper in her hand could link to her sister. Why would Monte go over the edge into the cave?

"Monte!" she called louder.

"Can I help you?" A man stood several steps above wearing blue jeans, a white Nike tee shirt, and sneakers. His reddish hair was dull and full of gray which also bristled on his face. His left eye drooped. He smiled at her, but his smile bore no relation to his eyes, which didn't reflect light but looked like two dark stones in his face.

"Ah . . ." she exhaled, recognizing immediately who she was confronting. She crumpled the wrapper in her hand and tucked it in her pocket where she pressed #2 SEND on her cell phone. "Ah . . . no . . . no . . . I was just testing the acoustics. 'Helloo-o!'" she called out, singing to the walls. She improvised further, "Mountain . . . Climb every mountain . . ." as if she'd been singing into the cave rather than calling her sister's name. She opened her guidebook. "It says the acoustics here are almost perfect in the upper caves. Have you visited before?"

The Elder moved toward her. His unrelenting stare made her think he knew exactly who she was, that she was fooling no one. She pressed #2 SEND again and again on her phone in her pocket. "I'm heading to the theater where I'm told the acoustics are even better." She steadied her voice as she moved down the stairs. She saw movement below the railing. Could it be Monte? She wanted to draw this man away so he wouldn't see her sister, if in fact, she was there.

"Arugula!" She called into the cave. "I thought it would echo," she explained, smiling. She was half a dozen steps farther down now, but the Elder had stopped on the platform where she'd been. "Arugula!" she shouted as loud as she could as she hastened her pace down the stairs.

"Arugula!" was the childhood alert for danger. After they'd reunited that day in Pompeii, she and Monte and Cal had agreed on the code word. She and Cal took extra care to include Monte after that, and they spent the next days plotting all the ways they might get lost or captured or in trouble and agreed the password, if such a danger should occur, was "arugula" . . . a word they'd all found hilarious when their father and mother ordered arugula salads. In the conspiracy of childhood, they kept calling, "Arugula!" to each other whenever they spotted potential villains in the coliseums of Rome or the side streets of Venice.

The Elder looked over the railing into the precipice. Samantha hoped Monte had heard her and knew danger was near and would keep herself from view.

From the bottom of the steps, Jim moved quickly toward her. "So there you are!" He took her in his arms and kissed her, a kiss that surprisingly stirred her as he pulled her close. "I thought I'd lost you. The kids are waiting below," he said. "Where's your mother?"

"Oh . . . she's still at the top. It's too much for her."

Above the Elder, turning in the other direction, Samantha saw two men she recognized from the restaurant in Rabat.

"Let's get the children, then I'll go help your mom," Jim said. Hand in hand they descended the stairs to the theater at the base of the Cathedral Cave, leaving Monte on the rocks, off piste.

CHAPTER THIRTY-ONE

AT THE TOP OF THE concrete risers in the Cathedral Cave, Stephen sat with the Beretta pistol hidden under a newspaper, his hand resting on its ridged handle. He lifted it, felt its weight in his palm. The gun was standard issue, similar to what he used in the Army. He wondered if Monte was here, if he would see her again before he left the cave and disappeared for good.

He now believed he could get away, though yesterday for thirteen hours tied up in a kerosene-soaked closet, he had waited for a match to strike. He'd strained to free himself but managed only to pull the ropes tighter. Finally, he'd forced himself to lie still, to listen to his own heartbeat. He felt his life, his fate was no longer in his hands. His mind reached for some other power to help. Was there a power? Could he yield to it, yield his anger, his mistakes, his colossal misjudgment without losing himself? He didn't know, but for a moment lying tied up in a space no larger than a tomb, he glimpsed what it might be like to do so. And then he passed out. He was awakened by shouting: "Is anyone here? Anyone up here?"

He sat now at the top of the cave watching the first tourists arrive in the theater and cross the proscenium stage. Why had they been allowed in? Wasn't anyone in charge? He wanted to tell them to leave. The paths in the upper cave all led to this theater. Floodlights reflected off the rocks. In front of the stage concrete risers with rows of red plastic chairs climbed upwards. A father and daughter holding hands arrived on the stage. Two teenage boys raced each other up the risers toward the exit.

Stephen sat in the last row behind a column so that he could see the stage but not be seen. Emerging onto the proscenium, the two men who had tied him up appeared. They slipped into the shadows on either side. Stephen's muscles tightened in anticipation. He put his hand back on the gun. He was tempted to shoot them before they spotted him, but they were far away. If he didn't drop them both with the first shot, he'd be in jeopardy and jeopardize others. He watched as they made their way slowly to the risers on either side. Where were Jim and Samantha? He could still leave. The men hadn't seen him. He was sitting near the exit. He could take the pass codes and flee. He checked the magazine of the pistol and released the safety.

The music swelled, bouncing off the walls and the limestone that hung from above like a troubled sky. He could flee or he could stay and find Monte. Samantha was right, the kidnapping of Monte had not been random. When he met the sisters that night in the hotel dining room before the Festival, he'd recognized Samantha Waters, who answered his question: "Have you been here before?" by telling him they'd spent their early years in Spain with the American Embassy. After dinner he'd gone on the internet in the hotel business center to find out more about these two women. He discovered Anne Montgomery Waters was an officer at the U.S. State Department. He didn't know there would be an attack, but the Elder had had him sell short into European and especially Spanish markets. When the first bomb went off, he called those he knew were nearby. They facilitated his exit. He could have stepped away then. His engagement with the Elder so far had been limited to a few meetings, financial advice, and the execution of trades—poor judgement, perhaps, but nothing criminal, at least nothing he couldn't unwind or explain. But he had pressed forward—why? Not simply for access and a book, but to see his own limits, find the dividing line between good and evil, heaven and hell—did it exist?—was that a fiction? Or did he just want to prove himself by outwitting the powers that be? To take the apple, gain the knowledge, make the money, get the story, and disappear behind the veil.

He couldn't entirely explain his behavior even to himself. It was only after Monte was raped by the Elder that he grasped that the consequences of what he'd done had sent him way over a line. He realized what would happen to her if he didn't intervene. Because he was drawn to act, he ceded to her a measure of power over his conscience. From that point, his mission became to close down *Les Guerriers de l'Enfer,* and he persuaded himself that had always been his mission.

These thoughts raced through his head as he saw Jim and Samantha approaching up the center aisle. They hadn't seen the enforcers below them. Jim suddenly turned and raced down the steps in the other direction. Samantha moved toward Stephen as the heavyset man lumbered up the risers on the right and the other man, who'd just spotted Stephen, accelerated up the left, reaching for his gun.

Samantha moved into Stephen's row. "I think Monte is—" she started.

"Get down!" Stephen shouted, pushing her to the ground, scattering red plastic chairs. With deadly accuracy he fired first to his left, then to his right as he threw his body on top of Samantha's to shield her.

The shots rang out, echoing off the walls, shattering the ethereal flutes with the burst of exploding gunpowder and metal. Stephen held Samantha down until he was sure there was no response from the two men who lay sprawled on the stairs. Screams from the few tourists resounded as the parents ran with their children out of the cave.

"Monte . . ." Samantha cried. "We've got to get to Monte!" She struggled up from among the fallen chairs. "Monte's trapped." Samantha turned around. "Where's Jim?"

Hurrying down the risers, Samantha crossed the stage back to the steps. Stephen followed her until two security guards shouted from the top of the risers, "Stop!"

"Here . . . take the gun." Stephen slipped it into Samantha's bag. "The safety's off. Be careful. I'll take care of the guards." He turned, raising his hands. As Samantha mounted the stairs toward the upper cave, Stephen walked slowly toward the guards, smiling.

CHAPTER THIRTY-TWO

THE ELDER HAD stayed behind when Samantha left, but Monte had heard Sam's warning and knew to stay out of sight.

"I know you're down there," the Elder shouted.

Monte saw his face peering into the darkness. She cowered behind the rocks. His voice was like a bolt that locked down her soul.

"My little whore . . ." he cajoled as he tried to provoke her to show herself. He shot in the direction of the clothes she'd left on the cave floor.

The shot snapped her to attention. It was that shot Jim had heard when he'd turned and raced back up the stairs. A plan suddenly flashed into Monte's head. She began to whistle. She whistled quietly at first and then louder and louder—*From the Halls of Montezuma to the shores of Tripoli; We fight our country's battles in the air, on land, and sea.* She whistled as a dare, as a provocation this battle hymn of the United States Marine Corps. If she could rouse the Elder's rage, which trumped his intelligence, if she could get him to come after her, she thought she could prevail. She knew what to do.

"Whore!" he called.

She didn't respond. To react was to give up the advantage. This was how he operated, getting others to pursue and expend their resources. She kept whistling, then she began to sing softly: *If the Army and the Navy ever look on Heaven's scenes, they will find the streets are guarded by United States Marines.* She relied on her hubris, her affront being too much for him. She wanted him to swing at her pitch.

He started to climb over the railing to come after her. He stepped onto the wet stones as she'd done the day before. She slipped her rope over the rock above her, creating a grip. He fired in her direction.

"Monte!" She heard Samantha shout as she ran up the metal stairs.

"Stay back!" Monte warned. "Stay back! Call for help."

As the Elder moved toward her, he began to lose his footing just as she'd done the day before. He stumbled on the wet stones and grasped at the walls for a handhold just as she had, but there were none. He reached for the rope Monte had set as a lure and extended his hand to grasp it, but as he stretched toward it, she jerked it back, throwing him off balance. He skidded down the rocks. There was nothing to hold onto. He had no power here. Instead of sitting down as she had, he tried to assert himself. He saw her and lunged toward her. She nodded, acknowledging his dilemma. "Sit down," she said quietly, but he didn't follow her advice. Instead, he pitched forward, wavered, hesitated, and then plunged over the edge. He plummeted thirty feet to the floor below. As he descended, he shouted upwards into the dark cavern, but his words were indecipherable.

Monte called after him. "Welcome to hell!" There was no response. "Sam . . . Sam . . . Now I need help!"

Samantha hurried to the railing. Jim, who'd heard the first shot but run back up the other stairs, also arrived. From his pack, he took out a rope and began tying it to the rail then threw it toward Monte, but she couldn't reach it.

"I'll take it to her," Samantha said.

"I'll do that."

"I don't have the strength to pull us both up, but you do." Samantha dropped her bag on the platform. She pulled out the gun Stephen had given her and handed it to Jim, who flipped on the safety and tucked it under his shirt. He secured the rope around her waist. Samantha could hear the police hurrying down the metal stairs on the nearby path. She swung herself over the rail and started down the rocks. She was wearing rubber-soled sneakers, but she couldn't get traction. She pressed on the sides of the cave wall to steady herself. Jim anchored his feet against the barrier to brace himself and secure her. As she slid on the wet stones, Jim held the rope taut and kept her balanced.

"Monte . . ." she called. Monte was still twenty feet below.

"I'm here . . ." Monte was wedged into a crevice in the wall out of sight.

At the bottom of the cave Samantha saw a pile of clothes. Was it moving? She inched her way toward Monte's voice. The cave had no lights in this section, only the reflected glow from the lights above. She peered through the darkness, feeling her way along the rocks.

When she finally reached Monte, she gasped. Monte looked like a wraith. Her hair had turned white. Did she know this? "Monte . . . Monte . . ." Her voice broke.

"Easy . . ." Monte said. "I'm okay. Really. I'm better than I've been for a long time."

Samantha hugged her then quickly tied Monte's cloth rope around them. She placed Monte ahead of her on the rope Jim was holding so she could balance her sister as they started back up the rocks. Jim couldn't pull them straight up, but he could anchor them and give them the leverage they needed as Samantha helped Monte climb out of the cave.

"What time is it?" Monte asked urgently as they struggled to ascend.

"I don't know. Around ten. Do you think he's dead?" Samantha looked at the bottom of the cave. "Could he have survived the fall?"

"He has nine lives. But he's finished even if he isn't dead. There's no exit down there. He's superstitious. He knows he's arrived at the gates of hell."

When they reached the top, Jim put his arms around Monte and lifted her over the railing, then he helped Samantha climb to the safety of the steps. "You two have to leave," he insisted.

"What time is it?" Monte asked again.

"Ten twenty. Bomb-sniffing dogs have arrived. From what Stephen tells us, explosions could go off any minute."

"They're set for noon," Monte said. "I heard men talking last night." Then she asked quietly, "Is Stephen here?"

"They tried to kill him," Samantha told her. "He shot, and I think killed, the men pursuing him," she told Jim. "I left him back at the exit to deal with the security guards. He's unarmed."

"You need to leave!" Jim insisted.

"How futile," Monte said. "If you've cleared the cave, the only ones who will die will be them. This is the Rock of Gibraltar. The Rock will hold."

"Unless they blow up NATO's munitions," Jim said. "Or unless it's a nuclear device."

"Whatever it is, it will receive worldwide publicity," Samantha said.

"Yes. That is the point," Monte agreed. "The story is the point."

CHAPTER THIRTY-THREE

As they emerged from the cave, Monte blinked into the daylight. She'd been in the dark so long she couldn't see at first. Slowly, the blue sky and the pines on the hill came into focus as if nothing had transpired in the last twenty-four hours. A monkey approached on the path with his hand out.

"Where's Safi?" she asked.

Jim pointed down the hill. "Get to town as quickly as you can. I'll find him and bring him to you, but you need to leave in case there's an explosion."

Police in padded vests were still rushing through the exit. "We think we found the bombers in the harbor. A small fishing boat spotted them and reported to the harbor police."

"Tayri . . . ?" Samantha asked.

"I don't know," Jim said. "Go back to Zahara. I'll meet you at the hotel as soon as I can."

"Zahara's here?" Monte asked.

"She's staying with a friend of mine," Samantha said.

Monte leaned against the side of the cliff and took a long swallow from the water bottle Jim had given her. He'd also given her two packets of glucose and a protein bar he had in his pack, telling her to get sugar and salt into her body. At the bottom of the cave last night, she'd managed to catch some water dripping from above and pooled on the ground, but she was dehydrated.

"Can you make it to the cable car?" Samantha asked. "I'll try to find us a ride. The funicular will stop operating soon."

"I'd like to walk."

"I don't think you're up to it." It was already 10:45 a.m.

"It's downhill. I'd like the air and the view just for a while." Monte looked out at the sky and the sea. "I left everything at the bottom of the cave." She stretched out her arms. "I feel free for the first time in a long time. I wish I could wake up to this view every day."

Samantha glanced around for a taxi, but there were none. She was anxious to get safely away. She wanted to find out what happened to Stephen and Tayri and make sure Zahara was all right. She wondered how Jim would get out. But Monte seemed to have passed to the other side of crisis or was too exhausted to hurry. Instead, Monte ambled down the path.

"Given the credit you'll get for capturing, even killing, the Elder, I imagine you can write your own ticket and work wherever you want," Samantha said.

"I'm thinking of retiring." Monte dropped bits of the protein bar Jim had given her onto the ground for a family of monkeys following them. "The monkeys need to get down the Rock too," she said.

Samantha watched her sister as though observing a stranger. Monte had never shown any interest or sympathy for the animal kingdom. "Monte, we've got to hurry."

"I should have told you I was raped," Monte said. "But you've figured that out by now. How is Zahara?"

Though Samantha wanted to push her sister along, she also wanted to let her have this moment. "She's fine. She's perfect. She's waiting for you. I wondered if Stephen was the father, but he said he's not."

"Stephen . . . Safi . . . never raped me."

Monte gazed back toward the horizon. She looked twenty years older: her white hair cropped close like a man's or fashionable woman's; her skin, without makeup, brown and weathered; her wide green eyes carved into their sockets. She bent over slightly as she walked. She no longer looked, or even sounded, the same. Her voice scraped against the air like someone who'd been sick, but it held steady.

"He violated me by bringing me there. He took advantage, emotional advantage, but he didn't force me. In the end, he helped me and protected me from the others."

"So the child could be his?" Samantha asked as they turned the corner to see the funicular descending the mountain.

"Yes. But I think her father is the Elder's bodyguard, a man I saw only a few times. He wasn't brutal like the Elder, who tried to hurt me and put a knife to my throat and cut me. His bodyguard was almost apologetic, but the Elder insisted, and he followed orders."

"Monte . . ." Samantha put her arm around her sister, who didn't flinch this time. With Monte's hair sheared, Samantha now saw the scar on her neck shaped like a crescent moon. "I didn't know . . . How did you go on?"

Monte's gaze fixed on the sea and sky and the adjacent continents as Samantha hurried her along. "Tayri came and stayed with me. Safi brought her. Safi brought me books. I read. I escaped in my mind. I studied ancient Greek. Herodotus. The Persian wars began with the abduction and rape of kings' daughters. Once I tried to run away, but when I was brought back, they almost killed me. The Elder came into my tent with his lawyer who was wearing a suit in the desert and stood silently by while the Elder stripped me and chained me to the tent pole. He lectured me about the filth that women, especially women like me, were in the world. He would have raped me again,

but a guard told him Safi needed to see him. The Elder and his lawyer left. He told his bodyguard to finish for him, but after the Elder
left, the man handed me my clothes and left without touching me.
It turns out I was already pregnant by then, but I didn't know. If he
or the Elder had raped me again, I probably would have lost the baby
and also myself. I considered taking my life, but I kept thinking
about Emma and Craig."

"And Philip?"

"Not Philip. I had to let him go."

Samantha kept her arm around Monte's shoulders. Monte hadn't
talked to her so openly in years.

"I think Philip had already decided to let me go. Before you and I
met at the Festival, Philip told me he wasn't coming with me to
Indonesia."

Monte leaned now on her sister as Samantha accelerated their
pace. The road curved around the pine trees. They were halfway
down; they were the only people on the path. Samantha again
checked her watch; it was after eleven o'clock. She looked up and
down the slope for a car. She could see the town below.

"I don't know what happened before you left," Samantha said,
"but I think Philip still loves you."

Monte looked at her sister whose hair had pulled free from its tie
and was disheveled around her face. Her freckles roamed her nose
making her look like a fresh-faced kid. Her mouth was broad, her
aquamarine eyes large and inquiring. Feature by feature she wasn't
that beautiful, but the whole—the easy smile, the beckoning gaze—
she had always shined in Monte's eyes. Samantha was a romantic in
spite of her reporting on conflicts around the world, Monte thought.
"I think Philip has someone else," Monte said.

"I lived in your house. I never saw him with another woman
though that doesn't mean there wasn't one. Have you asked him?"

"When I got back, that wasn't where I wanted to begin, nor did he. Maybe we should have."

Samantha hesitated. "He did go out regularly on Tuesday nights."

"He plays bridge on Tuesday," Monte said. "I don't know what will happen with us."

"What would you like to happen?"

"I don't know that either."

They walked for a few minutes in silence. They were nearing a checkpoint. The monkeys had abandoned them once the food ran out. Monte's pace, which at first was steady, faltered. They arrived at Jews' Gate where the monument to the Pillars of Hercules stood—two large bronze-colored discs, one proclaiming "The Ancient World," the other, "The Modern World," each supported by columns. A roadblock turned traffic back. Monte sank onto the steps of the monument.

"*Non Plus Ultra*," she read. She knew the story of the twelve labors Hercules had to perform in penance for his sins. One of the last labors sent him crashing across the Atlas Mountains in Morocco, smashing through the isthmus and creating the channel they now overlooked connecting the Atlantic and Mediterranean with land in three directions. But to the west was nothing but endless ocean. "No wonder the ancients thought the world ended here," Monte said. "But there was something beyond . . . America."

"What?" Samantha stood above her.

A guard walked over. "You need to get down to town," he warned. "Shall I get you a taxi?"

Monte was covered in sweat though the air was cool.

"Yes, please," Samantha answered.

Without objecting, Monte climbed into the white minivan and leaned her head back on the seat while Samantha gave the driver the hotel name and address. As the taxi wound down the road, Samantha told Monte, "They tried to kill Stephen. Jim found him tied up in a closet. Stephen came to the cave today to stop them and to find you."

"Yes . . ." Monte said, staring out the cab window as houses appeared. She looked up at the white Rock Hotel on the cliff with its terraces and colonial façade. Farther down, they drove past an ancient Moorish tower from the time when the Moors conquered Gibraltar en route to Spain.

"Do you think Stephen will contact you?" Samantha asked. "What will happen to him?"

Monte looked over at her sister, who couldn't help asking questions. "I doubt he'll come to me. He knows he'd be arrested. I don't have control over what will happen to him, but I can't imagine him in prison for the rest of his life. Now that the Elder and his henchmen are gone, he's safer."

"What will you do if he does come to you?"

"With the Elder dead, or at least captured, I'm not as worried about him, though people will look for him if he's taken their money. I doubt Jim will bring him to the hotel. I can't imagine the cave's security guards were his match. I would guess he's already gone."

"He came back to help you," Samantha repeated.

"You're a romantic, Sam. He came back for the money."

The taxi made its way past the harbor and turned onto the cobbled streets of the Old Town. As it pulled up to the hotel, Monte started to cough and then to shiver.

Samantha paid the driver and helped her sister out of the cab. "It's all right," she said softly. "You'll be all right." Samantha supported her under her arm. "You want me to get you a room, and you can get some rest before you see Zahara?"

"Yes . . . please."

Samantha registered for a room as an extension of her own registration. "A room near mine with the best view you have," she told the clerk.

The bellman offered to get Monte food—a toasted ham-and-cheese sandwich and a glass of milk, Samantha's suggestion—from a nearby pub though Monte said she wasn't hungry. Samantha took her to a room on the same floor as hers and Jim's. She helped Monte climb onto the high four-poster bed. She told Monte she would leave a key on the nightstand, but she would also lock the door outside so no one could get in. There might still be a threat if any of the Elder's men knew she was there. She'd given Monte's name as Anne Montana, the secret name Monte had chosen as an eight-year-old; Samantha's secret name had been Tammy Madrid. Samantha said she'd return with food and a nightgown, but before she could expand on her plan, Monte stretched out on top of the flowered bedspread and fell asleep, her boots still on. Samantha unlaced the boots and set them on the floor. She pulled a blanket from the closet and covered her sister. She drew the curtains, leaving just a crack so that when Monte woke, she'd know if it was night or day. She left a note under the key with her room number. She hung a Do Not Disturb sign on the door.

In her own room Samantha called her friend Allison whom she knew from their reporting days covering the war in Iraq together. Allison had married a retired British colonel and settled here and now had two children and did public relations work. Samantha was surprised at her yearning to see her niece. Allison said Zahara was sleeping and said she could stay until four. Next Samantha called the police to find out what was happening and to inquire about Stephen and Tayri and Jim, but the small peninsula services were overwhelmed, and no one could answer her questions.

Samantha returned to Monte's room with the ham-and-cheese sandwich and a glass of milk, which she left on the nightstand. At noon she went outside and looked up at the Rock. She heard—or thought she heard—a distant intake of air, like a plane crashing through the sound barrier, but there was no smoke, no evidence of an explosion. Maybe something had happened on the other side of the Rock. Back in her room, she turned on the local news, but nothing was reported. She called Jim, but he didn't answer. She waited; she was not good at waiting. She changed into jeans and put on a nylon jacket with a hood to go out. She again checked on Monte, who was sleeping deeply. She left another note telling her she was going down to the harbor and to call if she woke up.

The streets of this British outpost appeared undisturbed on a late summer day, like a seaside English village preparing to close up for the season. Samantha looked over her shoulder, aware that the Elder might have others working with him who hadn't been killed or caught. She pulled up the hood on her jacket. As she walked along the quay, she checked her watch. It was already two. There were no signs of explosions near the water. The story in Gibraltar might be about what didn't happen. She wondered how many attacks around the world had been foiled since 9/11. Success for Jim was measured by what didn't happen; whereas her job was to report what did.

When Samantha returned to the hotel, the bellman handed her an envelope that had been dropped off for her or her sister. She pulled out a flash drive. "Who left this?" she asked.

"He didn't offer a name, just gave me twenty quid to be sure it got to you or your sister."

She stepped outside and looked up and down the narrow street. Tourists and residents were strolling in and out of the antique and souvenir shops and sitting at cafés in the late afternoon sun. "When did he leave it?"

"Just after you left."

She took the envelope to her room where she pulled out a note. "Do with this as you please . . . maybe you or your brother can write the book." The note was unsigned. She put the flash drive into her computer. It contained Stephen's interviews and notes on the life and finances of the Elder. She copied the flash drive onto her computer and then onto her own flash drive so there would be multiple copies since Monte would have to turn this over to the authorities.

She called Jim again, but he still didn't answer. Where was he? She worried something had happened to him. It was 3:45 p.m. She returned to Monte's room where Monte continued to sleep, though she'd turned over and now faced the window. Samantha left a third note. "Call me as soon as you're awake. I have something for you."

Samantha went to pick up Zahara, who had slept half the day too, according to her friend Allison. "But when she was awake, she was a charmer, so alert, watching everything."

Zahara greeted Samantha with arms and legs wiggling. Samantha took her into her arms and held her close, enjoying the soft body next to hers and the recognition Zahara showed at seeing her. Together they went into the Old Town where the shops were open and people sat at outdoor cafés. As Samantha pushed the stroller, she watched passersby on the street, alert for anyone suspicious. In a children's clothing store, she bought Zahara two outfits then hurried across the road to Marks & Spencer and bought clothes for Monte.

When she returned to the hotel, Monte was still sleeping. She delivered the new clothes, dinner, and another note. Jim still hadn't come back to the hotel, and her calls to his phone had gone unanswered. No one was answering the government phones now that the offices were closed for the night, and emergency lines were clogged. She called the hospitals, but Jim wasn't listed as a patient.

With Zahara and Monte here, she couldn't go out. She called Alex in Spain to see if he had any information, but Alex wasn't answering his phone either. She wasn't sure if her concern for Jim was professional—after all she wasn't writing this story, she reminded herself—or personal.

CHAPTER THIRTY-FOUR

FROM AN UNMARKED TRAIL high among the pines, Safir had watched a wisp of a woman with white hair shuffling down the hill. Could that be Monte? She was leaning on a tall woman with long chestnut hair so it must be Monte. He watched the two women descending. They didn't seem in the hurry he was. He worried Monte was in danger with the Elder's men still on the Rock. She'd come here for him, but she must know he wouldn't turn himself in.

It had been easy for him to get away from the security guards in the cave. He'd moved up the risers, bent down to the pocket of the dead man and retrieved his passport, wallet, and papers. As a guard accelerated toward him, he again raised his hands. "Just wanted to confirm the bastard's dead," he said in Spanish and English. He pulled out his old U.S. military ID he kept in his wallet and his U.S. passport and explained that the men at their feet were international criminals. He told the guards an operation was underway to secure the caves from terrorists planting bombs. Surely they'd gotten a call telling them to clear the cave and get down the mountain. Yes, they had, so his story was credible, but they were nervous. He told them they should take credit for the bodies. Maybe they could even collect the reward. He didn't want it. He had to go.

As he made his way along the ridgeline, he looked out on the water and wondered if he would be able to find a different life. He needed to disappear, take a new name. The possibilities for him were both open-ended and closed. If he got away, if he ever settled, he'd have to find his world within. He'd told his mother she wouldn't hear from him for a long time. To her credit, she didn't ask questions. She let him tell her what he wanted, then she would tell his father, who asked too many questions, usually filled with judgment. But his father had another family so mostly he left him alone. He would be alone wherever he landed, but he couldn't think about that now.

He followed the sisters until he saw them get safely into a taxi, then he took the direct route and sprinted to town. He calculated there were still at least half a dozen operatives on the Rock so he moved cautiously through the alleyways. He had three flash drives shoved deep into his pocket, one with his notes on the life and finances of the Elder and the others with the bank accounts and codes.

He made his way to the local Marks & Spencer. Fortunately, the Elder's men hadn't looted his cash so he could buy a backpack, underwear, three tee shirts, two trousers, a sweater, jacket, shoes, and a cap. He couldn't risk using a credit card, which could be tracked. He changed in the dressing room, storing Jim's clothes and everything else in the new backpack.

He went to Samantha's hotel and watched from across the street until he saw her leave by herself. His cap pulled down on his head, he approached the porter who also substituted as the bellman at the front door. He took a slip of hotel paper, scribbled a note, then sealed it and a flash drive into a hotel envelope. He gave the man twenty pounds to deliver it to Samantha or Monte Waters. Only Samantha Waters was registered.

He had one more task before he could leave. He headed to the bank where he and Kenneth kept the real accounts. He and Kenneth had gotten both sets of books in order. Rainer didn't know they'd recently lost millions as markets were starting to fall globally. Instead, they gave him the second set of books and told him they had been selling short into the U.S. markets, which had been whip-sawed in a mortgage crisis.

The Elder and Rainer didn't operate in a political or ideological framework. They operated as criminals. The Elder had side deals with everyone—traders of drugs and diamonds, and arms. If his partners found out about the money he was skimming from them, he would be their target. Safir had told Rainer he was moving accounts to Dubai. Rainer liked living in Dubai so he'd signed all the documents. Safir gave him a map of the accounts and put Rainer's name on the latest and largest trust in Cyprus. A corporation in Turks and Caicos was beneficiary where its directors, Rainer's relatives, lived and from which they could move the corporation instantly if there were inquiries. The funds from the corporation and trust flowed into the Dubai account from which Rainer, on the Elder's behalf, could draw. There were similar trusts in over a dozen countries.

Safir lived in this web of fearful invention. He knew he was play-ing a dangerous game, but he still thought he might prevail though the space for maneuvers had closed. He planned to bankrupt the Elder and his network, take a commission for his trouble, then dis-appear. He wouldn't deliver accounts to Monte after all. It would expose him and endanger her. He would get Kenneth's funds to his sons then he would hide the rest until the time was right . . . for what he didn't yet know . . . for charitable distribution? Perhaps. At least that was what he told himself. He had abandoned his plan to have an adventure and write a book. That scheme had been caught short by the reality of Monte. Soon he would start his journey, shedding himself as he went until he could finally stop and assess what was left and, from there, begin again. Could he find another life? He didn't know. He trusted Monte would find hers. She was perhaps already on her way.

CHAPTER THIRTY-FIVE

WHEN MONTE FINALLY AWOKE, the sun was lighting the sky outside. She didn't know how long she'd slept, but from the notes on her bedside table—four in all—and by the cold sandwich and the baguette with butter and jam and chicken and choices of milk, orange juice, soda, and thermos of coffee, she guessed she'd been asleep almost twenty-four hours.

Samantha had also left on a chair by her bed the evening paper, a nightgown, a toothbrush, toothpaste, new underwear, a pair of new black jeans, and new green sweater, shirt, socks, and a bottle of bubble bath. The latter made her smile, that her sister remembered this small luxury she loved.

She opened the curtains so she could watch the sun fill the sky. She sat up in the bed and lay the newspaper open, using the classified section as a placemat. She spread the butter and jam on the baguette and piled on the chicken and began to eat. She didn't remember when she'd been this hungry, though she couldn't eat more than half because she filled up quickly. She drank the orange juice first. She finished off her first meal in two days with the thermos of coffee. She read through the evening paper, which Samantha had already previewed in her last note, which told her explosions had gone off on the far side of the Rock, killing two people in suicide vests who'd also set the explosives. She assumed they were the men she'd heard, which meant the wife of the one would never have the baby she wanted, at least not by that father. Another man trying to abort the explosion was seriously injured and in critical condition, the paper reported.

She didn't call Samantha. Instead, she lay there after the meal letting her mind wander and rest, savoring what it felt like to be on a high soft bed with a full stomach and the daily threat she'd lived under for more than a year lifted. Finally, she got up to take a hot shower, using Samantha's lemon-scented bubble bath as soap. She washed her hair and face and stepped out of the shower into the sunlight. For the first time she looked into the mirror and saw what Samantha had seen. Her hair was completely white. Was that even her face in the mirror? She'd heard about such transformations in times of great stress or fright. She barely recognized herself. She understood why Samantha looked so stricken. She ran her fingers through her hair and smiled. She liked the odd crown of white; it made her look experienced, even wise. Tayri once beckoned her out of the desert and into the tent by telling her that she was being prepared, that she would find courage and lead others. She still didn't know what she was preparing for or where or how she might lead anyone. First, she had to figure out where she was going.

She dried off with the thin white towel in the bathroom and put on the black nylon underwear and stylish jeans and white shirt and soft green virgin wool sweater Samantha had brought her. Samantha had bought a size too large, but Monte felt herself filling up inside with her sister's care.

She was sitting in the armchair staring out the window at the rooftops of Gibraltar and the bay in the distance, wearing her new clothes and matching green socks, when Samantha tiptoed in at 9:00 a.m.

"You're awake! How long have you been up?" Samantha asked. "Why didn't you call?"

"I was gathering . . ." Monte turned around and saw her sister in the doorway with a diaper bag over her shoulder and Zahara in her arms. Zahara was wearing a pink tee shirt and pink overalls with Minnie Mouse on the bib. She started kicking her legs when she saw Monte.

"I'm sorry to surprise you with her," Samantha said, "but Jim never came back last night. I had no one to leave her with."

"It's okay." Monte hadn't seen the baby in over a month.

Samantha stepped toward Monte expecting her to take the child, but Monte didn't reach for her so Samantha sat with Zahara on the bed. "She's such a good baby," Samantha said, "not that I have any to compare her with, but she takes what's given her and works with it. She only cries when she's hungry or scared."

"Yes . . ." Monte said. She looked back out the window. "I was sitting here thinking about her. And you." She turned back around. "I can't take her, Sam. I can't. I don't know how I'm going to put my life back together as it is, but I have to focus on Craig and Emma. I can't ask them to understand what happened to me. I don't want to. I don't know about Philip and me. I don't feel a bond to her. I'm sorry. I don't. I don't want her to be hurt. I know I can't just leave her, but if I take her, then everyone will know what happened. And she'll spend the rest of her life with that story attached to her. What kind of start is that for a child? She deserves more too."

"What are you suggesting?" Samantha asked. She was holding Zahara in her lap on the bed. The child leaned against Samantha's chest in order to sit up, grasping Samantha's fingers for balance.

"You . . . you would be such a good mother. I know you would. You could just say you decided to adopt a child. I know I can't really ask you . . . Only if it's something you want, but you once told me you'd thought about adopting a child if you didn't have one of your own."

Samantha lay Zahara down on the bedspread. Zahara was smiling and began exploring her toes, her legs stretched out in a split above her head. She reached for Samantha. "What about . . . about the father?" Samantha asked though she wasn't entirely sure what she was asking.

"He was . . . I can't tell you for sure who he was, but I told you I think he was . . . I think he was the guard, and in at least one moment afterwards, he was not unkind. That's about all I can say. She will have to find her own way and figure that out. You could help her. And you would love her. I know you would. And she would love you and help you. You both would be so lucky. But there is time to think about that."

* * *

Samantha booked flights for them out of Gibraltar to London that morning. She wanted them to get off the Rock as soon as possible. Jim called as they were packing.

"You're alive!" Samantha exhaled.

"Yes, I am. I'm sorry I didn't call."

"Good to hear from you." Only as she said that did she realize how relieved she was to hear from him. She explained her plan, and he agreed they should leave right away.

"I'll meet you at the airport," he said.

*   *   *

From the window in the airport lounge Samantha and Monte watched Jim speed onto the runway in a police car. The airport's single runway, perched at the foot of the Rock, was bisected by Winston Churchill Avenue, which ran to the border of Spain. When a plane took off or landed, barriers were wheeled out to block traffic.

Samantha, Monte, and Zahara met Jim in a private office in the lounge. A shadow of a beard spread on his tan cheeks; his hazel eyes were heavy, his thick dark hair uncombed, but a smile broke across his face when he saw them. He embraced Samantha and then Monte. "The Elder is in custody," he said.

"He's alive?" Monte asked.

"They don't think he'll make it. He's unconscious under heavy guard in the hospital."

"Be careful," Monte warned. "Others may come for him."

"We know."

"His own men or those whom he owes and want to kill him," Monte elaborated.

"What happened?" Samantha asked. "I couldn't reach you or get any news from the hotel."

"We were lucky. Two of the elite from the British 301 EOD—Explosive Ordnance Disposal—unit were in Gibraltar in transit and came to help. They sent a 'wheelbarrow' robot down the tunnels. The robot found two large bombs with activated timers. The technicians dismantled them. If they'd detonated, they might have ignited the NATO munitions, and the whole Rock would have shaken."

Jim sat on a chair beside Samantha as she fed Zahara. "The bomb-sniffing dogs found the two suicide bombers in another area," he

said. "It was harder to dismantle a human bomb. That requires negotiating and language skills so Moha suited up and joined the EOD
team and tried to talk the men back, but the bombers were panicked
by the dogs. Here were two men with bombs strapped to their chests,
and they were afraid of dogs. The EOD team walked the dogs back.
From the end of the tunnel Moha kept talking to them, but he didn't
have enough time. The bombs detonated. The dogs and EOD team
had reached a safe distance, but it took an hour to get Moha out. The
men were killed. Moha was rushed to the hospital. They'd also
planted bombs inside the walls. The Rock was damaged with limestone collapsing and closing off one tunnel. It turned out their
bombs had been set to go off first so that security police and munitions teams would have been on-site when the main explosion happened. We were lucky we found the other bombs."

"What about Safi? Where is he?" Monte asked.

Jim glanced from Samantha to Monte. He frowned, and his
expression hardened, but his voice reached out to her. "By the time
I got to the security guards in the cave, he was gone. He'd persuaded
them to let him go. I don't know where he is. I went to the hospital
and stayed through the night with Moha." Jim turned back to
Samantha. "I'm sorry. I should have called you."

"You're here. That's what matters." She smiled without reserve
and saw that Monte noticed. Jim returned the smile and reached out
and touched Zahara's hand and then hers.

They walked to the gate together where a dozen passengers were
queued up for the British Air flight, including a well-dressed older
gentleman with a red handkerchief in his pocket and a fine leather
briefcase. When he saw Jim and the police, he grew visibly nervous,
wiping his forehead with the handkerchief. He slipped out of the
line and moved toward the exit where Monte saw him leaving by the
side door.

"That's Rainer!" she told Jim. "That's the Elder's lawyer—Anton Rainer. I only met him once, but I'm sure that's him!"

"Get on the plane and get out of here," Jim said. He touched Samantha's shoulder then he and the police sprinted out the door onto the runway where the barriers were being wheeled out as a black sedan sped toward Spain.

PART FOUR

CHAPTER THIRTY-SIX

Standing at the railing on the Watergate balcony, Samantha and Monte leaned on the balustrade, shoulders touching, heads together. The early summer sun skipped off the waters of the Potomac.

Inside Lala and Ma-jo's apartment a party was about to begin. Lala turned 104 tomorrow, and Zahara was two years old today. Everyone had been instructed to come dressed as a monster.

"Was this party yours or Mother's idea?" Monte asked dryly. Her white hair had grown, but she still kept it clipped short and swept across her left eye.

"I told Mother that Zahara had started waking up with nightmares about monsters. She said she remembered that phase with you, and she had an idea to help."

"Emma also wakes up and comes in, but I'm already awake, and the monsters are sitting around chatting with me."

"Still?" Samantha asked.

"I never was a great sleeper, unlike you and Cal, who sleep the sleep of the innocent."

"Does Emma also go to Philip?"

"Usually to me."

Monte had moved back into her house in Northern Virginia, but she'd told Samantha that she and Philip kept separate bedrooms. She wasn't certain how, or even if, she was going to stay in Washington; however, for now she'd shifted to the State Department's Language School where she taught Foreign Service officers advance courses and was herself studying Mandarin Chinese.

"You still planning to go to China?" Samantha asked. Monte hadn't mentioned this possibility to the rest of the family, but Samantha knew she was restless.

"I need another year of language to be useful." Monte didn't say useful at what.

"And Philip?"

"I don't know. Lambent and Taylor have offices in Hong Kong so he might consider moving."

"How are you two doing? Are you trying?"

Monte smiled wryly. She sat down on the lounger, stretched out her legs, lowered her sunglasses, and let the warm sun embrace her. She'd remained a petite size and had taken to wearing black, which set off her snow-white hair. "Are *you* trying?" she asked.

Samantha joined her on the other lounger and pulled down her sunglasses. She was dressed in a red tee shirt and red jeans in an effort at being a dragon for the party. On the deck by the chair were a pair of gold wings that could belong to a dragon. Also by the chair sat her briefcase.

"Yes, I'm trying like crazy. I go to work late, get home early, then work past midnight after Zahara's asleep. I've learned to get by with six hours sleep." After a year's sabbatical, Samantha had shifted from reporting news to hosting a weekly international affairs show based in Washington so she didn't have to travel as much.

"You are a better mother than I've ever been," Monte said. "Zahara is lucky."

"I love her," Samantha said. She pulled her briefcase onto the chair and began digging through it. "I am the lucky one. Here . . ." She pulled out a manila envelope and extracted a galley. "You know, Philip helped us with the financial forensics for this." She offered the galley to Monte.

Non Plus Ultra—Nothing Beyond:
Crime and Terror in the Wilderness

By Samantha A. Waters and Calvin A. Waters

Samantha turned to the dedication page:

To our sister, the courageous Anne Montgomery Waters.

Monte opened the galley and started the introduction. She flipped to the table of contents and opened to the chapter entitled: "Stephen/ Safir: The American." She scanned through more pages then paused and looked up. "Can I keep this?"

"Please. Final corrections are due in two weeks. Tell me if we've missed anything."

"When do your stories run? I assume your producers are happy?"

"Ecstatic. They'll run on our network and in *The Economist* the same week before publication—drugs, diamonds, and arms trafficking and the links between them and terrorists around the world. We'll conclude by showing how the money is laundered."

"So you got the story after all."

"Only because you gave us your blessing and Stephen gave us his notes and interviews. I still feel odd not crediting him."

"Those were my terms. In any case you've been able to corroborate everything, right?"

"Everything but the Elder's interviews. But he opened the door and gave us the leads. Writing the book let me go deeper into the story than any broadcast. Cal and I are already planning our next book."

Monte read the epigraph on "The American" chapter, a passage Stephen had copied out in his journal:

"The words of his mouth were smoother than butter, but war was in his heart; his words were softer than oil, yet were they drawn swords." —Psalms 55:21

Monte shut the galley. "I wonder if Safi will ever see the book."

"You've never heard from him?" Samantha set her case back on the ground.

"I told you I wouldn't. I turned everything over to the government. People are still looking for him."

Samantha wanted to ask if Stephen spoke Chinese, but the question came from the journalist, not the sister, and she was making up time as a sister. Monte was trying too. Monte had finally settled into a role she could handle as an aunt to Zahara. Her children loved their cousin. Having a younger girl in the family had brought Emma out of herself. She liked to play with Zahara, sharing stories, dressing her up and telling her what to do though Samantha saw already the day would come when Zahara would assert her own voice. She was precocious with a vocabulary of a three- or four-year-old, according to her preschool teacher. She was tall for her age with almond-colored skin, wavy black hair, and penetrating green eyes.

Samantha and Monte didn't know what had become of Stephen except for what Jim told Samantha. Stephen Carlos Oroya/ Safir

Brahim remained on Interpol's wanted list, along with the lawyer, Anton Rainer, who got away. Jim and Samantha Skyped at least once a week. Jim was in North Africa where he and Moha continued to track down the Elder's network around the globe. Jim had told Samantha that Stephen had succeeded in bankrupting *Les Guerriers de l'Enfer* and their patrons. Intercepts received had been full of recriminations and vicious comments blaming the Elder, who had hovered in a coma with round-the-clock security at the Gibraltar hospital for two months before he died. How much Stephen had skimmed from the Elder's accounts, Jim couldn't say, but the U.S. government was pursuing him with agents from the Departments of Treasury, Defense, State, and the CIA. Jim speculated he'd hidden away a sizable part of the fortune and was letting it sit for now.

"He's not in a rush," Jim said, "but he will be caught."

In spite of Monte's and Jim's analysis, no one else trusted Stephen's sympathies. There was particular venom because he held a U.S. passport and citizenship and trained in the U.S. Army.

On the surface Monte had returned to the family. She was solicitous toward her mother, who'd accepted Zahara with a surprising grace that impressed everyone. "She is one of God's children," their mother had declared and that was the end of it. Their father accepted the new member of the family as he might accept anyone seeking asylum.

As Samantha and Monte stared out at the river, Samantha asked, "Are you happy?"

Monte looked over at her and smiled as though she understood the larger question. "I don't ask that anymore, at least about myself. Are Emma and Craig happy? I ask that all the time. They seem happy so I am."

"Is that enough?"

"For now. What about you? When is that guy coming?"

"What guy?"

"Jim—the one who helped us in the cave. The one you told me kissed you? The one who calls you." Samantha laughed. "You said he might be moving here?"

"He's assigned here next month. But why do I think you already know that?"

Monte raised her eyebrows, which were snow-white arcs on her small face. "Are you still seeing that diplomat Ma-jo set you up with?"

"I go to events with him sometimes . . . nothing more."

"Does he kiss you too?"

Samantha laughed again. "Time to go in."

"Why won't you tell me?"

"You never asked me these things before. Are you gathering information? I'm too old to be dating."

"You're never too old unless you're married like me."

"Why can't you and Philip start dating again? Seriously, isn't it worth sorting things out with Philip?"

"Why is it you, Cal, and I haven't figured out marriage the way Mom and Dad did? Mother asked me that the other day."

"What did she say?"

"She asked if I thought it was her fault or Dad's fault that none of us was happily married. I told her it was the times. I'm trying, I told her. She took my hands in hers and said, 'Then you'll succeed, Monte. You've always succeeded when you put your mind to something, though this time it's your heart you'll have to release, not your mind. Don't be afraid.' Then she hugged me." Monte threw up her hands and shrugged.

"That makes me happy," Samantha said.

"I've messed up with her, haven't I? Holding . . . I don't even know what against her for years . . . my own insecurity . . . that she didn't know me or didn't love me as much as she loved you and Cal."

The sliding door opened, and their mother, dressed in a green jumpsuit as the Loch Ness Monster, called them in. Samantha and Monte uncurled from the loungers and the world they shared outside and joined the family inside.

The landing was set up like a stage. In the living room Lala sat semi-reclined on the sofa in her navy velour tracksuit. She'd been to the beauty parlor, and her thin gray hair swept off her face, framed by a gold headband. A big gold watch hung around her neck. Lala said she had come as the monster she feared the most these days— Time. This confession unsettled Samantha and Monte who wanted to believe Lala would live forever.

Marjorie, dressed as a ghost in pink chiffon, sat on the other sofa, her gray-blonde hair in a pageboy with two wings swept back on the top, the style she'd worn for sixty years. Beside her sat an elderly, distinguished man with a head of silver hair, a former Ambassador to Portugal, a widower who'd recently moved into the apartment next door.

Their mother asked their father to dim the lights and close the curtains. As the room darkened, Samantha took a seat beside Lala and lifted Zahara, dressed in red as a baby dragon, onto her lap. Monte perched on the footstool by Ma-jo. Philip stood by the door to the terrace near Monte with a handheld spotlight.

Zahara started clapping as the music began with her favorite song: "The Mice Go Marching." "The mice go marching quietly by, shh! shh! . . ." She sang the words. Then the next verse, "The mighty monster marches by Kaboom! Kaboom!"

Mother announced the play: "*Goodbye, Monsters!* is being per-formed this afternoon for the first time for Zahara Waters and Lala Waters on the occasion of their birthdays." Everyone clapped.

"Once upon a time a long time ago, before there were people, there were m-o-n-s-t-e-r-s!" their mother began in a deep voice. "Monsters thought they owned the earth . . ." The four older grand-children stomped around like monsters who owned the earth.

"But monsters, even those who look scary, are not too smart, not as smart as people, and certainly not as smart as children. If a mon-ster visits you, what should you do?" Mother asked.

Annie, Cal's youngest daughter, stepped forward. "Ask the mon-ster its name. What is your name?"

"Loch Ness," Mother growled.

"Ask it what it wants," Craig, Monte's son, added. "What do you want?"

"I want to eat you up!"

From the side of the stairs Emma, Monte's daughter dressed as the Cookie Monster, ran in with a plate of cookies. "No, eat these instead!" The four cousins surrounded Loch Ness and gave her a cookie. The sudden conversion of the other monsters was unex-plained, but Zahara sat credulous. The play abruptly broke up as Emma called to Zahara, "Don't be afraid!"

"Come up with us," said Mannie, Cal's older daughter who, at fifteen, had let it be known she was too old for these skits.

The audience clapped. Cal flipped on the lights, and Zahara ran up to the stage.

She sat on the floor next to Emma, her favorite cousin. Samantha and Monte watched Zahara then glanced at each other. They didn't know if the time would ever come to tell her the truth about what had happened to her mother, but they agreed that what happened to

Monte and what would happen to Zahara had separate trajectories. They hoped the intersections would be benign.

Philip, who was standing beside Monte, was also watching. He put his hand on Monte's shoulder. Since they'd come back to the States, Philip hadn't demanded an accounting, and Monte was grateful for that.

Dad clapped. "Brava for Grandma! Did I ever tell you I met your grandmother when she was a secret agent?" Dad was dressed as a Cyclops in brown slacks and a brown turtleneck with an eye pasted on his forehead. "She was working in West Berlin. I fell in love with her as soon as I saw her. That's how I became a Cyclops." He pointed to his one eye. "From then on, she was all I could see."

Their father was a romantic, they all knew, though a difficult one. Samantha, Monte, and Cal exchanged glances. He'd referred to their mother's early career as a secret agent before. "Is that true, Mother?" Monte asked.

Lacey Waters flipped her tail at her husband and said to her children, "Someday when you're all grown up and the embargo on secrecy has expired, I'll tell you about my life before I met your father."

Lala sat forward on the sofa. She reached out for Zahara to come to her. "Since it's my birthday, I want to tell you how I get rid of my monsters. But first I want to say how happy I am to share my birthday with Zahara Waters, who comes to our family from a place that only she knows, just like I come from a place that only I know, and everyone comes from their own place, but we are bound together by love and history. Do you know what that means?"

Craig raised his hand as though this was a test and he knew the answer. Lala continued, "To get rid of a monster, first you have to look the monster straight in the eye. Then you say to it, '*Mushkeegan!*'"

she shouted in a frail voice. "Usually that will make it go away. It goes away because it doesn't know what else to do."

"What is *Mushkeegan*?" asked Annie.

"It means . . . well, it doesn't mean so much as it is. It holds in it all the love you have in your heart. That's what I do every morning. I stand in front of the mirror and say, 'Mushkeegan! Mushkeegan! Mushkeegan!' until I'm brave enough to face the day. You're littler than me," Lala said, touching Zahara's head, "but I can see already you've got a powerful heart. You're going to get rid of a lot of monsters in this world. We are so lucky you are part of our family."

CHAPTER THIRTY-SEVEN

IT WAS ONE THIRTY in the morning as Samantha slipped Zahara into her car seat and drove across the river to Virginia. She didn't call in advance. Monte would want to know why she was coming, and Samantha needed to talk face-to-face.

She'd just hung up with Jim, who'd moved to Washington last month. "I think you should tell her before the news gets out or someone calls her," he said. "Shall I come by later tonight?"

Jim had rented an apartment in Foggy Bottom near the State Department, only a mile from Samantha. He stopped by several nights a week for dinner or a walk along the river with Zahara in the summer evenings. "I'll call you, but yes," Samantha said.

Zahara fell back asleep as they approached Memorial Bridge. There was no traffic at this hour. The night air was silky. Stars erupted in the sky. Were her mission less urgent, she would have pulled over to watch the moon shining on the Reflecting Pool in front of the Lincoln Memorial. She would bring Jim here on Saturday night to walk around the water and sit on the white marble steps of the Memorial. They were taking their relationship slow, or rather Jim was taking it slow as if he knew to give her plenty of room. They talked about her meeting his son soon. He kissed her goodnight with passion, but then left her with Zahara each evening. On Saturday night Zahara was sleeping over at her cousins'.

As Samantha pulled into the driveway of the red brick house in Alexandria, she phoned Monte's cell. "I'm outside. Can I come in?"

In green silk pajamas Monte opened the front door and stepped onto the porch. Petite, her hair askew, she looked like an elf in the moonlight. Inside, Samantha lay Zahara on the worn brown leather sofa in the living room and covered her with a knitted afghan, then followed Monte into the adjacent den.

Philip appeared in the doorway in a plaid robe. He'd trimmed down; his gray-brown hair fell in thin strands on his head. In his deep-set brown eyes, Samantha saw his strength. His eyes didn't look away; he took in facts, analyzed them, drew conclusions. "Everything all right?" he asked.

"I need to speak with Monte," Samantha whispered.

He glanced at Monte, who nodded. She and Philip had moved back into the same bedroom last month after Lala's birthday party.

Monte had told Samantha that Marjorie and Lala had invited her over for lunch the next day. "Life spins by so fast, you don't realize," Lala said as they ate sandwiches on the terrace. "You look up and ask, where did it go and what have I accomplished?"

"The only thing sure is how much you've loved," Ma-jo added as though they had rehearsed the conversation especially for her. "The rest is paperwork."

"People miss that," Lala said. "They get too busy with the paperwork."

Marjorie then gave her a worn leather portfolio that had belonged to her grandfather Montgomery. "He carried it to all his meetings," she told Monte. "I want you to have it."

Monte had accepted the case but told Samantha she worried that Ma-jo and Lala were giving out advice and heirlooms.

"I went home and talked with Philip and moved back in. I can't explain why, but a barrier broke. Philip didn't ask why. He's not pressing me the way he used to. I appreciate that. I think he may still love me, though I'm not sure why."

"He does love you," Samantha had said. "I watch him watching you. I think he's intimidated by you sometimes."

"I loved him once," Monte said. "Beneath all my anxiety and impossible self, maybe I still do, in spite of . . . well, we're all loved in spite of something."

"Are you sure about going back together?" Samantha had asked.

"No. But there are compelling reasons to try."

After Philip left the den, Monte turned to Samantha. "It's Safi, isn't it? They've killed him." Her voice was matter-of-fact, as if stating what she already knew.

"In Bali. Agents surrounded his house. He'd apparently been living there for over a year in a small villa on the beach under the name of Sam Montgomery."

Monte lifted her eyebrows, acknowledging the adoption of their names and his destination of Indonesia where she'd been assigned but never gone.

"Jim told me the police urged him to give himself up. Everyone wanted him alive, but he told them he wasn't spending his life in prison. He told them to step back and then the house exploded. He'd obviously prepared for that moment. Jim was told it exploded inwards upon itself like a demolition site so no one outside was hurt."

"He trained in munitions in the Army," Monte said.

"That's what Jim told me. He said very little was left."

"Did they identify his body?"

"I didn't ask. I assume. I wanted to get here to tell you before anyone else did."

Monte stared across the modest den with its pine furniture and bookshelves and tweed reclining chair. "Thank Jim for letting me know." She peered out the window toward another horizon. She wondered if it was possible he'd escaped, but she didn't ask. In the desert where the land changed with each wind, where whole armies disappeared in sandstorms never to be seen again, she'd let go of the need for certainties. She'd once wondered if she would disappear and be lost on the flat hard earth or among the dunes. The sand dunes were said to sing when wind passed over them, songs from invisible animals and djinns hidden within, but she'd never heard the singing. She'd gone to the dunes only once, the night they escaped. They rode the camels all night as Tayri navigated by the stars, then before light, when the sun would bake the earth and those searching might see them, they arrived at the rolling mountains of sand. Tayri led them to a gully where the dunes cast a shadow. There they rested. She had fallen into a deep sleep there with Zahara tucked beside her, and she missed whatever music may have played.

On the other side of the ocean now, she lay awake some nights listening for the music that had eluded her. Some people said they found truth in the desert. Others reported finding faith. In that space where there was nothing, she'd discovered the stars and the moon and the immensity of the universe. And she had discovered her mettle. She'd held on. Gradually fear had fallen away like the skin of the old serpent that slithered off to find the shade of a rock.

"*Truth is not political,*" she'd told Safi.

"*Then what is it for you who works on behalf of your country's interests?*" He lay with his head in her lap.

"*Not anymore. You've seen to that.*"

"*You will go back soon.*"

"*That is a lie you keep telling me. I will not be allowed to leave . . . or to live.*"

"*I won't let them kill you.*"

"*You are a liar. You are lost, Stephen Carlos Oroya Safir Brahim.*"

"*Then you must help me get found.*"

"*Perhaps I am lost too.*"

Samantha put her arm around her sister. "Are you okay?" she asked.

"Safi once gave me a passage in ancient Greek from the Bible," she answered. "*God hath not given us the spirit of fear but of power and of love and of a sound mind.* He asked me if I thought that were true or false."

"What did you say?"

"I told him it was irrelevant unless I had access to the power. He asked me, 'What if it is there for the taking?'"

Samantha watched her. They were closer than they'd ever been— the memories and hurts of childhood, the ambitions of careers, the competitions—all now muted.

"Is Zahara still coming over Saturday night?" Monte asked.

"Yes, she's looking forward. So . . ." Samantha asked, "is it there for the taking?"

Monte looked at her and smiled slightly. Her white hair fluffed on her head like the crown of some exotic bird; her white eyebrows outlined her searing green eyes. She didn't answer at first, then she said, "Yes, I think it is. It waits inside."

AUTHOR'S NOTE

I first visited Santiago de Compostela, Spain—the opening scene in *The Far Side of the Desert*—in 1993 as a delegate to PEN International's 60th Congress. The PEN Congress coincided with the Festival of St. James and the Camino de Santiago where tourists and pilgrims gathered on the plaza in front of the massive Baroque and Romanesque cathedral. The PEN Congress was an entirely separate event, but the festivities overlapped in the square.

Salman Rushdie made a surprise visit to the Congress, one of his first since the fatwa had been issued against him. At that Congress I was elected the Chair of PEN International's Writers in Prison Committee, the division of PEN that spearheads PEN's human rights work on behalf of persecuted writers worldwide, so I was one of a small group who greeted and shared dinner with Rushdie. I mention these events because it was there I began contemplating what it would be like if one had to disappear or was disappeared, either by choice or coercion. That question is central to the opening of *The Far Side of the Desert* and also informs another novel of mine. What happens when all the familiar props of life are taken away?

There are many events, much research, and intertwining threads that develop in *The Far Side of the Desert,* but the seed of imagination began in Santiago de Compostela and at the end of the Camino on the rugged cliffs of Galicia facing west over the Atlantic. It is here the ancient Romans thought the world ended, a spot they called the Cape of Death because the sun died there and because ships wrecked on the rocks that jutted out into the sea. The Romans saw nothing westward and could imagine nothing but terrors so they declared *Non plus ultra*: *There is nothing beyond.*

Imagining what is beyond, discovering what holds and what falls away is the journey of the two sisters Monte and Samantha Waters who are from an American diplomatic family. The outer frame of the story includes drug and arms trafficking, money laundering, and financial manipulation—a membrane of crime that smothers large parts of the globe. But the core is the characters and the journeys of their hearts and minds.

BOOK CLUB
DISCUSSION QUESTIONS

1. What differences and similarities do you see in the sisters Monte and Samantha Waters? Do these characteristics change for either of them during the book?

2. Do you think that Monte could have prevented her kidnapping—or better protected herself? Do you think Samantha would have gotten kidnapped?

3. How do the "characters" of Stephen Oroya and Safir Brahim contrast? Do they have a common motivation?

4. What was Cal's primary role in the story?

5. How would you describe Monte's relationship with her husband and children? Had that changed by the end of the story?

6. How important are family history and the interactions with Edgar and Lacey Waters in the story?

7. Who is the Elder and what motivates him? Is he a kind of "Azazel"?

8. Why does Monte go after Stephen/Safir in the end?

9. Do you think Stephen/Safir survives?

10. What is the significance of history and myth, especially the myth of Hercules?

11. What is the significance of the journey to the Rock of Gibraltar and the caves?

12. Stephen/Safir gives Monte a Biblical quote: *"God hath not given us the spirit of fear but of power and of love and of a sound mind."* He asks her, "True or false?" What is your view?

13. What do the grandmothers Ma-Jo and Lala mean when they tell Monte, *"The only thing sure is how much you've loved . . . The rest is paperwork."*

For more information about *The Far Side of the Desert* and Joanne Leedom-Ackerman, visit her website at: www.joanneleedom-ackerman.com.

NOTE FROM THE PUBLISHER

We hope that you enjoyed *The Far Side of the Desert* by Joanne Leedom-Ackerman. If you did, we'd like to recommend her previous novel, *Burning Distance*, another international thriller with strong family bonds.

Burning Distance begins when Lizzy West is ten years old and her father's plane explodes over the Persian Gulf—initiating her journey through the dark world of arms trafficking and covert political forces against the background of the Gulf War. Against all odds, a modern-day Romeo and Juliet love story emerges in a world seething with secrets, betrayals, international intrigue, and competing loyalties.

"*Burning Distance* opens with a mystery, glides into a love story, and unfolds into a political thriller. Set against the backdrop of 1980s and '90s global politics . . . this is a story of war, family, history, politics, and passion. Joanne Leedom-Ackerman's evocation of the era is pitch-perfect!" —Susan Isaacs,
New York Times best-selling author

We hope that you will enjoy reading *Burning Distance* and look forward to more Joanne Leedom-Ackerman novels.

For more information, please visit
www.joanneleedom-ackerman.com

If you liked *The Far Side of the Desert,* we would be very appreciative if you would consider leaving a review. As you probably already know, book reviews are important to authors and they are very grateful when a reader makes the special effort to write a review, however brief.

Happy Reading,
Oceanview Publishing
Your Home for Mystery, Thriller, and Suspense